David Shepherd w:
near Lancaster, in 1942.
School in Derbyshir
Durham. After Univers
Linlithgow, West Lothian and a student at
Theological College in Edinburgh. From 1968-1979, he
was Chaplain of St Paul's Cathedral, Dundee and
Anglican Chaplain in the University of Dundee from
1973-1979. Since 1979, he has been Rector of
St Mary Magdalene's Church, Dundee.

Eight detective novels have now been published:

Who killed Sophie Jack?
Murder Within Tent
Slaughter at the Polls
A Christmas Cracker
A Mishap in Majorca
A Prospect of Rye
Murder on the Mallaig Express
Buried in Baptism

Copies are available from:

**Meadowside Publications
14 Albany Terrace
Dundee DD3 6HR
Telephone 01382 223510**

**Further details can be obtained from our website:
http://www.crime-fiction.com**

BURIED
IN BAPTISM

A DETECTIVE NOVEL
BY
DAVID SHEPHERD

MEADOWSIDE PUBLICATIONS
DUNDEE
2006

Meadowside Publications
14 Albany Terrace, Dundee DD3 6HR

© *Meadowside Publications, 2006*

Printed by
Prontaprint,
Dundee, Scotland

*The Characters portrayed in this
novel are all imaginary and bear
no intended resemblance to any
person alive or dead.*

ISBN 978-0-9520632-7-8

Meadowside Crime
is a © imprint of
Meadowside Publications,
Dundee

CONTENTS

*The story is set in Grasshallows
in August, 1989.*

1. *A Child Of Our Time*

"I think I'll have Charles as a godparent. He's got the most gorgeous eyes . . . Makes me go weak at the knees . . ."

Sandra twirled her Biro thoughtfully over the form she was filling in. Her friend, Heidi, who was painting her nails deep crimson, looked up.

"Won't Jimmy be annoyed?"

"Oh, I'm having him as well. It says I can have up to three godparents. I'm going to have all my exes."

"Don't you think you should include your brother?"

Sandra scowled.

"Why should I? He never came to visit me in hospital. He didn't even send a card. When Mum told him I was pregnant, he said I should have an abortion. What sort of godfather would he be?"

Heidi blew on her nails.

"Well, he probably thought you were bringing the family into disrepute – having a baby and then refusing to marry the father . . ."

Sandra shook her head.

"I couldn't marry Ron. You know that. He's far too immature. He's got no thought of settling down."

"And yet you've put him down as the father! That's what you told the Registrar."

Sandra sighed.

"It's difficult to know which of them it was. It could have been any of them."

"You could always have a DNA test. Then you'd know."

"I'm not doing that. Just think! The test might prove it was Ron. Then where would I be?"

Heidi laughed.

"Much poorer."

"It's no laughing matter. I don't want any of them claiming Mark as their baby . . ."

"You still want to play the field?"

"I need time to let the whole thing settle down. To see which bloke I really want. Not which one is good for a one-nighter. I mean, if he pulls himself together, even Ron might be worth having."

"Stephanie told me he was thinking of joining the Army."

Sandra nodded.

"I know. The trouble is – he's just the type they're looking for. Strong, good-looking, enthusiastic. They're bound to take him."

"Then you'll be lumbered with Jimmy."

"He's unemployed."

"He's unemployable. Never gets up till lunchtime. He could never hold down a proper job."

"He's a good DJ. Everyone says so."

"Yes. But would he be a faithful husband? Could you trust him? He's always picking up birds at the disco. You know that." Heidi looked at her friend. She looked sad and disappointed. "Never mind," she said. "He always says he loves you most."

"He probably does."

"You've got to admit – you do encourage him."

Sandra laughed.

"I've got to keep all my balls in the air."

It was clear that Sandra's love life was in a mess. She had always had lots of boyfriends. In fact, never in her life had she been without them. Lads were always phoning her up to see if she was free to go out. She must be one of the most popular girls in Grasshallows.

It wasn't that she had the looks of a fashion model or the sex appeal of a movie star, but she was tall, slim, with short-cut gold hair. She had a fresh face, a warm smile and a good sense of humour. She was an attentive listener but also had a fund of racy jokes which could make people howl with laughter. She was fun to be with – and it was also said she was a fairly easy lay. So – she was extremely popular.

But having the baby had made a difference. There was no doubt about it. She couldn't hide the fact that she was pregnant – and some of the lads had shied off. That was the true test of loyalty – the faithful few who still went out with her in those final months before Mark was born.

Of course they didn't know whether the baby was theirs. But they kept in with the young mother-to-be for fear they might be accused of deserting their own child.

And there was another reason.

Sandra was Bert Stone's daughter. And you didn't offend a member of the Stone family.

If you did, you could be quite certain that one or more of the family might take it out on you some dark night.

The Stones were a formidable family in Grasshallows. They drank together, fought together, stuck together. The police were familiar figures on their doorsteps – charging various male members with being drunk and disorderly – or committing an assault.

So Sandra's friends continued to rally round, showing great interest in the baby, taking the young mother out – but at the same time wondering how, even at this late stage, they could avoid matrimony.

Sandra was conscious that, by joining the Army, Ron was ratting on her; but she took his decision in her stride. So long as he contributed sixty pounds a week in maintenance for young Mark, she would let him go. If he was in the Army, she would always know where to find him. He was a "convenient" father even if he was not yet a "desirable" husband.

Sandra fully intended to sow her wild oats for a little while longer; but her father had made it clear there must be no more mistakes like Mark. She must take proper precautions, or, as her brother had said, she would indeed bring shame and embarrassment to the whole family.

But Mark had not proved an embarrassment. He had been very popular. He was a quiet, good-looking baby. People kept staring at his small, pink face trying to decide which if any of his features was theirs. But at this stage, it was impossible to tell.

Now the moment had come for baptism – the first great public event in young Mark's life. The family would be arranging a special party at Uncle Tom's house. The blessings of Christianity would be bestowed on the baby at St Benedict's. People would then wet the baby's head with copious draughts of lager, heavy and bitter – with perhaps a generous measure of Famous Grouse or Johnny Walker thrown in. It would be a wonderful drunken binge.

The Church didn't mean much to the Stone family. But it was the "done thing" to have the kids baptized and the daughters married. It was a moment of lip service to higher things, imperfectly understood. A few quid would go into the collection plate. "Conscience money", Sandra's dad called it. But soon it would be forgotten in the welter of food and drink which followed.

Sandra was coming to the end of the form.

"Does Jimmy have any religious convictions?"

Heidi laughed.

"I think he once appeared in a juvenile court for pinching money from an alms box in St Benedict's!"

"Well, he should feel quite at home, visiting his old haunts."

Heidi did not think her friend was approaching the baptism with sufficient seriousness. She uttered a word of caution:

"I don't think any of them are suitable as godparents," she said.

"Who cares?" said Sandra. "It's only for a day!"

2. *See The Conquering Hero Comes*

The Reverend Blazer felt quite excited about the baptism. It would be his first. He had been appointed as Assistant Curate of St Benedict's in June and given full pastoral responsibility whilst the Rector was away. Canon Murray had gone off to the Mediterranean for a Hellenic cruise. Members of the Theological Faculty in the University would celebrate and preach whilst he was away. But this baptism was the first real piece of business that had come Edmund's way – and he was determined to make the most of it.

As soon as he heard about it, he went out to 28 Coronation Gardens to see the family. He chained his bicycle to the garden fence (after all, this was Henslea!); he took off his cycle clips

10

and knocked at the front door.

He received a warm welcome from Mr Stone.

"Come in, lad. We're glad to see you."

Mr Stone was particularly glad to see it was not Canon Murray. Many harsh words had passed between the two men and Bert had made many rash promises – none of which had been kept. This young man would know nothing of the family background.

He took him through to the living room and settled him down in a large, comfortable, leather armchair.

"The ladies'll be down in a minute. They're upstairs seeing to the baby." Bert Stone smiled cheerfully. "Can I get you a drink? A glass of my own home-made beer? Beautiful stuff. Go on – it'll put hairs on your chest."

The Reverend Blazer looked as if he could do with a few hairs on his chest.

Mr Stone carefully dispensed a pint glass of rich, succulent home-brew; but for himself, he opened a can of Carlsberg Special.

Edmund did not think to ask why – until he drank his first mouthful. The beer was immensely strong – very malty – and not particularly pleasant to drink. He had a few more sips and put the glass down on the table beside him.

"Do you make it in large quantities?" he asked politely.

"About five gallons at a time. I get the yeast from my work. When I've nothing else to do, I lay down a few jars. We use it mostly for parties," he added.

(In fact, they used it when people had got fairly tipsy and it wasn't worth wasting the good stuff . . . But he didn't say that.)

He looked at Mr Blazer speculatively. It could be quite a good wheeze getting the young reverend completely plastered.

Bert smiled at him warmly.

"You will be coming to the party, won't you?" he said. "It's at my brother Tom's house."

"You're having a party after the baptism?"

Such things were unknown in Mr Blazer's world. Canon Murray would never have been invited to any party given by the Stone family. Even had he been invited, he would have refused. The ensuing publicity would have been little short of disastrous.

"You'll be getting an invitation from Sandra."

"That's very kind."

"You're new to Grasshallows, I hear."

The Reverend Blazer gave Mr Stone a potted summary of his life which more than confirmed his naivety and inexperience.

By the time he had finished, Sandra and her mother were down with the baby.

Mr Blazer had never handled a baby before. In fact, he had rarely looked at one all that closely. But this being his first customer, he made sure he examined him with great interest.

He was small, pink, with a tiny button nose. The eyes were closed but he was told that they were blue.

"No," said Mrs Stone. "Grey. Just like his father."

She looked reproachfully at her husband.

Edmund gazed a little longer at the white woollen package with its placid, sleeping face – and asked the obvious question:

"And who is his father?"

Mrs Stone smiled.

"Ronald Middleton. Lovely lad. Comes from a good home. He's terribly proud of the baby. Comes over every day to see him."

Mr Stone tried not to choke on his beer.

Ron Middleton did not come from a good family. His parents were divorced and living with their partners. As for coming over to see the baby, they'd be lucky if they saw him more than once a week.

His wife's exaggerations bordered on total deceit.

Edmund suddenly became terribly serious.

"So you're not married?"

"Not yet," said Sandra sweetly.

"Didn't want to rush into it," said Bert.

"The baby came as a bit of a surprise," said Mrs Stone indulgently. "We thought it was better to wait till the baby was born before we got round to thinking about a wedding dress. Not easy getting married when you're six months gone."

The Reverend Blazer looked with warmth and compassion at

the young mother cradling her child in her arms. Of course she would want to look at her best on her wedding day. To avoid the shame of a large, unsightly bulge. Especially when she was so slim and elegant.

Sandra looked at him with a heart-melting smile which completely captivated Mr Blazer.

"Such a beautiful girl," he thought.

He hoped Mr Middleton was worthy of her.

Thinking that the two of them might be his first wedding couple, he said:

"But you will be getting married?"

"Of course," said Mrs Stone.

"Unless a better offer comes along!" said her husband.

"Oh, Dad! What a dreadful thing to say!"

Mr Stone got up and went off into the kitchen to get himself another can of Special.

"Drink up, lad," he urged. "Then I'll get you another."

Betty Stone looked anxious.

"Oh, he's not given you his home-brew, has he? It's very strong."

"I'm enjoying it," Edmund lied.

He continued to look adoringly at the daughter of the house in her white top and cherry pink trousers. She had such soft, gentle lips and wondrous grey eyes.

Mr Blazer was not quite sure yet what he was – straight or gay. But the sight of Sandra and her baby gave him a powerful impetus in the direction of heterosexuality.

"What are you calling the baby?" he asked.

"Mark," said Sandra, with a firm look at her mother which said quite clearly: "Don't mention the other names!"

"Oh, how splendid!" said Edmund. "Calling him after the first evangelist."

Sandra looked blank.

Mr Stone returned from the kitchen.

"The first what?"

"The first of the disciples to write a Gospel. Of course, *he* wasn't a disciple. But he wrote down what St Peter told him to write. In Rome," he added helpfully. "But many people think he was the young man in the garden who ran away with no clothes on."

Mr Stone began to wonder what sort of rubbish they taught people in theological colleges these days.

"Which garden?" he asked. "Not in ours, I hope. We don't want any young men running around naked in our patch! What'd the neighbours think?"

"Dad!"

The Reverend Blazer realized that the Stone family had very little knowledge of scripture. Points of detail which he took for granted obviously meant nothing to them. They probably thought he was trying to tell them he was gay. He blushed with embarrassment.

"It's an incident in the Bible. On the night before our Lord died, a young man was present in the Garden of Gethsemane where he was betrayed. The soldiers tried to seize him; but he escaped, leaving his clothes in their hands. Many people think that was St Mark."

Mr Stone took a swig of Carlsberg.

"Oh, I see," he said.

"But we're not calling him after him," said Mrs Stone. (As if they would ever call their grandchild after some unknown streaker.) "We're calling him after Mark Santer, the champion tennis-player. Sandra has a real soft spot for him, don't you, love?"

Sandra smiled another enigmatic smile.

"I don't know if he's going to be a tennis player."

"He's certainly not going to be a 'vangelist," said Mr Stone forcibly. "We're having none of that sort of thing round here!"

Sandra looked thoughtfully at Mr Blazer.

"You're not married, are you?"

The young clergyman blushed again.

"No."

"Any girlfriends?" asked Mrs Stone more indulgently.

"I had one at university; but she went abroad. We lost touch."

"What you need is a nice steady girl," said Betty Stone.

"Someone like Heidi," said Bert mischievously.

"No! Not someone like Heidi! She's a loose woman. Don't

listen to him!"

Mr Blazer returned to the business in hand.

"Now when were you thinking of having the baptism?"

"August 13th," said Mr Stone. "That's the only date our Tom can manage. We phoned round the family and that's the date that suits them."

"Is there anyone else being baptized on the 13th?"

"No. You're the only one."

"Have you had a lot of experience – baptizing babies?"

Mr Stone asked the question knowing full well what the answer would be.

"No. Actually, this will be my first baptism."

"You won't drop him, will you?" said Mrs Stone.

"I'll be very careful."

The young curate looked at Mark with great respect and pride. His first baptism. He was sure it would be a moving and uplifting experience.

"He's not heavy, is he?"

"Eleven pounds, four ounces," said Sandra. "We had him weighed this morning. He'll just fit into your arm. Would you like to practise holding him?"

Mr Blazer gathered the small package into the crook of his arm. The baby promptly – and audibly – filled his nappy.

"Better not do that on the day," said Mrs Stone.

Sandra made no effort to take Mark back, so Edmund sat there, staring down at the now malodorous infant.

He realized then – if he had not realized it before – that babies are not just sweetness and light.

"There's also the question of godparents," he said. "People normally have three. Two men and a woman for a boy; two women and a man for a girl. And they must all be practising members of the Church."

This was dangerous ground. Two of the godparents were lapsed Catholics and the other had vague Methodist connections through a grandmother.

Heidi? Well, Heidi was Jewish – a Jewish atheist. Less said about that, the better! To cover her embarrassment, Sandra made a big fuss taking the baby back from Edmund. Then she smiled sweetly.

"I was wondering if I could have four godparents. Three men and a woman. Would that be all right?"

The Reverend Blazer was delighted.

"Of course," he said. "If you want four, you must have four."

"That's the spirit!" said Mr Stone. "The more the merrier! Drink up your beer, young man, and I'll get you another."

Edmund smiled politely.

"No. I'm fine."

But was he? At one end, he felt light-headed. At the other, a tingling sensation which suggested rapidly approaching diarrhoea. Certainly a quick departure was required – before he disgraced himself. He could hardly ask the Stones to use their toilet.

But Betty Stone sensed his embarrassment.

"If you've got the runs, you can use our bathroom. It's upstairs on the left." She laughed. "We know what Dad's booze can do to people."

Mr Blazer thanked her for her kindness – and within a few moments he was obliged to take advantage of her offer.

Whilst he was upstairs, Mr Stone chuckled.

"Got a weak bladder has our Edmund!"

Mrs Stone upbraided him.

"You didn't ought to have given him that home-made stuff. You know what it does to people. Poor lad, he could have had an accident."

Sandra didn't say anything. She knew her dad liked playing tricks on people. Especially the young and gullible. She continued to cradle the baby in her arms.

"D'you think there'll be any trouble over the godparents? Jimmy's a Catholic; and so's Ron."

Mr Stone winked.

"What the eye don't see, the heart don't grieve over. So far as we're concerned, they're all good Protestants. Pillars of the Church of England." He belched loudly. "If they keep their mouths shut, he'll never know."

The Reverend Blazer came downstairs feeling much better. But he didn't sit down again, even though Mr Stone pressed him to have another half pint – and Mrs Stone, to have a nice cup of tea. Even Sandra's obvious charms failed to detain him.

"I'm sorry," he said. "I must go and say Evensong."

Mr Stone admired his devotion. At this time of day, most lads of his age would be stopping off for a pint and a game of snooker. But he was going off to sing for his supper.

"Well," he said, putting a reassuring arm round Edmund's shoulders, "remember this, lad. You're always welcome round here – any time you want. You can come and have a bite with us, see the baby, have a pint. We're really glad it's you who's doing the service. We'll all be there on the thirteenth."

The Reverend Blazer put on his cycle clips and once again felt an unpleasant tingling in his loins. Very quickly, he leapt on his bike and, with a final wave, cycled rapidly down Coronation Gardens, hoping against hope that he would reach the church in time. He made a mental note never to touch Mr Stone's home-made beer again.

3. *Love Of Three Oranges*

When Sandra returned her form to the church, she enclosed a stunning photograph of herself and the baby. The overpowering sensuality of this picture proved highly distracting to Edmund. He placed the photograph on his desk and as he worked away, his eyes constantly flickered in its direction.

Therefore, the contents of the baptismal form did not receive quite the scrutiny they deserved. The religious allegiance of the godparents – and the inclusion of Miss Heidi Houston – were all open to question. But love is blind . . .

When she was told that her name had been included, Heidi was horrified. "But I've already told you – I don't want to be a godmother! You know what I'm like. Everyone knows what I'm like. Even your dad calls me a 'corrupting influence'!"

"He should know!"

"So he should. I haven't forgotten that kiss under the

mistletoe last Christmas. Lifted me right out of my high heels!"

Sandra smiled.

"He hasn't forgotten about it either. He keeps telling people."

"Perhaps I'll get another at the party?"

"Better not let Mum see you. She'd blow her top."

Heidi smiled.

"I promise to be good."

"That'll be the day!"

"Wait till the Reverend Blazes sees me in my low-cut, gold dress with everything peeking out! Wait till he smells my 100% perfume! He's going to be absolutely knocked out."

Sandra laughed.

"It'll make Karl jealous."

(Karl was Heidi's current boyfriend.)

"It'll make him bloody furious."

"Well, I'm wearing my black lace outfit. Fish-net stockings and the six-inch heels."

"At the church? You can't."

"Well, I'm thinking about the party afterwards. I want to make sure they look at me as a woman – not a mother. I want to get all their hormones bubbling. This is my big comeback."

Heidi shook her head.

"This is bad news for Mr Blazes."

"Blazer!" said Sandra. "Edmund Blazer."

"Oh, we're on first name terms, are we?"

"Almost."

"And what are Charles, Ron and Jimmy going to say about that?"

"I think he's quite sweet. I've never had a clergyman before." She smiled dreamily. "I want to see if he can resist temptation." She laughed. "I think he's already beginning to crumble . . ."

"And you call me a 'corrupting influence'?"

"You know, he was very good with Mark. A natural. Of course he pooped the moment he got hold of him; but he sat there as if nothing had happened. He's a really good-natured bloke, but he needs to live a bit. I've sent him my photograph."

Heidi shook her head again.

"This baptism has all the makings of a first-class disaster. You're letting a Daniel loose in a den of lions. The Stones will eat him for breakfast. And if my Karl lays into him, he'll be carried out horizontal."

"Well," said Sandra, "we want a bit of fun. As long as they don't lay him out before the baptism . . . It doesn't matter what happens afterwards. I can be discreet. I can keep my mouth shut."

"That'll be the first time."

"Don't spoil it," said Sandra. "If I want to have a little cuddle with Edmund, I shall. But you'll have to cover for me. Tell them I'm breast-feeding – or something."

"Breast-feeding the vicar?"

"What I do with him's my business. He may turn out to be quite hopeless . . . On the other hand . . ." She looked out of the window, still daydreaming.

Heidi decided to bring her down to earth.

"Is he going to pay £60 a week for Mark?"

Sandra laughed.

"He could make a contribution."

"I don't see why not, " said Heidi. "Everyone else is!"

4. *Water Music*

Sunday August 13th dawned bright and sunny. It had all the makings of a perfect summer's day.

The Reverend Edmund Blazer had read through all his notes on "Baptism" and rehearsed the ceremony several times in his mind. He could scarcely wait to perform his first act of initiation.

Once he had got rid of the morning congregation with the visiting preacher and celebrant, he felt very much in command. He lit the paschal candle, poured about five gallons of water into the mediaeval font, made sure there were at least one hundred orders of service, not forgetting a large brass collection plate beside the door.

He put on his beautiful, snow-white cotta, hemmed with at least six inches of lace, and then an embroidered gold stole. Although he was only a deacon, he wore it like a priest. It looked better that way.

He placed a neatly-ironed purificator on the edge of the font together with a large scallop shell with which to administer the sacramental gift of holy water. Then he genuflected twice in front of the Lady Chapel aumbry before extracting the oil for chrism. He looked round carefully to make sure everything was ready. It was.

Long before the magic hour of one o'clock, Edmund was at the door to welcome his congregation. But they showed a strange reluctance to come inside.

He reckoned it was probably because it was a warm afternoon and it was more pleasant standing on the grass. Besides, many of them were smoking. Edmund wondered if there was any rule preventing people from smoking in a graveyard.

There were quite a lot of children, he noticed. About nine or ten of them – two in fluorescent pink and green dresses with red, heart-shaped sunglasses. They seemed to be totally out of control. Where were their parents?

Mr Stone was the first to make a move towards the church. He was in a smart blue suit with a rather racy pink tie depicting Marilyn Monroe at her famous moment in "The Seven Year Itch." Underneath was the motto: "Nihil Carborundum Illegitimae", which even Edmund, with his poor grasp of Latin, could easily translate.

Mr Stone came forward with a cheesy grin.

"I need a slash."

"A slash?"

"The little boys' room."

Edmund still looked quite blank.

"The toilet, you jerk!"

"Oh, yes – if you come this way."

He led Mr Stone across to the south aisle to the choir vestry where there was a rather antiquated lavatory.

When he returned to the church, he was pleased to note that members of the Stone clan were beginning to drift into the building. Unfortunately, that included the two girls with the fluorescent dresses who were running up and down the north aisle, screaming. The smaller one had a particularly piercing shriek.

Edmund tried to round them up but they ran away in the direction of the high altar – still screaming.

"What wonderful acoustics you have!" said a tall young man in a grey suit.

Edmund comforted himself with his Lord's command that one should not rebuke the little children – but it was difficult not to think they would benefit from a clip round the ear.

A young man with long hair walked past, listening intently to his Walkman. Even five feet away, one could hear the thudding bass.

"This is a church!" said Edmund.

"Get lost!" said the youth.

Two of the ladies stopped to admire the lace on his cotta. "It must have cost you a great deal."

"About seventy pounds," said Edmund modestly.

"Bloody poof!" said a rather macho young thug with tattoos on both arms.

Edmund was beginning to get a trifle worried. They didn't seem a very devout congregation. He had expected them to be respectful, passive, appreciative; but, if anything, they seemed rather aggressive.

An elderly woman pressed a plastic bottle into his hands.

"Water from the River Jordan," she said.

"What d'you expect me to do with it?"

"Baptize the baby with it!"

Edmund was affronted.

"Certainly not! It might contain cholera – or some other impurity."

"Father Ryan always uses it at the Catholic Church."

"Well, we're not Catholics!"

The woman standing beside her said: "Don't argue with her! She's blind. And her son died in the Falklands!"

Edmund looked acutely embarrassed and twisted the bottle of water round and round in his hands wondering where he could lose it. He turned away.

"What a liar you are, Cis!" said the "blind" woman. "Fancy telling all those porkies to the minister!"

The Reverend Blazer returned despairingly to the font where he was accosted by a small man with a black beard, clutching a video camera.

"Where d'you want me to stand?"

"To stand?"

"I'm the video man."

The video man!

This was a horrifying prospect. This man was intending to film the baptism. If anything went wrong, the evidence would be there for all to see. He could be a laughing stock. Edmund was sure Canon Murray would not permit a video to be used during a service.

"Have you done this before?"

The man grinned.

"Hundreds of times. I'm from Munn's, the Photographers."

It meant nothing to Edmund.

"Well . . ." he said anxiously.

"If you make any boobs, we'll split the £250."

The video man winked maliciously.

"The £250?"

"Send it to ITV. 'You've Been Framed'. They'll love it."

"You can't do that!"

This was even worse. The whole nation . . .

He was interrupted by a distant metallic crash – followed by screams from near the high altar.

Edmund put down the bottle of water and hurried down the aisle.

One of the little girls had undone the catch holding the processional cross in position. It had fallen – but fortunately (or unfortunately, depending on your point of view) it had missed both the children.

Two of the chancel tiles were badly cracked and the little brass Christ was split in two. It seemed a fearsome omen.

"She did it!"

"No, I didn't."

Silently – sadly – Edmund picked up the cross, put it back in its holder and picked up the broken fragments. The children, cowed by his silence, ran back to their mother.

Things were going from bad to worse.

As he returned to the west end of the church, he noticed someone lighting a cigarette from the paschal candle.

He flew over to the offender.

"Put that out immediately! This is a church!"

"- - - - off!"

Mrs Stone smiled indulgently.

"It's a bad habit. He's tried to give it up – but he can't."

"Well, he can go outside and smoke!"

Edmund was almost in tears.

"Best to say nothing," said Mrs Stone. "You wouldn't want to provoke a fight."

"A fight?"

"Some people burn on a very short fuse."

Mr Stone was once more at his side.

"Don't you have any lavatory paper in this place?"

Lavatory paper!

Mr Stone kept a straight face. "Had to use a few sheets of music," he said. "Hope it doesn't matter."

Mrs Stone saw the look on Edmund's face.

"He's joking, love! Don't take him seriously."

Edmund relaxed.

He looked round anxiously.

"Is the baby not here yet?"

Mr Stone looked towards the door.

"No. Sandra's always late. She'll be doing her make-up or changing her dress. Could be another ten minutes."

Could he endure another ten minutes?

Would the church survive another ten minutes of the Stone family?

Two children were climbing over the stone effigy of Blessed William of Grasshallows.

But before he could haul them down, there was a deep blast

of a trombone on the sixteen foot pedal of the recently restored organ. The blast was followed by several others. Two boys were sitting at the console, pulling out the stops and pressing the pedals.

Edmund marched with grim determination up to the organ.

"Get off the organ immediately!"

"I play the organ," said the youngest boy.

"He's got a Yamaha," said the other.

"Get out!"

"We're not doing anything wrong!"

Any thought of child protection had quite departed from Edmund's mind. He dragged the boys kicking and screaming off the organ and threw them out of the organ box. He was helped by Mr Stone who twisted their ears with sadistic pleasure.

"You godless little bastards!"

"I'll tell my dad on you!"

Edmund switched off the organ and breathed a sigh of relief that no damage had been done.

Whilst he was busy at the organ, Cis recovered her bottle of water from the River Jordan and poured it into the font. It left a slightly oily swirl.

"Must have been the olive oil," she said.

Edmund returned to find not only polluted water but also a dog end and cigarette ash in the baptismal shell. Someone had also taken the silver container with the oil of chrism.

He could not control himself. He began to weep. Everything was completely out of control. He took the shell away to get rid of its vile contents and give it a clean wash.

Whilst he was away, Sandra arrived with the baby and Heidi. As promised, she was wearing a black lace, see-through dress, fish-net tights and very high heels. Heidi was in her low-cut, ankle-length, gold dress. Her cleavage left very little to the imagination.

The baby, Mark, was completely eclipsed by these two young women. He was wearing a sailor suit and blue sandals. He was smiling and bubbling happily.

"I gave him a small dose of valium before we set out."

24

"That should keep him quiet."

When Edmund emerged with his pristine baptismal shell, things seemed to have settled down. Everyone was crowding round the baby. Edmund handed out the service sheets and encouraged everyone to gather round the font.

"Godparents?" he shouted. "The godparents over here."

The tall young man in the grey suit took his place.

"I'm Charles – and this is Ron."

"Pleased to meet ya."

Ron was a tall, wholesome young man with a dumb face and bright blue eyes.

" . . . and Jimmy."

Jimmy was the long-haired youth who had been listening intently to his Walkman. He was wearing dark glasses so it was impossible to see his eyes.

He was also chewing gum. More alarming was his T shirt, emblazoned with the word "Satan" and sporting a horned, grinning devil in bright scarlet.

Edmund smiled a false smile.

"Cool!" said Jimmy.

Whether he was speaking to the curate or describing Heidi was not clear. But she swept into position beside the font rather as the Queen of Sheba must have swept into the court of King Solomon.

"I'm Heidi," she said.

Edmund was overwhelmed by her striking appearance. He was also intoxicated by her perfume. Gusts of it enveloped the entire congregation.

"What have you got on, babe?"

"A touch of Jungle, big man."

"It smells like at least half a bottle."

"Near enough." Heidi glowed. "But it's a deeply spiritual occasion, isn't it, Mr Blazer?"

She gave him one of her dark knowing looks.

"I hope so," he muttered.

In fact, Edmund was beyond caring. He felt totally demoralized. Terrified of what was to come. The unsuitability of the godparents was only too plain.

A small girl handed back his silver vessel containing the oil. "It's not lip salve!" she said accusingly. "It tastes horrible!" A little boy tugged at his stole.

"Are you an angel. Mister?"

The red light appeared on the video camera. The bearded man smiled.

"Camera's rolling!" he said.

5. *The Rite Of Spring*

Whether it was the presence of the video camera or not, the Stone family instantly became more orderly – and concentrated on the service. Even the children were better behaved.

Edmund swallowed nervously.

"You have brought this child to baptism . . ."

Why? Why? Why? he wondered.

He reeled off the duties of parents and godparents. Things he was sure they would never do.

"It is your duty to bring up this child to follow Christ. Are you willing?"

The godparents replied: "We are willing."

"Liars!" thought Edmund.

But they listened to his words and joined in the prayer. There were no giggles, no wisecracks, nothing embarrassing. He could hardly believe his luck.

He reached the baptismal promises.

"Do you turn to Christ?"

Edmund looked at the T shirt with Satan.

"I turn to Christ."

"Do you repent of your sins?"

This came as a bit of a shock to the godparents. Hell, no, they quite enjoyed their sins. The baby was the living proof of their collective guilt. Ron shuffled his feet. Jimmy, being a Catholic, was used to perjury. Charles looked at Heidi as if she was the most notorious sinner present. But Heidi held her head up high. If she was going to be a godmother, she would act her part to

26

perfection. Sins? What sins? Sandra looked at her father with an indulgent smile.

There was a rather ragged reply to the question.

"I repent of my sins."

"And do you renounce evil?"

No problem there. Everyone would happily renounce evil. Sin was fun – but real evil, as purveyed by Stalin, Hitler, the SS and the IRA – sure, they were against it. So, with full confidence, they were able to say: "I renounce evil."

The Reverend Blazer moved on to the blessing of the water. He knew that, being a deacon, he wasn't supposed to bless anything. That was a job for a priest. But, in for a penny . . . He blessed the water, noting the oily swirl – and wondered where it had come from. He confronted Heidi who was now holding the baby.

"Name this child."

"Mark Charles Ronald James."

The baby was looking very peaceful in its drug-induced sleep – with its head on one side, close to Heidi's right breast. Edmund's eyes were more on the breast than on the baby.

He pulled himself together.

This was not the moment to be entertaining carnal thoughts. He took the child into his arms. It seemed heavier than he had expected. He held the infant tight and carried it over to the font.

This was the dangerous bit. Any slip now . . . He mustn't drop the baby . . . Everything must be done with dignity . . . He hoped the baby wouldn't poop – or cry. But Mark was well and truly sedated. He sleepwalked into his Christian inheritance.

Edmund poured scoops of water three times over the baby's forehead.

"Mark Charles Ronald James, I baptize you . . ."

So far, so good.

No chance of drying the baby's forehead. The purificator had fallen into the font. He tried to open the silver vessel containing the oil with one hand. It was awkward but he did it.

"I sign you with the sign of the cross."

He remembered being warned that if the baby moved his head, there was every danger of implanting a swastika rather

27

than a cross. But Mark did not move. There was a warm, contented smile on his face.

And so, back to Heidi.

Their heads were close. His arm brushed against that magnificent right breast. He was conscious of it; so was she. Her perfume was overpowering.

And now for the candle . . .

Where was the candle? Panic! It should have been sitting next to the paschal candle. Had it been stolen?

He coughed apologetically.

"Has anyone seen the baptismal candle?"

An unknown child came forward and sheepishly handed over the box and candle.

"Thank you," he said.

"Little thief!" he thought.

He lit the candle and went over to Sandra. Another heart-melting moment. The soft, pink lips, the grey eyes, the perfect face. Madonna and child.

He put the candle into her right hand.

"Receive this light. This is to show that Mark . . ."

Pause to get it right.

" . . . Mark Charles Ronald James has passed from darkness into light."

And so to the concluding prayers and blessing.

Without a hitch.

The Reverend Blazer breathed a sigh of relief. At least the service had gone all right.

Mr Stone echoed his feelings.

"Well done, lad! You did him proud!"

Everyone gave him a round of applause. Even the babes in arms stopped nibbling the service sheets and waved their tiny limbs enthusiastically.

Sandra kissed all the godparents. Heidi handed over the baby thankfully to his grandmother. Edmund encouraged the young thief to blow out the paschal candle. She succeeded at the third blow.

The video man switched off his camera.

"Well done!" he said. "That was good!"

Edmund began to feel proud. Perhaps it hadn't been such a disaster after all?

"Lovely service. Of course, Canon Murray doesn't allow video cameras into the church . . . Can't see why not . . . Splendid advertisement for the old heap! That's what I say!"

Edmund smiled shyly.

At least he would not be embarrassed even if Canon Murray did see the video.

But perhaps he congratulated himself too soon. The children had now reverted to type and were once again shouting and screaming. They had turned the service sheets into paper aeroplanes and were hurling them down the aisle.

Heidi came up to him.

"Have you ever had a woman?"

"Er . . . no."

"But you'd like to, wouldn't you?"

Her eyes twinkled with mischief.

"Of course you would. You're a very passionate person. We must get together and talk about it."

With that, she slipped away.

Sandra was even more direct.

She put her arms round Edmund's neck and gave him a big kiss.

"That was great!" she said. "You took the service beautifully. I knew you would." She looked at the baby nestling in her mother's arms. "Wasn't he good? Didn't even cry." (She said nothing about the valium.)

Close behind her was her brother – a ferocious young man.

"It's a disgrace!" he said. "A bloody disgrace! This baby should never have been baptized."

A little earlier, Edmund would have been inclined to agree with him but now he was not so sure. Sandra was a devoted mother.

She turned on her brother.

"Shut up. Alec! If I hear another word, I'll put Karl on to you."

As if to prove her point, the rather unpleasant skinhead with tattoos on both arms, appeared suddenly at his side. He caught the flash of a knife.

29

Mrs Stone had been right to warn him of the dangers of violence – even at a baptism.

Edmund turned away and spoke to the godparents.

Rather hypocritically, he said: "It's nice to have you here at St Benedict's."

Jimmy stopped chewing his gum.

"Last time I was here, mate, I was lifted. I got a year's probation for breaking into those alms boxes."

He resumed chewing his gum.

Edmund turned to Ron.

"I hear you're off to join the Army."

Ron grinned.

"Time for a sharp exit!"

Edmund was disappointed.

"I was hoping you might be my first wedding."

(Though, of course, after the baptism, he was not quite so sure.)

Ron sneered.

"Not if I can help it."

"But you are the father of the baby."

"Am I?"

Edmund was confused.

Charles came to his aid.

"Sandra doesn't know who the father is. It could be any of us. That's why she chose all three of us as godparents. She wants all of us to play our part."

"Well, you can play your part. I'm going!"

The Reverend Blazer felt terribly disillusioned.

"I can't believe it . . . I didn't think . . ."

Ron poked him in the stomach.

"The trouble is . . . you don't know the Stone family. You're a newcomer to Grasshallows . . ."

Charles added: "You've a lot to learn."

Edmund felt shattered. It was bad enough not to be marrying the baby's father. But not even to know who the father was! He felt betrayed. Cheated. He should have been told. Not knowing this had made him look a complete fool.

He went over to Mr Stone to give him a strong piece of his mind.

"Mr Stone . . ."

But as he spoke, there occurred one of those little tragedies which can mar any public occasion. A young man in a black suit collapsed. He had been looking a little bit strange during the service – his eyes rolling and his mouth twisting. Now he had had a fit and was foaming at the mouth.

Edmund turned to see what had happened.

"Epilepsy," said Bert Stone. "Had it for years."

He looked contemptuously at the Reverend Blazer. "Why don't you go and lay hands on him?"

"Lay hands?"

"Heal him. Give him a faith-healing touch."

"How?"

"Your boss did it."

"Canon Murray?"

"No. The Big One – upstairs."

Edmund looked helplessly at the poor man.

"You could at least say a prayer with him!"

Edmund turned in anger. He felt Mr Stone was yet again taking the mickey out of him.

"Look here!" he said.

But Bert was busy taking a swig out of a silver hip flask. "Want a drink?"

"No."

Mr Stone screwed back the top.

"See you at the party."

He walked off.

Edmund was left with the two women and the man who was lying flat out on the cold stone floor. He offered to get him some water, but was told it was not necessary. It was only a question of time before he came round. To be helpful, he held one of his hands and, in the quiet of his mind, he offered up a rather garbled prayer.

It was amazing how quiet the building was now that everyone had gone. A blessed calm which made the baptism seem like a bad dream.

Whilst he was kneeling on the floor, Edmund ran through his mind all the things he had to do. Empty the font. Put the oil

31

back in the aumbry. Take the broken pieces of the brass Christ to the jeweller to see if it could be repaired.

He must put away the service sheets which had not been nibbled. Collect all the paper aeroplanes. Put the collection in the safe.

He had heard all the coins rattling in the collection plate. (Always a bad sign!) Probably there would be a lot of coppers and five penny pieces. It might not even cover the cost of the candle and the baptismal certificate. It was certainly a lot of work for very little. He wished now that he had said: "No." Not been so eager. Truly, it had been a baptism of fire.

The poor man eventually opened his eyes and looked around him.

"Took a turn, did I?"

"Now, Eric, just wait a minute. Take your time."

Slowly, he was helped to his feet and over to the door. Edmund saw him safely out of the building; then he returned to the collection plate.

It was empty.

He knew money had been given; but someone had swiped the lot. He walked back to the font. To his disgust, a small paper boat was floating on the water. Savagely, he crunched up the boat and pulled out the plug. The oily water drained away.

He was no longer hurt; he was angry. Why had they done all this to him? The whole thing had been a mockery. Both he and God had been treated with complete contempt.

A final indignity awaited him. The paschal candle had been nicked! There was the stand – but no candle. He looked at it with cold fury.

He had already decided that he would not go to the baptismal party. As if he would wish to spend any more time with such dreadful people! But these final blows to his pride made him change his mind. He would not let them get away with it. He would go and tell them exactly what he thought of them. Especially Mr Stone. He would find out who had stolen the collection and the paschal candle. Honour demanded that he should get them back. If not . . . if not . . . he would go to the police.

6. *Orpheus In The Underworld*

There was no doubting where the party was being held. For as soon as you entered Harrogate Drive – one of the more select havens of the nouveau riche in Grasshallows – you could choose to follow either your nose or your ears. An entrancing smell of grilled meat wafted down the road; and the steady thump of a disco guided you in as surely as a flightpath leads directly to the runway. As you got closer, the sound of children screaming and the swaying turrets of a bouncy castle brought you right up to the front door.

It was an impressive house set in a large area of lawn and trees. The contrast between this and the council house in Coronation Gardens could not have been more marked. Uncle Tom was obviously a great deal richer than his brother – and much more generous with his hospitality.

The first thing that Edmund noticed was the table of drinks on the patio. They were being served by waiters in white jackets. The barbecue, which was going full blast outside the double garage, was being supervised by a portly man wearing a red cummerbund. Flags and pennants were fluttering all the way up the drive. Baskets of fuchsias and petunias hung at every corner of the house. There were happy sounds of laughter and glasses clinking – obviously a very successful party on a beautiful summer's day.

Edmund hesitated.

Was this the place – or the time – to create a scene? To start shouting the odds about a stolen collection or a missing candle? Perhaps they didn't really matter that much.

He made his way up the drive. As he reached the house, a grey-haired man in a blue shirt came out to meet him.

"Father Blazer, how good to meet you! So glad you could come." He smiled a warm welcome. "I'm Sandra's uncle Tom."

Edmund shook his hand warmly.

"Service didn't go too badly, did it?"

"Well . . ."

"I know, I know. Some of the family are complete peasants! Their children quite uncontrollable. Didn't do any damage, I hope?"

Uncle Tom was used to dealing with the general public; buttering up important people, calming ruffled feathers and settling disputes before they reached the point of open violence.

The Reverend Blazer found himself telling Uncle Tom about the cross, the candle and the collection plate.

Uncle Tom immediately reached into his back pocket and pulled out his wallet.

"Would a hundred pounds cover it?"

"More than."

"Take it, lad. And don't worry any more about it."

He pushed five twenty pound notes into the curate's hand. "Now take your jacket off and relax." His eyes twinkled. "I know there's at least one young lady in there dying to meet you."

It was always a good policy to make young people feel they were the centre of romantic attention. If all else failed, one of the waitresses might give him a cuddle.

Edmund thanked him effusively.

"Don't say any more about it. Come in and meet the family. Grace will get you a drink. What's it to be?"

"A gin and tonic?"

"A gin and tonic for the Reverend, Grace. Plenty of ice."

Edmund found himself swept into the house on a wave of goodwill.

"And this is my brother, Raymond, and his good lady. Works for the Post Office. A shop steward. Strong Labour man . . ."

* * * *

Ron threw back the last of a pint of lager.

"Your pin-up's arrived!"

"My pin-up?"

"The vicar."

"Oh, Edmund, you mean. He's not my pin-up. You are. I'm looking forward to seeing you in uniform. Will you be wearing a kilt?"

"Not in the Middlesex."

"You might have been better in a Scottish regiment. You have the legs for it."

"Among other things!" said Heidi cynically.

"So what's the attraction of this vicar, then?" asked Ron. "Your dad told me you'd sent him your photograph."

"No, it was a photograph of Mark. I thought he'd like it. It was his first baptism, you know. Very special."

"You're not thinking of marrying him?"

"Good heavens, no! I'm not marrying anyone. I told you."

Ron looked sly.

"Well, if I'm paying for the baby, I shall expect a few backhanders."

"You'll get them!" said Heidi. "No doubt about that."

Sandra radiated love and affection.

"When you're settled in Germany, Mark and I'll come over and spend a week with you."

"That should be a right turn-off!" thought Heidi.

Ron said: "Your vicar friend seemed to think we were getting married."

"I'm sure he'd love to do it."

Ron was suspicious.

"Have you told him something you haven't told me?"

"I told him what I told you. We both need time."

Ron smiled to himself.

"You've got all the time in the world."

He turned on his heel and went off to the bar.

"He's ratting," said Heidi. "Definitely ratting."

Sandra nodded.

"I know."

* * * *

The waitress came up to Bert Stone with a tray of food.

"Well, Grace, fancy seeing you here! Just like old times."

"Canapés, sir."

"Hors d'oeuvres'd be more up your street."

Bert laughed.

Grace eyed him coldly.

"There's no need to be nasty."

"I was just remembering our happy times together."

"There weren't any happy times!" Grace looked around to make sure no-one was listening. "You raped me, you bastard!"

Bert laughed scornfully.

"Raped you? You were gagging for it."

If Grace could have thrown the tray of canapés at him, she would have done. Her hands were shaking. "You know it was rape, you dirty pig! I was going to go to the police, but you begged me not to . . . for the sake of your wife and family. Ugh! What a fool I was."

"It could have ruined your reputation."

"They would have put you where you belonged. In jail."

Bert was forgiving.

"You and I should get together again."

"No, thank you. I'm happier on my own. More than you'll ever be."

"It's never too late to kindle an old flame."

"You'll get your come-uppance one of these days, Bert Stone. You mark my words. You'll go too far. And when you do, I hope they castrate you – like a pig!"

She turned on her heel and moved on to the next guest.

"Canapés, sir."

Bert was licking his fingers.

"Thank you, Grace – you old cow!"

* * * *

Uncle Tom was moving through the downstairs rooms, trying to be the perfect host. Mrs Stone was walking up and down nursing the baby. Uncle Tom came up to her.

"Perfect baby. Never made a sound."

"It's not surprising he's quiet . . . she drugged him before he went to the church."

"Drugged him? How stupid can you get?"

"I didn't know what she was doing. She put it in his milk."

"Will it do him any damage?"

"I hope not. He's beginning to open his eyes. There!"

Mark opened his eyes and managed a faint smile.

Uncle Tom looked across the room to where Sandra was talking to Ron.

"The sooner she gets married, the better."

"But not to him."

"He seems a nice lad."

"Too young. Too immature. Besides, he's going into the Army."

Uncle Tom had strong views about that; but, being the perfect host, he didn't say a word. Instead, he asked: "Have you had anything to drink?"

"Just a Bacardi and Coke."

"Would you like another?"

"Not just yet."

Uncle Tom bent closer over the baby and held his hand.

"Hello, you little fellow. Waking up?" To the grandmother he said: "Any chance of us getting together later?"

Betty Stone looked round the crowded room.

"We'll see."

* * * *

Fortified by two gin and tonics, Edmund tackled Mr Stone.

"You deceived me!"

"In what way?"

"You told me that Ron Middleton was the father of the baby."

"So he is. If you go down to the Registrar's, you'll see his name on the birth certificate."

"But he says no one knows who the father is."

"It's ninety per cent certain. She was with him more than any of the others. He was quite willing to put his name to it. And he's paying maintenance."

"He also says he's got no intention of marrying Sandra."

"Hope for you yet!" said Mr Stone sarcastically.

"But you told me that they would be getting married."

"No, I didn't. I said: 'Unless a better offer comes along.'

37

Perhaps it will."

He looked speculatively at Mr Blazer. No, he could never tolerate this creep as his son-in-law.

"And then, the godparents! I've just discovered that two of them are Roman Catholics!"

"Are they?"

"Lapsed Roman Catholics!" said Mr Blazer emphatically.

"Doesn't matter to me."

"But they're supposed to be practising members of the Church. The Church of England. That's why they're godparents."

"I don't think they're practising members of anything . . ."

Mr Stone cast an eye over to Jimmy who had taken off his shirt and was working hard at the disco.

" . . . but they're good lads. All three of them."

"And Miss Houston's Jewish!"

"Who told you all this?"

"Your brother, Raymond."

"Oh, you shouldn't listen to him. He just opens his mouth and lets his belly rumble."

"She's not even a Christian!"

"She's a bloody good kisser!" Mr Stone laughed crudely. "You try her and see. I saw you ogling her during the service."

Edmund blushed.

"I think you've made a complete mockery of the Church and everything it stands for."

Bert sneered.

"You've got your money. What more d'you want?"

* * * *

Lapsed Catholic or no, Jimmy was enjoying himself immensely. The DJ is always the star of the show. All the girls come his way. The disco had been set up outside the French windows and was now blasting out over the lawn. Jimmy was on to his third pint, sorting out the tracks he was going to use later. Heidi brought him a plate of goodies.

"Thanks, babe. How's it going?"

"Fine."

"Love the dress."

* * * *

Inside the sitting room, one of the little boys who had been hammering the church organ suddenly caught sight of the Reverend Blazer. He turned to his friend who was scoffing a hot dog.

"Here's that man from the church! You better hide that candle."

The boy stuffed the rest of the hot dog into his mouth, picked up the paschal candle with greasy hands smeared with tomato ketchup and shoved it under the sofa.

* * * *

Uncle Donald was relaxing in a large armchair surrounded by several middle-aged women. Donald was Bert's other brother.

"Of course, I was married in St Benedict's."

"No, you weren't!" said his wife. "We were married at the Registry Office. You were divorced."

Uncle Donald pronged a large piece of grilled steak into his mouth.

"I was referring to my first marriage."

"That didn't last long!"

"Weren't you divorced twice?" asked one of the women.

"Mental cruelty, wasn't it?"

His wife sighed sadly.

"Tell me about it!"

Uncle Donald turned to the waiter.

"Get me another pint of bitter."

"That's your fourth!"

"Third, my dear."

His wife shook her head.

"The whole family are complete liars."

* * * *

Karl was also drinking heavily. There was nothing else to do. Heidi was busy with Sandra, making a fuss of the baby. It was not his scene.

He had a plate of sausages, steak and chips and a large iced lager. He was sitting at the dining room table on his own. He looked a complete misfit.

Charles, conscious of his responsibilities as a godfather, went over to him.

"I don't think we've been introduced."

Karl looked up at him. Bloody patronizing git! A toff in a smart grey suit.

But at least he was trying to be friendly. More than could be said for the rest of them.

He put out a large hand with the fingers tattooed LOVE and HATE. They shook hands. Charles sat down.

"You seem to like tattoos?"

"Had it done when I was in the Army."

"Really? Are you still in the Army?" Charles looked at the combat gear.

"No. I left a couple of years ago."

"What are you doing now?"

"Labouring. What are you doing?"

"I work in a bank. Barclays."

"And you're a friend of Sandra?"

Charles nodded.

"We've known each other since we were at school."

He looked at Karl.

"Where d'you come from?"

"Leeds."

"And you're Heidi's boyfriend?"

Karl's eyes lit up.

"Sure! Great girl! Real class."

"To you, perhaps!" thought Charles. "Down here, she's the sort of girl most mothers warn us about. Keep away from her! She's trouble."

40

"How long have you been going out?"

"'Bout eight weeks. Since I came down here. I met her and Sandra at Jimmy's disco."

"Oh, yes; great place."

"You've been there?"

"Once or twice."

At which point, the conversation faltered. There was not much in common between them. The silence was embarrassing. Karl looked at his plate – then at Charles.

"Aren't you having any nosh?"

"Yes. I suppose I should."

It was as good an excuse as any to get away.

* * * *

Bert Stone was in the kitchen, pouring out a glass of home-made beer for Eric. He had assured him that it had great medicinal properties – especially for those suffering from epilepsy. He looked forward to the results with cruel relish.

Cis, the friend of the woman who had supplied the water from the River Jordan, was getting her "blind" friend a glass of orange juice.

"I do like your tie."

"Got it for my birthday."

"It's Marilyn Monroe, isn't it?"

"Peeing down the drain! All the conveniences were closed!"

"Oh, you are dreadful!"

"Did you see the film?"

"The Seven Year Itch?"

"That's right." Bert Stone laughed. "I've been married seven years and I'm itching for it."

"Not with me you aren't!"

She hurried back to the sitting room.

"You've no idea what that awful man said to me!"

* * * *

Uncle Raymond now took pity on Karl.

"I hear you're a visitor down here?"

"Yes. I come from Leeds."

"You must be a Labour man?"

"Communist."

"Communist? That wouldn't go down well in the Army?"

"No. They threw me out."

"And why was that?"

"I beat up the sergeant."

Uncle Raymond laughed.

"I did much the same when I was in the Army. They put me in the glass house for ten days solitary."

He leant a little bit closer to Karl.

"See here. I could probably get you a job in the Post Office. Pull a few strings for you. Get you a flat if you wanted."

Karl smiled – a rare smile.

"That's great."

Uncle Raymond gave him a friendly wink.

"We Party men must stick together."

It didn't seem quite the moment to tell Uncle Raymond that he was actually a member of the National Front.

* * * *

Heidi found the Reverend Blazer sitting at a wooden table underneath a large chestnut tree. It was cool and shaded. Like everyone else, he was tucking into a barbecued steak with chips.

"Are you all right?"

"Yes, thank you."

His reply was stilted. She could tell he was annoyed. But Heidi would not have been Heidi if she had not been able to wrap men round her little finger. Very quickly, she found the cause of his unhappiness.

"It's all so wrong," he said. "The parents of the baby are supposed to be married – or getting married. And the godparents are supposed to be decent Christian people. Mr Stone completely deceived me. Ron says he has no intention of marrying Sandra and all the godparents are atheists. It was a complete farce. And it was my first baptism."

Heidi wondered where she should start.

"I didn't want to be a godparent," she said. "Sandra put my name down on the form. I didn't know anything about it. When she told me, I couldn't really say 'No'." She smiled apologetically. "It was for Mark's sake she did it. And I will try . . ." She gazed at Edmund with a look of utter sincerity. "I will make sure he's brought up as a Christian. I promise."

Edmund was moved.

"I'm sorry. I didn't mean to criticize you. It's just that I was told so many lies."

Heidi put a soft hand on his arm.

"It's been a very difficult time for all of us. Sandra getting pregnant. Her brother was very upset about it. He wanted her to have an abortion . . ."

"Oh, no!"

"Oh, yes. But I persuaded her to keep the baby . . ."

(It was a complete lie; but Edmund would never know.)

" . . . I didn't think it was right to have an abortion."

"Certainly not."

(The Reverend Blazer was a member of the Society for the Protection of the Unborn Child.)

"But she didn't want to rush into marriage until she was sure. So she put down Ron as the father and decided to have the other two as godparents."

Edmund looked distressed.

"So Jimmy could be the father?"

He looked at the half-naked savage prancing around on the lawn. Jimmy was now down to his blue underpants.

Heidi nodded.

"Or Charles?"

"He's really nice."

"It's all so sordid."

It was indeed. Even more sordid than Edmund imagined. Heidi was hard put to present it in its most favourable light. She took his hand in hers.

"Edmund," she said. "Can I call you Edmund . . .?"

"Of course."

" . . . Not everyone can keep up to the highest standards. We're all sinners. Isn't that what your Bible says?"

"Yes." He said it cautiously because he knew what she was going to say next.

"And our duty is to forgive people . . . not to judge them?"

Edmund nodded.

"For the sake of the baby – for Mark's sake – we all have to make an effort. It's him that matters. He hasn't done anything wrong . . ."

"Of course not."

(The Reverend Blazer conveniently overlooked the doctrine of original sin.)

" . . . so everyone's been doing their best – for him. Sandra's mum. Uncle Tom . . ." She looked round the lawn – the children leaping up and down in the bouncy castle, the baby in the pram, the portly man slaving over the barbecue. " . . .Uncle Tom's pulled out all the stops for him. It's a wonderful party."

"It is really."

Heidi put her fingers on Edmund's lips.

"Forgive," she said. "Just forgive – for me."

Being a gentleman, the Reverend Blazer could hardly refuse.

"Come on," she said. "Come back and join the party."

She took his hand and led him to the drinks table.

"You must have another drink."

"A glass of claret, please."

"A glass of claret for the Reverend."

She turned and put her arms round Edmund's neck and gave him a very long, sweet kiss. Nothing too passionate – but quite enough to set his pulses racing. He felt her body pressed close to his – and that perfume, still exceptionally strong. She let go – and gave him a dazzling smile.

To herself, she said: "And if that doesn't convert him, nothing will."

Edmund suddenly felt a great deal better.

* * * *

The video man put down his empty glass. He'd been

44

drinking nothing but champagne.

"A bloody good party, Tom."

"I like to see things go with a bang."

"Well, believe me, this was one was . . . A.1."

Uncle Tom smiled graciously. The man from Munn's was completely pickled.

"Would you like me to get you a taxi?"

The video man – with great difficulty – looked at his watch. "No. My wife's coming for me at 3.30pm."

"Lucky her!" thought Tom. Aloud, he said: "You should have told her to come and join us. The more the merrier."

"Oh, I don't think she would have approved. She knows what the Stone family is like. Your brother . . . she wouldn't want to meet him again." He laughed.

"Which one?"

"Bert . . . you remember?"

"Oh, yes. The indecent assault?"

"She's not likely to forget. It was her best friend!"

Uncle Tom laughed.

"Good job it wasn't on video!"

Which reminded Tom that he really must have a few words with his brother. He'd been meaning to speak to him for some time – and this was the time to do it – when he'd sunk a few and was feeling mellow. He found him out on the lawn watching the children leaping up and down in the bouncy castle.

"Eyeing up the future talent?" he asked.

Bert laughed.

"Bit young even for me."

Tom smiled.

His brother was incorrigible.

"I've been speaking to Betty. She tells me Ron's going off to the Army."

Bert shrugged his shoulders.

"Nothing to do with me."

"Well, I think they should marry and settle down. I'll help them get a flat. The kid needs a proper home."

Bert bristled with anger.

"He's got a proper home. Ours! I don't want her going off to bloody Germany and living in some frigging Army barracks in the middle of nowhere. She'd be far better off staying in Grasshallows with all her family and friends."

Tom looked at his brother thoughtfully.

"Are you hoping she'll marry someone else? Someone with money? Ron's not good enough for her. Is that what you're saying?"

Bert shook his head.

"No. Ron's just a lad. Give him time and he'll be fine. A couple of years in the Army and he'll settle down. But she doesn't know what she wants. She needs time to make up her mind . . ."

Tom laughed.

"Well, don't leave it too long – or I might marry her myself!"

The suggestion infuriated Bert. He was always conscious that, in the market of life, Tom had done better than he could ever do. He was the one with the money. He was the older brother who always knew best. After all the women he had had – the three wives – and countless mistresses – why should he now pinch his ewe lamb? His little daughter?

Bert saw red.

Maddened with drink, he let fly at his brother:

"You dirty little - - - -!"

The insults poured out like poisonous vomit.

Tom turned on his heel and walked back to the house. Bert pursued him angrily. Infuriated, he flung his empty beer glass at his head. It missed. Instead, it shattered on the patio, spraying the ground with broken glass.

Grace screamed.

"It's not safe round here! I should be paid danger money."

Bert would have pursued his brother into the house but as he approached the front door, he suddenly saw Eric's mother coming down the passage crying. This was the moment to make himself scarce.

"Are you leaving?"

Tom – once again the perfect host – despite the crunch of broken glass underfoot.

"Eric's had an accident."

"Another fit?"

"No, your brother . . ."

"Which one?"

"Need you ask? He gave Eric a glass of his home-made beer."

"Oh, dear!"

"He just couldn't get to the toilet in time."

"I am sorry."

"Donald's wife's helping to get him cleaned up."

"I am sorry."

He turned to the nearest waiter.

"Pour that home-made stuff down the sink. All of it!" Bert and his stupid practical jokes! Someone always got hurt. Poor Eric!

* * * *

But his brother was still at it.

He had beaten a retreat across to the disco where Karl was morosely drinking yet another pint of lager.

"Not looking after your lovely lady?" said Bert.

"She's too busy for me."

"I wouldn't say that. I'd say you've got competition."

"Oh, yeah? From who?"

"From the Reverend . . ."

Karl relaxed.

"Oh, I'm not bothered about him! He wouldn't know what to do with a woman. Not with someone like Heidi."

"Well," said Bert confidentially. "I saw them cosying up together. Kissing on the patio. They seemed to be getting on like a house on fire. If I were you, I'd keep an eye on them."

Suddenly, from inside the house, there were screams. People came flooding out through the French windows and on to the lawn.

Bert shouted: "What the hell's happening?"

"It's a fight."

"A fight?"

"The godfathers are knocking hell out of each other!"

The godfathers?

Mr Stone fought his way through the crowd to see what was happening.

Uncle Donald had managed to escape with his drink still intact. Just a few drops had spilled over. He looked at his glass with some surprise. It was still there. A bloody miracle!

He laughed cheerfully. To Cis, he said:

"No party in the Stone family is complete without a really good punch-up." He raised his glass triumphantly. "May the best man win!"

7. *The Ride Of The Valkyries*

"You're just mugs!" said Sandra's brother, Alec. "Paying out all that money and you don't even know which of you is the father."

Several pints and several chasers had loosened Alec's tongue. He had been speaking to Charles, but they had been joined by Ron and Jimmy, both of whom had been drinking quite heavily.

"How much are you paying her?"

"Sixty pounds a week," said Charles.

Jimmy nodded in agreement.

"Same here. It's quite a hefty sum."

Ron looked amazed. "I thought I was the only one who was paying. After all, I am the father."

"Who says?"

"Sandra."

"But she's told us all the same thing."

Jimmy shook his head.

"We're all in it."

"And she's netting one hundred and eighty pounds a week."

There was a thoughtful silence.

"I don't think she's getting all of it."

"No. Her dad's taking most of it. For housekeeping. She told me. Quite a nice little earner – ten thousand quid a year."

"I don't mind paying it," said Ron. "I'm willing to accept my responsibilities."

"But what if it turns out to be Charles' sprog?"

"We shall never know."

"She refused to have a DNA test."

"She doesn't want to know whose it is."

"So how long are you going to go on paying?"

Alec had a point. There was no harm each of them paying sixty pounds for the first few weeks of the baby's life. Prams had to be bought; cots, nappies and all the rest. But Alec was right. How long would they be expected to continue?

"Well," said Jimmy, "she says she wants to marry me – when I've got a job."

"That'll be the day!" said Ron.

"I've got the disco."

"That's not a proper job."

"Better than going into the Army. That's sheer escapism."

"Little boys playing at being soldiers. Covering their faces with cow dung. Crawling on their bellies through swamps."

Ron turned on Charles.

"That's rich, coming from you!" he snarled. "What d'you know about it? You're not even a man! You're a bloody pooftah! What did they used to write on the lavatory walls at school?"

Charles went red.

"I'm as much a man as you are. I've got a decent job. If she said 'yes' I'd marry her tomorrow."

Jimmy laughed.

"You've got to face it, Ron. There's only one thing holding her back. She doesn't want to marry you!"

"You're far too immature," said Charles. "She told me."

Ron put down his glass.

"I don't like your attitude."

"What are you going to do about it?"

"This."

Ron swung his fist in Charles' direction – but failed to connect. Jimmy tried to restrain him, but received a hefty blow on the ear.

"Hey, come on, man! That's no way to treat a mate!"

Jimmy hit him back – straight on the chin – not enough to

really hurt – just to sober him up. But nothing was going to stop Ron. He had been insulted. His manhood had been called in question. He flung himself at Charles, grabbed him round the neck, shook him and flung him on the floor. He kicked him in the stomach.

Alec tried to pull Ron away but only succeeded in tearing his jacket. Jimmy delivered another forceful blow at Ron's nose and drew blood. Ron picked up a chair and hurled it at Jimmy. By this time, people were screaming and running for cover. The peaceful atmosphere of the party was temporarily shattered. Glasses were knocked off tables and trampled underfoot.

Bert Stone leapt into the conflict, grabbing Ron by the hair.

"Leave him alone!" he hissed.

Ron shook himself free.

"Don't you tell me what to do, you money-grubbing bastard!"

He threw another wild punch in Bert's direction.

With years of experience behind him, the older man delivered a neat upper cut which landed Ron flat on his back on the floor.

Bert rubbed his fist tenderly.

"I don't think you'll have any more trouble from him."

Uncle Tom was quickly on the scene.

"What the hell are you doing?"

"Shutting him up. He was attacking these two lads."

He pointed to Charles who was getting to his feet, clutching his stomach – and Jimmy who was picking up a chair.

"Mental, man! Pure mental."

He walked back to the disco and looked through his lists to find the track: "Please don't treat me like a child."

"Who started it?"

"Ron."

Uncle Tom got down on his knees and helped Ron into a sitting position. He put an arm round him.

"Are you all right, lad?"

Ron nodded.

"Sorry. I just lost my cool."

"What were you quarrelling about?"

"Sandra."

Uncle Tom wiped his nose and mouth with a clean handkerchief, getting rid of some of the blood. He helped him into the downstairs toilet. Then he took him into the kitchen and made him a cup of coffee.

"The sooner you two get married, the better!"

"And have him for a father-in-law? Never!"

* * * *

Edmund did not witness the fight.

He had been upstairs with Sandra, looking at the baby. At least that had been the stated intention for their going upstairs. And they had certainly looked at Mark writhing around in his basket, gurgling and burping happily. But, of course, Sandra's real intention was to get to know Edmund a little better. To overcome his shyness. To see how far she could seduce him.

By this point, Edmund had consumed two large gin and tonics and several glasses of red wine. Oh yes – and one glass of champagne. It was perhaps a miracle that he was still capable of standing on his two feet. He was certainly light-headed and emotional.

Sandra turned all her charm on him.

"You were great," she said.

Edmund was open to any amount of flattery.

"No one could have done it better. The video man says it's come out beautifully. I'll get you a copy."

She was only inches away. An eager face. Clear skin. Those big grey eyes. And those ever-so-warm lips. How could Edmund resist?

She put her arms round his neck for a second time that afternoon – and sighed longingly. Then she shut her eyes and kissed him. It was a long, gentle kiss.

To steady himself, he put his hands on her hips. Then, as she pressed against him, he reached her spine. Finally, living dangerously, he touched her buttocks.

The kissing became more intense and she opened her mouth. This was new territory for Edmund. He responded as best he

51

could.

Then the baby started to cry. Edmund instinctively drew back.

"Don't worry about him!" she said brutally and pulled him closer.

Edmund felt . . . "This is wrong. I shouldn't be doing this. I'm being swallowed up." But it was all a new and vivid experience and he let her do what she wanted.

She pulled him down on to the bed and kicked off her sandals. Her dress rose up alarmingly to the very top of her thighs.

"It's O.K.," she said. "I'm on the pill."

"What about Mark?" he said breathlessly.

"He won't look," she said. "He knows when to close his eyes."

Almost on cue, the baby stopped crying.

She tore at his trousers.

"No!" said Edmund. "No!"

"Come on!" she said. "You'll enjoy it. Take my pants off and you'll feel like a real man!"

Whether Edmund felt like a real man – or more probably a sacrificial lamb, it was difficult to say. He was given very little time to think. She was determined to have him. He attributed his surrender to moral weakness whilst under the influence of drink. She got on top of him and rode him like a demented Valkyrie.

Whilst they were hard at it, her mother walked into the bedroom to see if Mark was all right. She had heard him crying. She looked at her daughter with some surprise. Poor Mr Blazer! What torments of guilt he would suffer! She hoped it was too soon for Sandra to get pregnant again! What a girl! She slipped out of the room without either of them noticing she had been there.

Sandra gave a final thrust and collapsed into Edmund's arms.

"Wasn't that good?" she said.

Edmund's first impression was that it had seemed very hard work. But it hadn't been unpleasant. If anything, it had been rather fun. Even though he had been a total ingenu, she had made him feel he was a man of some experience. And it had all happened so quickly.

He was kissed and caressed for another sixty seconds then she leapt to her feet, put on her pants and pulled down her dress.

She bent over Mark.

"There's a good little fellow. Didn't see anything, did you?"

Edmund followed her down the stairs in a daze.

* * * *

At the foot of the stairs, Heidi was standing with a look of curiosity on her face.

"Well, what was it like? Cordon Bleu?"

"Ploughman's lunch!"

Heidi laughed – then became serious.

"You missed the fight."

"Fight?"

"The godfathers came to blows."

"Did anyone get hurt?"

"Your dad knocked Ron out."

"Where is he?"

"I think he's in the kitchen. Your uncle Tom's giving him a cup of coffee."

Sandra flew to the kitchen.

Heidi turned to Edmund.

"She's a bit of a nympho, isn't she?"

"I suppose that would describe it."

"But did you enjoy it?"

Edmund was unused to being so honest about his private feelings – especially something as private as this. But he found it easy to talk to Heidi.

"Yes, I did," he admitted.

"She's been longing for you for ages."

Edmund was surprised. "Has she?"

"Yes. Ever since you came to see her about the baptism. She thinks you've got a lovely nature. So gentle and caring."

Edmund glowed happily.

He swallowed the compliment hook, line and sinker, without realizing that Charles, Jimmy and Ron had all been told much the same story. What Heidi really meant – but was too polite to say it – was: "Another mug!"

She smiled.

"Come and have a glass of champagne – to celebrate."

"I think I've already had too much."

"One more glass won't make any difference."

Edmund followed her over to the bar.

"Two glasses of champagne, please."

She passed Edmund his glass.

"To young lovers!"

"To Sandra!"

But Heidi was not going to be left out. It was not to be expected that Edmund would take her upstairs, but at least he could now give her a proper kiss.

Feeling more confident, Edmund put a hand round Heidi's waist and gave her a surprisingly passionate kiss.

"Another!" she said.

Edmund obliged.

How many more she would have received, it was impossible to say. But as they drew apart and Edmund took a swig of champagne, he was suddenly hit by a sledgehammer blow to his jaw. The blow threw him several feet across the hallway and he landed at the feet of Uncle Donald, who was being escorted out to his car, much the worse for drink.

"Another one down!" he chortled. "Reminds me of the good old days at *The Dun Cow*. Saturday night. Bodies everywhere!"

The assailant was Karl.

Following the warning he had been given, he had been keeping an eye open for the Reverend Blazer. He thought Mr Stone was just pulling his leg – there could be no possible competition from that quarter; but seeing the two of them drinking a toast together – and kissing so publicly – proved that Bert was right. All his deepest resentments and hatred for the rich, the middle-class and the Establishment in general – went into that blow.

Heidi was furious.

"You beast! Look what you've done!"

"Topped the bloody vicar!" said Mr Stone.

"I don't like you messing about with other blokes."

Once again, Uncle Tom was to the fore, trying to revive Edmund – but the young man was out cold and likely to remain so for some time.

"We'd better get him upstairs."

Charles and Jimmy came forward to pick him up.

Sandra emerged from the kitchen.

"Not another? What's happened?"

"Karl's just knocked out Mr Blazer. He was jealous. He saw us kissing."

Karl showed no remorse.

"He got what was coming to him. Your dad warned me what he was up to. That'll teach him to keep his hands off other people's birds!"

Sandra looked at Heidi. Both girls broke into uncontrollable giggles.

* * * *

It seemed that this was perhaps a good moment to bring the party to an end. There had been two outbreaks of violence – and tempers were still running high.

Uncle Tom suggested that the men should make their way up to the *Kirby Arms*. He would stand them free drinks for the rest of the evening. He phoned for a couple of taxis.

Bert Stone put an arm round Karl's shoulder.

"Well done!" he said. "That was a lovely punch."

Charles and Jimmy dumped Edmund in a back bedroom.

"Better take off his collar in case he chokes himself."

"I'll take his shoes off."

Edmund was left in peace.

Ron came up to Sandra – very apologetic about the fight.

"My sister's out tonight. Would you like to come round?"

She knew what he wanted.

"I'm still lactating!" she said.

Heidi went into another fit of the giggles.

"You'd be better going off to the pub with the rest of them," she said. "But no more fights."

The caterers were busy packing up the glassware before any more got broken. Uncle Tom gave Grace an extra twenty pounds for danger money.

"And tell your fancy brother to lay off me!"

* * * *

The two young boys managed to smuggle the paschal candle out of the house without anyone noticing. The two little girls in fluorescent pink and green dresses thanked Great-uncle Bert for their two-pound coins. He gave them each a big hug. He put a finger to his lips.

"Mum's the word."

"Thank you, Uncle Bert."

Betty Stone announced that she would be going home with Sandra and the baby. Heidi refused to go anywhere with Karl.

"You've ruined a beautiful party."

"You come up to the pub with us," said Uncle Raymond. "There's a new barmaid up there – just up your street."

"I refuse to be jealous."

"Will I see you again?"

"Perhaps."

Cis and her friend were among the last to go.

"What's happened to Father Blazer?"

"He's upstairs – having a lie down."

The lady who supplied the water from the River Jordan said: "Father Ryan'd never do anything like that. He knows how to hold his drink. He's a real gentleman."

Cis was still interested in the Marilyn Monroe tie.

"Is Bert still here?"

"No. He's just gone up to the *Kirby Arms* in a taxi."

"Oh, well. I'll see him at the bakery tomorrow."

Uncle Tom laughed.

"You keep your hands off his dough!"

* * * *

The Reverend Blazer slowly recovered consciousness. It wasn't so much the blow to the jaw or the crack on the back of his head as he hit the floor. It was an alcoholic mist which he moved in and out of – slowly coming back to life. The worst, perhaps, was over. The railway engines racing through the mind; the climbing out of a deep hole; the feeling of utter helplessness – wanting to move an arm or a leg but for nothing to happen. It was a horrible feeling which he had encountered once or twice before after a heavy binge at university.

Even when he opened his eyes, he shut them again. Another five minutes . . . Another ten minutes . . .

His senses told him that he was lying on top of a bed. It had a velvet cover. He felt it with his hand. There was no sound – not even the ticking of a clock.

He didn't know where he was; how he came to be there; what day it was; what time. But he was alive. He raised an arm.

When he opened his eyes again, he could see that he was in a small bedroom with reproduction furniture. A wardrobe and a dressing table. Pale green walls. No, on reflection, they were white walls. A window. A watery blue sky. Dark blue curtains.

He brought his watch up to his face.

6.25pm.

Gradually, it came back to him. The party. The baptism. Sandra. Heidi. Uncle Tom. And that thug who had hit him. He could remember the wild look in his eyes.

He put up his hand to his jaw. It was still aching. He opened his mouth and ran his fingers round his teeth. They were all still there. But sore.

He sighed.

A tear or two rolled down his cheeks.

What a mess! The baptism had been a complete farce. And the party had resulted in further humiliation. He had sunk his sorrows in drink. And they had just left him . . .

He sat up on the bed.

Oh, the headache! He put his hands to his head and rested his elbows on his knees. He groaned once or twice.

They had taken off his shoes – and his dog collar. Where was his jacket? Oh, it was on the back of a chair. Had he still got his money?

Hell!

He suddenly realized that it was Sunday. He was supposed to be at the 6.00pm Benediction. Not to take it – just to be there. Well, it was after half past six. He was too late. And there was no way he could turn up at the church like this. He was probably smelling like a brewery. He would just have to sneak back to his flat and say that he was ill.

He put on his shoes. It was an effort.

He stuffed his dog collar into his jacket pocket.

He stood up.

He was in a bedroom at the back of the house with a view over the lawn. The disco had gone; but the bouncy castle was still there. Everything looked peaceful and normal. He walked a few steps.

The toilet. He must go to the toilet.

He walked out of the room on to the upper landing. Deep pile carpet, it hardly made a sound.

But which was the toilet?

He opened one or two doors and looked in. More bedrooms. The third door he opened led him into what he supposed was the master bedroom. It was occupied. The curtains were drawn and there was a naked man and a naked woman lying on the bed. From the position they were in, it looked as if they had been making love and had then fallen asleep. He recognized the woman's dress and the man's shirt. Pigs! All of them.

He eventually found the bathroom but did not flush the toilet in case he woke up the couple. That would be even more embarrassing.

He went slowly down the stairs. Looked into each of the public rooms which had been so crowded, full of glasses, plates and people – now all tidy and cleared away. The caterers had gone; so had the barbecue and all the bottles.

He just walked out of the front door, down the front path and left Harrogate Drive – hopefully, never to return.

8. *Fanfare For The Common Man*

Detective-Inspector Raynes had just returned from his murder weekend in Mallaig. It had proved to be more than a mere game. A real, live body had been strangled and thrown off a train. Two of the weekend party had been arrested and charged with murder. He spent a pleasant half-hour telling Detective-Constable Carlisle all about it.

With some reluctance, he returned to the ordinary workaday world.

"Anything been happening round here?"

"Just the usual," said Carlisle. "Car theft, vandalism, two cases of shoplifting. And this morning, a missing person . . ."

"Male or female?"

"Male – aged about fifty."

"Scarcely worth bothering about!"

Raynes made himself a cup of coffee and sifted through the letters and papers waiting for him on his desk. They did not seem to be of any great interest. He picked up the heap of brown files and skimmed through them. Eventually, he came to the missing person.

"From Henslea?"

Carlisle nodded.

"Missing since Sunday?"

"Went to the pub. Never been seen again."

"Any insurance claim in the offing?"

"I really don't know. It was Sergeant Evans who went to see them."

"Ah! The ever-indispensable Evans!"

Raynes sipped at his coffee.

"Albert William Stone, 52. 28 Coronation Gardens. Occupation: Van driver. Last seen, 12.15 on the Monday morning."

The Inspector cast the file aside.

"Well, what d'you think has happened to Bert? Suicide? Murder? Loss of memory? Escaping from his creditors? Gone off with his fancy woman?"

Carlisle was becoming as cynical as his boss.

"I think we should assume the worst. The Stones are rather a rough lot. One or other of them's always in trouble. Usually drunk and disorderly. Can't resist picking a fight. I think Bert was had up earlier this year."

Raynes opened the file again.

"Yes. Saturday May 6th. An incident outside the *Kirby Arms*. Attempted assault. Fined fifty quid."

Carlisle looked at the Inspector.

"That's where he was last seen."

"Must be his local."

The younger officer shook his head.

"Not really. It's on this side of town. He'd have had to cross the river to get there. But it's a nice pub. Noisy . . . cheerful . . . bright and clean . . . I used to go there myself."

Carlisle sounded nostalgic.

Raynes reckoned that Mrs Carlisle kept a fairly tight grip on her husband. There was no chance of him going astray; let alone any prospect of him wasting money in a pub.

The Inspector ran an eye over Mr Stone's previous convictions. There were two indecent assaults – and one attempted rape.

"He's got quite a track record, has our Bert."

"They all have," said Carlisle. "Even the women. If you look them up in Records, you'll see they're all tarred with the same brush. Violence, abuse, drink . . ."

Raynes raised his eyebrows.

"We mustn't complain," he said patronizingly. "People like this are our bread and butter. Without such crooks and rogues, where would we be?"

Carlisle shrugged his shoulders.

Raynes smiled hopefully.

"So what d'you think's happened to Bert?"

"Fallen in the river? Swept downstream? His body'll probably be fished out at Olney. That's where they're normally found. Or he could have gone off into the Meadows for a 'quickie' with some obliging lass, had a heart attack and been left behind some bushes. A dog will probably find him."

"So you think he's dead?"

"People like Bert Stone don't run away. They may get knocked down or biffed over the head . . . But if they don't end up in hospital, I should think the river's our best bet."

"And so another member of the criminal fraternity bites the dust! Our statistics will fall . . ."

Carlisle sniffed disapprovingly.

"His funeral'll probably make up for it."

"Quite possibly," said Raynes. "But we haven't reached that point yet. We must visit the family – show some interest in poor Bert. Get a few pictures to stick on the wall . . . 'Have you seen this man?'" Raynes sighed. "Knowing my luck, he's probably sent a postcard from Ibiza. 'Having a wonderful time. Lots of booze. Plenty of birds. Back Sunday. Love, Bert.'"

Carlisle could already detect a tinge of disappointment in the Inspector's voice.

"You'd prefer something more dramatic?"

Raynes was honest.

"Of course I would. There's nothing like a good, juicy murder."

Carlisle was thinking of the Inspector's recent adventures in Mallaig. He shook his head.

"I should have thought you'd have had enough murders for one month."

* * * *

The journey to Henslea was not as swift as Raynes had hoped. A new gas main was being laid along Riverside Road. There were lights, single line traffic and long queues in both directions.

The Inspector sighed deeply.

"Why do they have to do all this work in August? At the height of the summer season – when the place is full of tourists? Why can't they do it in October?"

"I think it's already been delayed," said Carlisle. "They were planning to do it last year, but the local council didn't give them the go-ahead till May."

"It's a bloody nuisance."

He looked ahead.

"Go on! We can just do it."

But the car in front decided to stop. So they were left to fume for another two minutes. And even then, the car in front stalled.

Raynes exploded.

"Bloody women drivers!"

"It's actually a friend of yours," said Carlisle. "Rosalind Hayman. I recognize the car. She probably saw the police car right behind her and panicked."

"It'd be a pleasure to book her for something."

They reached Coronation Gardens shortly before 11.00am. A pram was sitting out in the garden; a dog lying beside it. As Raynes opened the gate, the dog began to bark and the invisible baby to cry.

Raynes smiled a grim smile.

"The perfect welcome!"

A tall young woman in a white T shirt and cerise stretch pants came out of the house to pacify the dog and comfort the baby.

"You woke him up," she said accusingly.

The Inspector shrugged his shoulders.

"Police," he said.

He showed her his identification badge.

"Oh, you've come about Dad?"

"He's not back yet?"

"No."

"Is it convenient to call?"

"Yes. Mum's in." She turned and yelled: "Mum! It's the police."

Mrs Stone appeared at the door.

She had dark lines around her eyes. She looked as if she had been crying. Raynes' first impression was that she was a woman who had begun to let herself go. A visit to the hair salon and a couple of hours with a beautician would make all the difference.

But as he looked at her face, he became conscious of her fine grey eyes and her broad sensual mouth. Mrs Stone could be a very attractive woman if she put her mind to it.

She looked suspiciously at the policemen.

"He's not back yet. You'd better come in."

Raynes followed her down the passage and into the living room. The house seemed well-furnished, clean and bright. The carpets were not cheap and neither was the furniture.

The daughter followed them in, carrying the baby. It had stopped crying.

Raynes settled into a comfortable, white leather armchair.

"We got your report this morning. I believe Sergeant Evans has been to see you?"

"Yes. He was most helpful."

Raynes grudgingly conceded a few Brownie points to his colleague.

"Your husband went missing on Sunday. Why didn't you report it before now?"

Mrs Stone shrugged her shoulders.

"We didn't miss him till Monday night. We thought he might be staying with his brother . . ."

The daughter was more blunt.

" . . . We thought he might have been lifted again. He'd had quite a bit to drink. Mum went to work on Monday morning. It wasn't till she came home that we began to get worried."

"Where does Mr Stone work?"

"At Hewitt's – the bakers. He delivers for them."

"And didn't they miss him?"

"They wouldn't have expected him back. Not till Tuesday, anyway . . ."

"They knew Dad. He often takes Monday off . . ."

" . . . Especially after a family get-together."

Raynes raised his eyebrows.

"What sort of get-together?"

"A baptism. We were getting Mark done."

The daughter smiled down at the baby.

"Mark Charles Ronald James Stone."

"A bit of a mouthful!" said Raynes, wondering whether this might be a good moment to open up a file on the baby as a future member of the criminal fraternity. (Like putting one's name down for Harrow or Eton.)

"Couldn't leave anyone out," said the daughter, bouncing the baby on her knee.

"And where was the baptism?"

"At St Benedict's."

"Canon Murray?"

"No. He's on holiday. It was a Mr Blazer. Nice young fellow." Raynes was sorry to hear that Canon Murray was out of the picture. He had been hoping to cross swords with him again.

"So Mr Stone went missing on Sunday night after the baptism? And you began to get worried on Monday night?"

"Mum phoned round the family. I went across to the pub. I asked whether anyone had seen him. But they hadn't . . ."

"We phoned the hospital."

"People said he'd just turn up."

"And you contacted the police?"

"Yesterday morning. And they sent Sergeant Evans round. He took all his particulars."

Raynes had forgotten to bring his file with him; but he remembered that Mr Stone was 52. He asked Mrs Stone if she had any photographs.

"Sandra's just got them back from Boots. Go and put the baby in the pram. He's settled now. And bring the Inspector the photos."

Mrs Stone took a framed photograph off the unit and brushed it against her thigh to remove any dust.

"That was him at our Silver."

"You've been married twenty-five years?"

"Twenty-seven now," she said proudly.

"And how many of a family?"

"Just the two of them. A boy and a girl."

Raynes looked at the photograph. It was pretty much what he had expected.

Mr Stone was a well-built man. About fourteen stone, he reckoned. Mischievous eyes, a nice smile – but a tough jaw line. Raynes could easily relate his looks to his record. A bit of a chancer. A bit of a boozer. A man who would not hesitate to get into a fight. But, nonetheless, a proud family man.

Sandra brought through two packs of photographs.

"They're mostly of Mark."

Her mother riffled through the packs and extracted four pictures of her husband. Once again, Mr Stone looked smart and well-dressed. He seemed cheerful and at ease.

"Quite a lot of people?" Raynes observed.

"There were over sixty people at the party. Most of the family came along."

Raynes reached out his hand for the rest of the pictures Some were blurred or dark. As Sandra had said, most of them were of the baby. She pointed out the godparents – all four of them; the new curate, Mr Blazer; her cousins; her friends. Raynes did not really take it all in.

Sandra was sitting on the arm of Raynes' leather armchair. The Inspector, being the sort of man he was, was conscious of her proximity. The slim thigh. The softly contoured bosom. The faint hint of Ivoire – not that he could have said what it was. But it captivated him. Made him feel slightly light-headed. He felt relieved when she moved away.

To Mrs Stone, he said: "We shall need to have one of those pictures . . . to show people . . ."

"To identify the corpse more like!" thought Carlisle.

"We'll get it back to you."

"We did give a photo to Sergeant Evans; but it was only a small one."

"I think that Silver Wedding picture would be excellent, We'll take a copy and Detective-Constable Carlisle will bring the original back to you tomorrow."

The framed portrait was duly put in a plastic bag.

Raynes resumed his questions:

"Has he ever done anything like this before?"

Mrs Stone looked at her daughter.

"Well, he was always a bit of a lad . . ."

"Don't mind me, Mum. We all knew what Dad was like."

"He liked the girls, Inspector. There's no point denying it. Couldn't keep his hands off them. Anything in skirts got him going. He had a good home . . . a lovely family, but that was his weakness."

"I noticed he had one or two charges."

Mrs Stone sighed sadly.

"It wasn't as bad as they made out. He just got a bit carried away. The girl admitted afterwards that she'd led him up the garden path. But he's mellowed, hasn't he? Not been quite so wild."

"Did he go regularly to the *Kirby Arms*?"

"All the family goes there. It's his brother, Tom, who owns it. Sometimes Bert helps them behind the bar."

"And that's where he was on Sunday night?"

"As far as we know, yes."

"He wasn't seen with any woman?"

"No. He went up with the rest of the lads. They all went to the *Kirby* together. I think Bert was the last to leave."

"Uncle Tom says he left about half past twelve."

"He didn't give him a lift home?"

"No. He was busy cleaning up."

"If you'd seen the amount they'd all been drinking, it wouldn't have been safe for him to have driven him home."

"It must have been quite a party?"

"It was."

There was a thoughtful silence.

"So he might have got a taxi home?"

"Or walked."

"If he had walked home," said Raynes cautiously, "he might have fallen into the river."

The Stones had already considered this possibility.

"We did wonder – but no one's found him, have they?"

"It could take a few days."

There was another silence.

"Did Bert have any enemies?"

Mrs Stone laughed coldly.

"Did he half! There's quite a few that'd like to get their own back on him; but they wouldn't dare. When he was young, he used to be a boxer. He never let you forget it. He was always ready to lift his arm. Got him into a lot of trouble."

66

"Had he had any recent quarrels with anyone?"

"Not that I know of."

Both Sandra and her mother shook their heads.

"No. He's been quite well-behaved lately."

"Ever since Mark was born . . ."

" . . . Given him a new lease of life. He really enjoyed being a grandfather."

"He did that."

Sandra laughed.

"Well, it'll be a long time before he has another!"

"If he's found alive . . ." thought Carlisle.

The same thought seemed to occur to everyone. The prospect of Bert being dead seemed real enough.

"Is there any insurance policy attached to his death?"

"Not that I know of."

"He used to pay that man who came round."

"That was just to cover his funeral."

"Well, you can't have a funeral without a body."

There was a longer silence.

"Did he have much money on him?"

"A few tenners. Enough to buy a couple of rounds . . . Sandra, go and look after that baby. It's crying again."

Raynes felt that the interview had come to an end. He stood up.

"It seems to me," he said, "that there are only one or two possibilities. He could have fallen into the river and been drowned. He could have wandered off somewhere and been taken ill. He could have been attacked. Or he could have gone off with someone – and stayed away for much longer than usual. But it seems unlikely."

Sandra returned with the baby.

"I think we're resigned to bad news, aren't we, Mum?"

"I'm afraid so."

Raynes promised to do all he could.

"We shall put out a nationwide alert. We shall search the river – and the outlying parts of the city. We shall speak to the taxi-drivers and ask whether any of them picked up anyone outside the *Kirby Arms* on Sunday night. Be sure we'll find him."

"You mean – his body?"

Raynes sighed.

"Yes. His body."

9. *The Banks Of Green Willow*

There was silence in the police car.

"You didn't give her much hope."

"There wasn't much to give."

"You'd think – if he'd been attacked, someone would have seen the body."

"Which makes the river more likely."

"What do we do?"

"Hire a couple of boats. Search the river all the way down to . . . where did you say?"

"Olney."

"We could offer a reward . . ."

"Put an article in the local rag . . ."

"But if we sit here for much longer, we shall get nothing done!"

Once again, they were held up by the traffic lights in Riverside Road. It was a hot summer's day and the Inspector's temper was getting shorter by the minute.

"Damn their eyes! Why don't they allow more cars through? Two or three at a time's ridiculous. I shall phone up the City Engineer."

Carlisle edged closer to the lights. He said soothingly: "An afternoon on the river'll make a pleasant change."

* * * *

Once they were back at police headquarters, things began to move. Three motor boats were hired and three teams of officers rapidly assembled to search for Bert's body.

There was no lack of volunteers. Anything was better than doing duty on the High Street, walking up and down the hot pavements, answering footling questions: "Where is Balliol College?"

"You're thinking of Oxford, ma'am. This is Grasshallows."

"Did Queen Elizabeth sleep here?"

"No. I think the traffic kept her awake!"

"Was *The Green Man* used in the film 'Tom Brown's Schooldays'?" and the perennial: "Where are the nearest toilets?" With the inevitable corollary: "You English policemen are so wonderful!"

At about half past three, they gathered together on the landing stage where the pleasure boats were rented out. There was a sudden stir of interest as the eleven officers, mostly in blue shirts, climbed into the boats, along with nets, poles, rakes and body bags.

News went round quickly that they were about to drag the river, looking for the missing man. It was all very exciting. For a couple of miles, they were followed by several boats of trippers, all armed with cameras and videos. At least the police were seen to be doing something. Raynes was conscious that it was a gross misuse of manpower, but it made a number of people very happy.

Raynes and Carlisle travelled in the central boat mid-stream, with the other two boats combing the left and right banks of the river. The water was very clear. They moved downstream – quite quickly whilst they were in the confines of the city, but more slowly once they reached open country.

There were many twists and turns in the river; there were bushes and overhanging trees; there were side channels and field drains which had to be checked. Now and again, an alarm was raised – a black bin bag full of rubbish – a water-logged pillow – a plank of wood; but the journey was quite unproductive. Two hours later, they reached Olney where there was a lock and a weir.

According to Carlisle, the few bodies that did fall into the river usually floated near the edge of the weir or were sucked into the lock. But the lock-keeper had seen no bodies in the river since March and nobody had reported a body in the lock. Bert was not in the river.

The officers trooped over to the local pub to have a pint before travelling home. It was called *The Cock Feathers* but Raynes felt it might be more appropriate if it was called *The Headless Chicken*. But there was a good atmosphere in the pub. One of the constables said to him:

"What do we do now, boss?"

"Search the Meadows. We'll do that tomorrow morning. Every bush, every ditch, for as long as it takes."

It took most of Friday morning.

But, like the river, it proved futile. A systematic search of the parkland, hedges, woods and culverts produced no sign of Mr Stone – though, as a tidying-up operation, it succeeded quite well. Items of clothing, bus tickets, used contraceptives, a walking stick, two pairs of spectacles, a child's paddling pool, a hammer and a kite were popped into plastic bags – but no body.

A separate team was engaged to inspect every garage and lock-up – particularly those near the *Kirby Arms* and in Henslea. This was a long job occupying most of the weekend – trying to locate the owners and arrange for them to hand over their keys. It was surprising how many garages there were and what strange things were stored there. Several prosecutions followed the investigation.

By the end of the week, all the taxi firms in Grasshallows had been contacted and their drivers asked if they had seen Mr Stone – or picked him up on the Sunday night. The answer was negative. The Inspector had to admit that Mr Stone had vanished into thin air.

10. *Cockaigne*

Whilst his officers were combing the Meadows, the Inspector called on Tom Stone in his elegant neo-Georgian mansion.

Tom had not expected visitors quite so early. He was still in his dressing-gown, reading the *Grasshallows Echo*. He did not need spectacles to read the banner headlines:

"Grasshallows Man Goes Missing. Police Hunt Widens."

The arrival of Raynes and Carlisle on his doorstep shortly after 9.00am emphasized the truth of the newspaper report.

"Coffee, gentlemen?"

"Thanks, Tom. I think we shall need it."

Mr Stone spooned three heaped tablespoonfuls of ground coffee in to the cafetiere and filled up the kettle. They sat round the kitchen table. Carlisle opened up his notepad and wrote down the date and the time.

"Are you the oldest member of the family?" Raynes asked.

"Yes. There are five of us. Four lads – and my sister."

"And Bert?"

"He's the youngest."

"So you must be about sixty?"

"Sixty-four, Inspector. And, by God, I feel it this morning."

"Are you married?"

Tom laughed.

"In between," he said. "I've had three. I'm just waiting for the latest divorce to come through."

"I see."

The Inspector did see. The house was extremely attractive – and showed many feminine touches; but the kitchen spoke of "bachelordom". Unwashed plates, a rather grimy stove, an ashtray overflowing with dog-ends, sugar out of a packet. There was the feeling that Tom was camping – rather than living – in the house.

The kettle boiled and the coffee was made.

Raynes took a welcome sip.

"So you are the oldest member of the family?"

"I am."

"And the richest?"

"I've worked hard for it."

"Always in the licensing trade?"

"Thirty-five years, next January."

"And you own the *Kirby Arms*?"

"I have three pubs," said Tom proudly. "I also own *The Dun Cow* and *The Raging Bull*." He smiled mischievously. "I called them after my first two wives!"

Everyone laughed.

Raynes had heard of *The Raging Bull*. It was a pub that was popular with the students.

"Where's *The Dun Cow*?" he asked.

"In Henslea. A bit rough. But it does all right."

"Why didn't Bert go there? It's a bit nearer home."

"The family prefer the *Kirby*. It's got more class. A better feel. Besides, if I'm around, they get fifty per cent off!"

"So after the baptism, everyone made their way up to the *Kirby* and rounded off the evening with a few pints?"

Tom nodded.

"It was a 'friendly'. Everything on the house."

"And who was there?"

"Bert. And Ron – he's the baby's father. And Alec . . ."

"Who's Alec?"

"Bert's son. Full name – Alexander. But they couldn't call him Sandy when Sandra came along. So they call him Alec. Not exactly blessed with charm. Bit of a sourpuss, if you ask me."

Tom lit a cigarette.

"Sandra seems a nice girl."

"She is. And very proud of her baby. We gave her a great party last Sunday. Biggest binge the family's had for many a year."

He noticed the unhappy expression on Raynes' face.

"Smoke getting to you?"

"I'm afraid so."

Tom stubbed out his cigarette.

"Sorry about that. I'm smoking too many of them. You were saying . . .?"

"The party was held here?"

"No room to swing a cat at Bert's place. Yes, we had it here. Drinks out on the patio. Barbecue beside the garage. A bouncy castle on the lawn. Hammocks under the trees. Plenty of beds if you felt a bit tiddly. I got in some outside caterers. Put on a lovely spread. Jimmy did the disco."

He laughed. "Only two complaints from the neighbours. I told them to come over and join us. I don't know whether they did. I'd rather lost count of things by that time."

"And after that, you all moved up to the *Kirby Arms*?"

"Yes. We took a couple of taxis. No point us trying to drive up there with you lads on the job!"

Tom's eyes twinkled.

"And Bert and Ron and Alec went with you?"

"More than that . . . Karl – that's Heidi's boyfriend . . ."

The name Heidi meant nothing to the Inspector.

". . . Heidi's godmother. A cracker. One hell of a cracker. She's got this skinhead in tow. Covered in tattoos. I thought he was a German. Looks like one. But apparently he comes from Leeds. Knows how to use his fists. He even knocked out the young Reverend . . ."

"Really?"

"It was quite uncalled for. He'd done nothing wrong. Then there was Charlie – nice lad. Works at Barclays. One of Sandra's friends. Jimmy couldn't join us. He had another booking later that evening. One of my brothers came along – Raymond. But the other one had to be taken home – smashed. So, there were . . . seven of us, all told."

"What time did they leave the pub?"

"I couldn't really tell you. I was quite busy behind the bar. We were short-staffed that night. All I can tell you is that Bert was the last to leave."

"What time was that?"

"After midnight." Tom shook his head. "I didn't think he was ever going to move. Quite frankly, Inspector, he was plastered. Totally plastered. I offered to get him a taxi – at about 11.00pm – but he was in no hurry to go. Once it got to midnight, I told him in no uncertain terms he'd have to leave. We were clearing up. I didn't think he'd have any trouble getting a taxi. If we hadn't been so short-staffed, I'd have got one of the barmen to give us both a lift home – but Bert's difficult to handle – especially when he's drunk as much as he did on Sunday. I didn't want to have an argument with him. I just told him to go. Last I saw of him was him standing on the pavement – still upright – swaying a bit. He shouldn't have had any trouble getting home."

"So what d'you think happened?"

"Lord knows! Vanished into thin air." He looked at the front page of the newspaper. "It says you've done the river . . ."

"We have. And this morning, we're searching the Meadows."

"No joy?"

"I'm not expecting anything. D'you think he's done a runner? Gone off with some woman?"

Tom pursed his lips.

"It wouldn't have been the first time." He reached for the packet of cigarettes – but then remembered the Inspector didn't like them.

"We'd have known about that by now," he said. "He wouldn't have done that to his family."

He shook his head sadly. "He really didn't look as if he was going anywhere when I last saw him. If he'd tried to walk home, he'd have fallen flat on his face. In fact, I wouldn't have been surprised if you lot had pulled him in for being drunk and disorderly."

"It wouldn't have been the first time," said Carlisle.

"No," said Tom. "He went on a blinder every few months . . . ended up quite legless. He was his own worst enemy."

"You felt sorry for him?"

"Not sorry. Just . . . annoyed. He never really tried to make a go of it. I gave him a couple of chances. A job behind the bar. But he mucked it up. Pinched money out of the till. He didn't have to do that. Then he started having arguments with the regulars. One of them led to a punch-up. I couldn't have that. I had to sack him."

"Do you think he was jealous of your success?"

"You've put your finger on it, Inspector. Envy, jealousy – call it what you will. The little green-eyed god. He used to needle me – but I tried not to rise to the bait. I knew it would only end in trouble. He used to be a boxer. So was I. But he was always ready to lift his fists."

"Had you quarrelled at the party?"

Tom laughed sadly.

"As a matter of fact we had. I'd suggested it was high time

74

Sandra got married. What with the baby and everything. Child needed a proper home. He said: 'He's got a good home. Ours!' But I said: 'No. She should marry Ron and settle down.'

"But he wasn't having any of that. He said Ron was joining the Army. What sort of life would that be for Sandra? In Germany, for God's sake! She'd be far better off staying here in Grasshallows with her mum and dad and all her friends. I said to him: 'You want her to marry someone else? Someone with money? Ron's not good enough for her. Isn't that what you're saying?' 'No,' he said. 'Ron's fine. But she still hasn't made her mind up. She'll decide in her own good time.' 'Well, don't leave it too long,' I said, 'or I'll marry her myself!' He got quite worked up at that. Told me I was a dirty creep – and a few other things I won't repeat." Tom smiled. "But he calmed down later."

"How much later?"

"Before he set off to the pub. We shook hands before he left the house. 'No hard feelings,' he said. Well, I know what he's like. Storm in a tea cup."

Raynes finished his coffee.

"So you have no idea what could have happened to him?"

"None whatsoever."

"And if he's dead . . . ?"

A look of warmth and humanity came into Tom's eyes. "You don't have to worry about the family, Inspector. I'll look after them. I'll see they're all right."

Raynes smiled.

"And you'll make sure Sandra marries Ron?"

Tom laughed.

"The alternative doesn't bear thinking about, does it? If I laid a hand on Sandra, Bert would kill me. Even from beyond the grave, he'd hunt me down."

Raynes stood up.

"I imagine her mother would have something to say about it as well."

Tom grinned.

"You bet she would!"

11. *Tristis Est Anima Mea*

The Reverend Edmund Blazer lived in a small, first-floor flat in a side street, just off the market place in Grasshallows. Raynes had decided that they should call on him at about 9.30 on Monday morning – on the assumption that Monday would be his day off. Raynes was hoping to catch the curate in his pyjamas, but Mr Blazer was already dressed and in his dog collar. He had attended the 7.30am Mass, eaten his breakfast and read the *Guardian* – as any right-thinking curate should.

The Inspector tugged at a rather ancient bell.

Edmund opened the door and looked warily at his visitors. They did not look like members of his congregation.

"Police," said Raynes.

"Oh?"

"May we come in?"

The flat consisted of a study-cum-living room, a bedroom with purple walls, a small kitchen and a bathroom. There was a strong smell of burnt toast.

A poster of Salvador Dali's "Christ of St John of the Cross" hung menacingly over the mantelpiece and a flyer for a pilgrimage to Walsingham lay on the carpet. There was a crucifix on every wall and postcards of Russian icons with bearded patriarchs raising two fingers in apostolic blessing. For Raynes, this was very much redskin territory.

He sat down in a large, corduroy armchair with his back to the window.

"I believe you are Canon Murray's curate?"

Edmund nodded.

"How long have you been in Grasshallows?"

"Since the end of June."

"And you haven't been sacked yet?"

"No."

The ghost of a smile appeared on Edmund's lips.

"Canon Murray's not back yet?"

"Not till next Wednesday."

"Well, that should give you time to let things settle down."
Mr Blazer looked uncertain as to what the Inspector meant.
"The baptism?"
"Oh, yes . . . the baptism . . ."
It was something he had been trying to forget.
"You baptized Bert Stone's grandchild . . ."
Edmund nodded sadly.
" . . . and attended the party afterwards?"
"Yes."
"I believe you had rather a bad time there?"
"It was a bit rough."
"You got knocked out?"
"Yes."
"By Karl somebody? Heidi's boyfriend?"
Edmund nodded glumly.
How much more had the Inspector been told?
"And who is Heidi?"
"She was one of the godparents."
"And why did Karl take it upon himself to hit you?"
Edmund sighed.
"Because he saw me kissing her. I'd been drinking a lot. It was a perfectly friendly kiss . . . There was no cause for him to be jealous."
The Reverend Blazer was so earnest, it was difficult to imagine him kissing anyone. Raynes tried not to smile.
"It seems to have been quite a party?"
"It was."
"Perhaps you could tell us all that happened after the baptism?"
"Well . . ."
It was difficult to know where to start. In Edmund's mind, both events were telescoped together as part of a single, ongoing nightmare. High spiritual endeavour ending in shame and humiliation. He had been guilty of a gross act of fornication with an unmarried mother whilst under the influence of drink – for which he had not yet been able to make his confession. But he wasn't going to tell the Inspector anything about that.
"Sandra invited me to the party. She wanted me to be there,

77

so I couldn't really refuse. I went round at about 2.30, I suppose. I had to tidy up the church – so I was a bit late. I was given a warm welcome by Tom – her uncle Tom. There were a large number of people there. Fifty or sixty people . . ."

"All the Stone family?"

"Yes. I didn't realize how many there were. I was introduced to Raymond . . . I think he works in the Post Office. And Donald . . . he was drunk most of the time. And, of course, I'd already met Mr Stone . . ."

"Who has now gone missing."

"Yes. I read it in the paper."

"He hasn't been seen since Sunday night."

"He was very full of life at the party. Trying to get people to drink his home-made beer."

"Pretty deadly?"

"Lethal! I drank some when I went round to his house to arrange the baptism." Edmund shuddered at the memory. "Never again."

"So who else was there?"

"Mrs Stone. The godparents. Various friends, I suppose. A lot of children. The caterers. A man doing the video . . ."

"Really?"

A video could be quite useful.

"Sandra's going to send me a copy."

Raynes noted that the Reverend Blazer seemed to be quite friendly with Bert Stone's daughter.

"I should like to see it."

"I think it was taken by an official photographer."

"Munn's?"

"Yes, that's who it was. A man with a beard. A black beard."

"We'll get a copy."

He looked at Detective-Constable Carlisle, who had already noted it down.

"And the godparents . . .? Who were they?"

"Well, there was Ron – Ron Middleton. He's the baby's father."

Edmund looked at the Inspector.

No. He obviously didn't know the background.

" . . . and Jimmy – Jimmy Watson. I believe he runs a disco. He was doing the disco at the party. And . . . Charles Costello. He works in a bank."

"And Heidi?"

"Heidi Houston."

"And what does she do?"

"I've no idea."

From the cold snap in Edmund's voice, the Inspector gathered that there was no love lost there.

"And do you think they'll be good godparents?"

Raynes was just being sarcastic. He was surprised by the severity of Mr Blazer's reaction.

"Certainly not!"

"You seem very emphatic."

"Well . . ." said Edmund again, " . . . Jimmy Watson is a thief. He apparently stole money from St Benedict's when he was a boy. Ron Middleton – the baby's father – has no intention of marrying the baby's mother. He's going off to Germany. Both of them are lapsed Roman Catholics. I'm told that Ron comes from a simply dreadful family. And Miss Houston's Jewish! A Jewish atheist!"

Raynes was much amused. Although not sharing Mr Blazer's rampant anti-semitism, he could quite understand his dismay.

"You didn't know this – before the baptism?"

"No. I was deceived."

"By whom?"

"The Stone family. I think I should have been told. They made out they were all good, upright Christian people."

Raynes nodded helpfully.

"I told Mr Stone what I thought of him."

"You blame him most?"

"Yes, I do. He seemed to have complete contempt for the Church – for me – for everything. I even saw him drinking from a hip flask in the church!"

Raynes began to think that the video might prove quite interesting.

"He told me that I'd got the money. What more did I want?

But . . ." Edmund paused. " . . . I didn't get the collection. It was stolen. So was the paschal candle. The processional cross was damaged. It was a nightmare."

The Inspector discovered that there was a deep undercurrent of fury in the young clergyman.

"And this was your first baptism?"

"Yes."

"I'm surprised you went to the party."

"I wasn't going to go – but I felt I just had to get these things back."

"And did you?"

Edmund's voice mellowed.

"Well, Uncle Tom was very kind. He gave me a very generous donation for the Church. But the paschal candle's gone. I don't know what I'm going to tell Canon Murray when he comes back. And the processional cross has damaged part of the chancel floor They broke the Christ figure – but I'm getting it repaired."

It seemed to have been a very dramatic day in the young man's life.

"And you spoke to Mr Stone at the party?"

"Yes. But it didn't do any good."

"He wouldn't listen to you?"

"No."

Edmund looked at the Inspector. He seemed an understanding sort of man.

"I felt used . . . In fact, I think the godparents felt much the same."

Raynes raised his eyebrows.

"Perhaps I shouldn't say this . . . but, apparently, no one knows which of them is the father . . ."

This did not surprise Detective-Constable Carlisle.

"That's why she chose all of them as godparents. Heidi – Miss Houston – told me they're all paying for the baby's maintenance."

"Including Heidi?"

"No. Just the men. They didn't know this. Ron thought it was just him. They had a terrible fight about it."

80

"When?"

"At the party."

Raynes looked surprised.

He looked at his colleague.

"Tom didn't say anything about this."

Carlisle shook his head.

"Not a cheep."

Raynes turned back to Mr Blazer.

"What actually happened?"

"Ron got knocked out."

"By whom?"

"By Mr Stone."

Raynes began to realize that there was more to this party than met the eye.

"At what time was the fight?"

"Oh, I don't know. Quite late in the afternoon. About four o'clock, I should think."

"Did you witness it?"

"No. I was upstairs . . . with the baby," he added hastily.

Edmund blushed.

Raynes thought; "Like hell he was! Far more likely, he was canoodling with Heidi!"

To Edmund, he said: "And where did the fight take place?"

"In the entrance hall. I'm told that Ron hit Jimmy and also knocked Charles down on the ground. He threw a chair at Jimmy and then Mr Stone weighed in and knocked him out."

Raynes thought about it.

And yet they all went to the pub together. Except for Jimmy – wasn't that what Tom had said? The possibility of a revenge attack began to figure in his mind.

"Did they kiss and make up?"

"I don't know. I didn't see any of this."

"What happened when you came downstairs?"

Raynes watched Edmund's reaction closely.

"I went for a drink with Miss Houston . . . and it was quite soon after that, that I was attacked."

"Quite a violent afternoon?"

"Yes, it was."

"So what happened then?"

"I really don't know. I suppose I must've been taken upstairs. I woke up to find myself in a back bedroom."

"It must've been quite a hefty blow?"

"Yes, but I'd also been drinking. Quite a lot."

For his own prurient amusement, Raynes asked:

"How much?"

Edmund calculated.

"Two gin and tonics. Quite strong ones. Two champagnes. No, I think it was three. And about four or five glasses of claret."

"It's a good job Canon Murray's away on holiday?"

"Yes."

Edmund bit his nails.

"You would have been sacked."

"If he'd seen the condition I was in."

"It's not on the video?"

"No."

"Just the service?"

Edmund nodded.

"So you woke up – eventually?"

"Yes. About half past six. They'd all gone."

He conveniently passed over the sleeping couple.

"So what did you do?"

"I went to the toilet – and then I just let myself out."

"And staggered home?"

"Yes."

"You didn't go to the *Kirby Arms*?"

"Certainly not."

"And you never saw Mr Stone again?"

"No. And I never want to."

"He could be dead . . ."

"Yes. I realize that."

" . . . which makes all the people at the party suspects . . ."

"I suppose so."

" . . . including you."

Edmund nodded gravely.

"So it's very important that you tell me anything you can

remember. Any tiny detail may help."

There was nothing Mr Blazer could add.

"I think I've told you all I can. Most of the people at the party were complete strangers. I'd never met the godparents or even Sandra's brother – or her uncle. There was a man who had epilepsy – he had a fit at the church."

"The caterers?"

"There was a man with a red cummerbund doing the barbecue. A waitress with a scraggy neck. I think she was called Grace. There were two other waiters and a younger waitress. I think she was called Yvonne."

"You'll have the address of the godparents?"

"No." But then his face lit up. "Of course I do."

He leapt up from his chair and went over to his desk. From a heap of papers, he drew out the baptismal form over which Sandra had laboured. He gave it to the Inspector.

Raynes ran his eye over the form.

Sandra was nineteen, going on twenty. Occupation: Mother. Her mother was Elizabeth Stone: nursing auxiliary. The godparents were Ronald George Middleton: Storeman. Army in brackets. James Arthur Watson: unemployed. Charles William Costello: bank clerk. And Miss Heidi Houston: hairdresser. In response to the questions: "Are you baptized . . .? Are you confirmed . . .?" each one was neatly ticked and each of them were declared to be bona fide members of the Church of England – including Heidi.

"A bit misleading?" said Raynes.

"Deliberately so."

"And you trust Sandra?"

"Not now."

Raynes looked pointedly at the stunning photo of Sandra and her baby on Mr Blazer's mantelpiece.

"She gave me it."

"Of course she did," said Raynes. "If there weren't any flies, fish wouldn't rise, would they?"

The Reverend Blazer looked hurt.

"It's not like that. I feel very sorry for her. Everyone seems to have let her down. And now her father's disappeared. It must be very hard for her."

Raynes said no more. As he gave the form a final casual glance, he suddenly noticed that Heidi Houston lived in Greenway Gardens – his street. He was No. 5. She was No. 58. It must be one of the bungalows at the far end.

He handed the form to Carlisle.

"D'you mind if we keep this? Detective-Constable Carlisle will take a copy and return the original."

"I don't think I shall be needing it again."

Raynes smiled.

"If you would like to take my advice, I would suggest you keep well away from Henslea . . . well away from the Stone family. At least till after the funeral."

12. *L'Apres-midi D'un Faune*

When Raynes and Carlisle returned to their car, it was to find it decorated with a parking ticket. The Inspector tore it into small pieces.

Carlisle smiled.

"Make sure you don't get caught for dropping litter."

"Another word from you, young man, and you'll be walking back to the office."

Carlisle could tell his boss was in a good mood.

"Well, we learnt quite a lot there that we didn't learn at Coronation Gardens."

"The plot thickens."

"Indeed it does. A baptism from hell. A fight. Mr Stone knocking out one of the godparents. All of them paying maintenance but none of them knowing who the father is. And then that baptismal form – a complete tissue of lies. Everyone conned by that elegant young woman."

"Including Mr Blazer."

"Besotted. Totally besotted – but you can see why."

Carlisle laughed.

"I thought you looked quite starry-eyed when she came and

sat beside you on the armchair."

"She certainly has . . . presence."

"Call it sex appeal."

"A capacity to deceive."

"And you're looking forward to seeing Heidi Houston?"

"Very much so. And the video."

"That'll be extremely useful."

"We'll call in at Munn's."

They visited the photographers' – but Mr Beamish was out on another job. They promised to deliver a copy of the video to the police station before five o'clock.

"Where to next?" asked Carlisle.

"Well," said Raynes thoughtfully, "I think it's still a bit early for Jimmy. DJs are rarely up before noon. I think we'll call at the bank and see Mr Costello. It'll give him a nasty jolt. Which one did he say it was?"

Carlisle looked at his notes.

"Barclays."

"We'll go back to the office and have a cup of coffee whilst you phone up and find out which branch he works in. Demand an immediate appointment. Strike whilst the iron is hot."

* * * *

Charles Costello was waiting for them in one of those depressing little rooms where bank managers habitually browbeat their customers, forcing them either to reduce their overdrafts or, instead, to take out extortionate loans.

But, this morning, the boot was on the other foot. Mr Costello was looking pale and anxious. The Bank did not like its junior staff attracting police attention and his line manager had warned him that, if it turned out to be anything serious, it might endanger his prospects of promotion.

Being, as he was, at the bottom of the pile, this was disheartening and perhaps even the Inspector realized that it might have been kinder to have seen the young man at home.

"You were at the *Kirby Arms*?"

"Not for long. I had one drink – then I left."

"What time would that have been?"

"Just before six. My mother was watching 'Songs of Praise' when I got home."

Raynes was reminded that Charles was the Methodist godparent. He looked a very earnest young man.

"How did you get involved with the Stone family?"

"I was at school with Sandra."

"I see. Childhood sweethearts?"

"Not really. We went to the same discos . . ."

" . . . And shared the same bed?"

Charles' face coloured.

"Only once or twice; when her parents were out working and we had the house to ourselves."

"Proved rather expensive, hasn't it?"

Charles nodded sadly.

"How much?"

"Sixty pounds a week. About one third of my wage."

"And you don't even know if you are the baby's father?"

"No. I asked for a DNA test – but she refused."

"Seems unfair?"

"Very."

For the first time, the Inspector detected a touch of anger in the young man's voice.

"So why are you paying?"

"Fear."

"Fear?"

The young man looked down at the small table with its black leather surface – and sighed.

"You don't argue with the Stone family, Inspector. Not if you want to avoid trouble. Mr Stone made the position quite clear. It was my responsibility to pay for the pram, the cot, the nappies – and to support Sandra."

"But you resented it?"

"Yes. Because he was pocketing all the money. It wasn't Sandra who was getting it. He's a complete crook. But I've known that for years."

"What school were you at?"

"Henslea Comprehensive."

86

"So this job must be very important to you?"

"It is."

Raynes looked at the young man in his standard white shirt and dark blue tie; the fine face and the large, soulful eyes – and felt sorry for him.

"I believe there was a fight at the baptismal party?"

Charles nodded.

"Who started it?"

"Ron. Ron Middleton. He's quite a tough customer. Going off to join the Army. We were arguing – about the maintenance money . . ."

"Does he object to paying it?"

"We all do. But he's in a difficult position. It's his name on the birth certificate. He has to pay." Charles paused. "I suppose I provoked him. I told him he was too immature to marry Sandra – he didn't like that. He got me round the neck and flung me on the floor. He also kicked me in the groin."

"Painful?"

"Well, he actually got me at the top of my thigh. I've had a huge bruise."

"And what happened next?"

"Well, I didn't really see what happened next. Mr Stone laid into him and knocked him out."

"And yet you all went for a drink together?"

"I didn't really want to go. It was Uncle Tom's idea. Kiss and make up, I suppose. Anyway, there was no chance of seeing Sandra. She was going home with her mother."

"You still have a soft spot for Sandra?"

"Oh, yes."

"If you found out the baby was yours, would you marry her?"

"If she'd have me. But I don't think she wants to marry anyone at the moment."

"And if the baby is someone else's?"

"I think we have to find out."

Raynes nodded his approval.

"I think this has to be done – as a matter of urgency. Until we know for sure who the father is, this row is going to go on and on."

"My parents are very upset about it."

"I'm not surprised."

Raynes returned to the main lines of his investigation.

"So who was in the *Kirby Arms* when you left?"

"Mr Stone . . . Ron . . . Karl . . . Alec . . . Tom, of course. He was busy behind the bar . . . and Raymond, his brother. He was getting at me for working for a capitalist institution."

"Who does he work for?"

"The Post Office, I believe."

"And was there a friendly atmosphere at the pub?"

"Not really. Alec was getting at his father. I think he hates him. He's always needling him. Not quite to the point of violence; but near enough to make everyone thoroughly uncomfortable."

Raynes said nothing.

"It was particularly bad last Christmas. I think he was jealous of all the attention Sandra was getting. His dad tried to soft-soap him by buying him a motor bike."

"Did he succeed?"

"I think he did. But when he's been drinking, Alec's still a pain."

"And he was particularly bad that night?"

"I've seen him worse."

Raynes asked the obvious question.

"D'you think he'd have done anything to hurt him?"

Charles shrugged his thin shoulders.

"If anyone got hurt, it'd be Alec. I don't think he'd have dared take on his dad. I believe he and Ron sloped off to the snooker club."

"And Karl?"

"He went off with Raymond. Raymond had been promising to get him a job. They looked as thick as thieves."

"He didn't go back to Heidi?"

"He may have done. In fact, I think she said he did. But she was very angry with him for knocking out the curate. She read the riot act to him. He seemed quite subdued after that."

"And Mr Stone? How was he?"

"Well, he was really angry with his brother, Tom. It was

something Tom had said. That if he didn't marry Sandra off to Ron, he would marry her himself. I'm sure he was only joking; but Mr Stone wouldn't let up. He said Tom was a creep, a parasite, a paedophile . . . trying to entice his daughter away with all his money and his big house. He kept saying: 'He thinks he can buy people; but he can't buy me.' A lot of nasty things were said; but Tom kept out of his way. I got tired of it. At the first opportunity, I left."

The Inspector looked closely at the bank clerk.

"So what d'you think has happened to Mr Stone?"

Charles hesitated.

"I did wonder if perhaps he'd gone off with the barmaid. I saw him stroking her thigh as she served the drinks. He was always making up to other women. I don't know how his wife puts up with it . . ."

"And then?"

" . . . Then I thought that perhaps the barmaid's husband might have got back at him. But I'm told he left the pub alone at midnight, when they shut up shop. It's all very odd."

"And where were you at midnight?"

"In bed." Charles Costello permitted himself a faint smile. "It'd been quite a day, Inspector. I'd drunk a lot more than usual; I'd been in a fight; I was still sore. And I was fed up."

"Fed up?"

"Of all the Stone family. They're such a twisted bunch. Arguing, fighting, cheating, drinking, womanizing – it makes you feel . . . dirty . . . being with them."

"And yet you're still thinking of marrying into them?"

"Oh, Sandra's different. She's a wonderful girl. And now that Mr Stone's gone, things are bound to be better. Much better. He was a terrible corrupting influence."

"And you think he's dead?"

"I hope so."

There was a long silence in the small room. Charles Costello had made his feelings perfectly clear. Like most people, he feared Albert Stone; was glad he was dead. It appeared that even his own son felt the same. If the investigation became a murder inquiry – as seemed increasingly likely – the list of possible suspects was daunting. Including this young man who had no alibi.

Raynes broke the silence by thumping his fist on the table. "Back to work, Mr Costello! Thank you for your help. If I have to see you again, I shall see you at home. I apologize for any inconvenience our visit may have caused. When I next see Sandra, I shall press for a DNA test. Then we shall know where we are."

As he and Carlisle left the bank, the manager intercepted them.

"I hope Mr Costello's not in any sort of trouble?"

"Not at all," said the Inspector confidently. "He's a very fine young man. A great asset to the Bank. Should go far."

The manager looked relieved.

As they reached the pavement, Raynes turned to Carlisle:

"Oh, the lies I have to tell!"

His colleague smiled.

"I think you meant it."

13. *The Planets*

Even by half past one, Jimmy had scarcely surfaced. He arrived at the door, bare-chested, wearing a pair of loose brown underpants, a rosary slung round his neck. It was a chance to see the whole man, tattoos and all.

He squinted at Inspector Raynes and Detective-Constable Carlisle.

"Hi, chaps! What's cooking?"

"Police," said Raynes.

"Thank God! I thought you were from the Council. Come to evict me."

"No. We're just here for a friendly chat."

Jimmy laughed.

"Pull the other one."

He shimmied down the passage.

"Give me a break whilst I get decent."

Raynes and Carlisle entered the living room-cum-kitchen. It was mostly bare boards. A couple of hard chairs and a sagging sofa. Clothes, towels and boxes of records lay scattered across the floor. There were several dirty plates and mugs. A bluebottle buzzed menacingly round a black bin bag. Housekeeping obviously came low on Jimmy's list of priorities.

He returned, wearing a pair of jeans, a brown belt and a dark blue T shirt, but still in bare feet.

"You guys want a coffee?"

"No, thanks," said Raynes.

"Well, I've got to have one."

The unshaven DJ went through the rigmarole of filling a kettle, opening cupboards, finding a mug, the Nescafe and the sugar.

Eventually, he perched on a stool.

"Now what've I done this time? Buggered a traffic warden?"

Raynes smiled.

"No," he said. "It's Bert Stone . . ."

"Sandra's dad?"

"We're still looking for him. Have you any ideas?"

"Sure." Jimmy took a swig of coffee and wiped his mouth.

"Aliens!" he said.

Raynes assumed that Jimmy was joking, but he swiftly discovered that the DJ was an ardent believer in close encounters of the third kind.

"They just come and grab people. It happens all the time. They need to regenerate their genetic stock – using humans as breeding material to create super beings. I should think Bert Stone was as good a choice as any."

If one accepted the basic premise, Raynes was inclined to agree.

"They just nicked him on his way home," Jimmy continued. "He was easy meat. You don't get any warning. Just a beam of light, then they scoop you up. You lose all sense of time. The CIA know all about it; but the press is gagged. You guys probably know all about it but you're sworn to secrecy. That's why you go round asking these damn-fool questions – pretending, but all the time you know he's on the way to the silent planet."

He reached for his tobacco pouch and lighter.

Raynes was quietly amused.

"I'm not aware of any alien activity – at least not around Grasshallows. Nor am I aware of any official cover-up. To us, this is a terrestrial problem. We're still expecting to find Bert Stone down here."

"It's gonna be a long search, chaps. I wish you luck."

He rolled his cigarette and lit it. Raynes was sure it contained some illegal substance.

He tried another angle.

"You weren't at the *Kirby Arms* on the Sunday night?"

"No, man. I was doing a gig."

"Where?"

"At the *Raging Bull*."

"That's one of Tom Stone's pubs?"

"Sure."

"Does he get you quite a few gigs?"

"Not enough to live on. Things are pretty rough when the Uni's closed down. The Students' Union's my bread and butter. Four nights a week. Lots of cool chicks . . ." He grinned. "I like 'em young."

Raynes looked thoughtful.

"Like Sandra?"

Jimmy's eyes lit up.

"She's great, man!"

"And do you hold yourself responsible for her pregnancy?"

Jimmy stretched out his lanky, brown body.

"Highest sperm count in Grasshallows! That's me!"

He laughed.

Even Detective-Constable Carlisle grinned.

"D'you think you're the baby's father?"

Jimmy shrugged his shoulders.

"Who knows? Could've been. I think I've got a bit more going for me than Charlie or Ron. She wanted to marry me but her father wouldn't let her. Said. I was a lousy drop-out . . . immature . . . irresponsible . . . You know the sort of thing parents say. But . . ." Jimmy stubbed out his cigarette and drank

92

the final dregs of his coffee. " . . . I work every night. Every night I can get work. I run my own business." He pointed to the poster on the wall. "Osiris. The Sacred Eye. Vibes of Eternity. It pays for all my bad habits." He grinned.

Judging by the smell, Raynes reckoned there was a hefty dose of cannabis in his reefer. He admired Jimmy's brazen contempt for the forces of law and order. But he wasn't going to be side-tracked from his investigation.

"Did you feel any . . . animosity against Mr Stone?"

Jimmy looked surprised.

"Hell, no! He was a complete tosspot! If Sandy wanted me, she could have me. She knows the score. We could shack up together; eat some decent grub; get the place ship-shape."

He started rolling another cigarette. "She always tidies the place up when she comes round. But she hasn't been round lately. Other fish to fry . . ."

"Ron?"

"No. That bloody vicar chap. She's gone overboard."

Raynes returned to his original line of thought.

"So if not aliens, who?"

"Difficult to say, man. One moment, he's on the pavement outside the *Kirby*, pissed as a bloody newt. Next minute, he's gone. You don't get it neater than that."

"Did he show any signs of . . . anxiety . . . during the baptismal party?"

"No way. He was as bright as a button. Stirring up everyone – 'specially Ron and Karl. I saw his game. He wanted to provoke a fight. He was wild, man. Really let fly. Socked Ron really hard. That fired him up. He even tried to pull Grace – but she gave him the brush off."

"Grace?"

"Yeh. Hippie dame. Lives in a caravan."

Raynes looked at Carlisle. A vision of scouts and black bra straps flashed before his eyes.

Carlisle underlined the name twice. No doubt they would soon be paying a return visit to Picton Dale.

Jimmy looked at the young policeman.

"Are you writing all this crap down?"

"Some of it," said Carlisle, thinking how bizarre the interview would appear when recorded in cold print.

"Well, you can't pin anything on me!"

"What about the wacky baccy?" said Raynes.

"Oh, go on! Everyone's doing it. Half the kids at Uni are stoned on it. Pull me in and you'll have to pull in half the adult population of Britain. It's social, man!"

"Grace . . .?" asked Raynes.

"I don't know her surname; but she works for Tom at functions. Nice dame. But she really hates Bert."

"Why?"

"He raped her."

"At the baptism party?"

"No. Years ago. She's never forgiven him. She told me that if she had a knife, she'd have sliced off his John Thomas. And she meant it!"

"Really?" said Raynes, mentally noting another possible suspect.

"Bert's been asking for it for years. He thinks he can grab any chick. But people are frightened of him. He's a boxer, you see. Knows how to use his fists. Felled Ron with a single blow. He'd do the same to me if he got half a chance. No one's going to pinch his little princess!"

"Did he ever threaten you?"

Jimmy laughed. "No way! I steered clear of him. I just talked rubbish when he was around. He thinks I'm just a mindless jerk. I let him believe it."

"So you think that if he'd been attacked on Sunday night, he'd still have been able to stand up for himself?"

"Sure thing! No one'd have got Bert down. He'd have had them flat on the ground – even when he was half pissed. No, that's another good reason for believing it was aliens that lifted him. Once they'd zapped him with their cosmic ray, he'd have been putty in their hands. Sick as a parrot. Totally disorientated. Now he's probably deep frozen and on his way to some distant planet forty million light years away." Jimmy's eyes lit up with a warm, inner light. "A great shock to the folks in Galaxy 389; but a great relief to all of us down here."

94

The smell of cannabis was beginning to overwhelm the Inspector and he was sick of being dive-bombed by the aggressive bluebottle. If Jimmy could suggest nothing more positive than aliens, it was time to move on.

He sighed and looked at Carlisle.

Enough was enough.

"Thank you, Mr Watson, for helping us with our inquiries."

The DJ leapt to his feet.

"Call me Jimmy, Inspector. Everyone does. Anything more I can do for you guys, you've only to ask. If you need a disco for the Police Christmas Dance – just give me a ring." He handed over a grubby piece of cardboard. "That's my number. If you want a charity disco for the widows and orphans ..."

"There aren't any!" said Raynes coldly.

Jimmy looked at him sadly.

"Relax, man! Let it all hang out! You've only got one life. Chill!"

"Thank you for your advice. I shall keep it in mind."

As he shut the door behind them. Jimmy breathed a sigh of relief. He had had a narrow escape.

14. *Onward, Christian Soldiers*

Ron Middleton was a cocky, arrogant young thug. He had short, spiky hair, a button nose, pale blue eyes and cauliflower ears. He had all those unpleasant traits of character which Raynes hoped the Army would soon knock out of him. They met in his sister's flat in Henslea – not far from Coronation Gardens.

"When are you joining up?"

"I have to report to the barracks on October 1st."

"Which regiment?"

"The Middlesex."

"A famous regiment."

"Is it?"

Raynes raised his eyebrows. Ron obviously had a lot to

learn.

"And, at present, you're working as a storeman?"

Ron shook his head.

"I'm on compassionate leave."

"Caring for the Stone family?"

"Yeah."

Ron had a shifty look.

"And you're a storeman with . . ."

"Car parts firm. Riverside Road."

"I see."

Raynes looked across at Carlisle as if seeking inspiration.

"The *Kirby Arms* is not far from Riverside Road?"

"No."

"D'you go there often?"

"Yes. Quite often."

"You went there on the night of the baptism? The night Mr Stone went missing?"

"Yes."

Ron was wary.

"Wasn't that a bit odd, considering Mr, Stone had just hit you? Do you often go for a drink with people who've knocked you out?"

"It's the first time I've ever been knocked out."

Raynes stroked his chin – but said nothing.

Ron explained – unwillingly: "It wasn't my idea. It was Tom's. He was trying to patch things up. I wanted Sandra to come round here – my sister was working – but she wouldn't. She went off with that Jewish bitch. She thought it would be a good thing if I joined the others at the pub. So . . ." he ended rather lamely, "that's where I went."

"Not much fun?"

"No. I spent most of the time talking to Alec – Bert's son. Once we'd had a couple, we went off to the snooker."

"Till when?"

"Now you're asking! Eleven or so. I was quite knackered. Long day. Had a skinful. Had to be at work at seven."

"You didn't go back to the *Kirby* to have it out with Bert?"

"Not much point." Ron gave a wry smile. "Didn't want to be

96

knocked out twice in one day."

"Has he ever hit you before?"

"No."

"But you know his reputation?"

"Alec told me what he was like. Used to beat the living daylights out of him when he was a kid. Normally when he was drunk."

"Is Alec a good friend of yours?"

"Yeah."

"And presumably, it was through Alec that you met Sandra?"

Ron nodded.

"And how long have you been . . . friends?"

"About two years – on and off."

"You weren't at school with her?"

"No. I went to the Catholic school. Thomas More."

"And she thinks you're the father of the baby?"

"Does she hell! It's all a big con."

Raynes raised his eyebrows as if this was news to him. In fact, he was rapidly tiring of the whole question of Mark's paternity.

"That bastard . . ." Ron stabbed the air with his fist.

"That bastard went down to the Registrar's and put my name on the birth certificate. Then he came back to the house and treated me to a couple of Carlsbergs and said: 'Congratulations, lad! You'll make a splendid dad!'

"Well, I was quite chuffed. Proud, you know. He's a nice little kid. They say he has my nose. But then, in the next breath, Bert said to me: 'You'll have to take your responsibilities like a man.' I didn't know what he meant. Not then, anyway.

"A couple of days later, he said to me: 'Babies cost money, lad. Nappies, milk, prams, clothes. You just go down to the supermarket and see what nappies cost! About a fiver a day! Who's going to pay for it? Me? It's your baby, lad. Your responsibility. And who's going to maintain our Sandra? She can't work. You'll have to cough up, lad.' He always called me 'lad'.

"So I said: 'How much?' And he said; 'Sixty quid a week!' And I said: 'That's half my bloody wage!' And he said: 'You should have thought of that before you started screwing our Sandra!'

"So I spoke to her and she said: 'You'd better do it; just to keep the peace. You know what Dad's like.' But it upset me, I can tell you. I didn't want to settle down; I couldn't afford it; and I certainly didn't want him for a father-in-law. No way!"

"So that's when you decided to join up?"

"Yes. I was passing the recruitment office one lunchtime. You know. 'Join the Army. See the World'. And I thought: 'Yes'."

"Sandra didn't object?"

"No. Not as long as she gets her money." Ron shook his head sadly. "They're all so bloody greedy. I didn't know – not till the party – that I wasn't the only one paying sixty quid. That the other two were in it as well. I ask you! Three blokes all forking out for one baby! And him just raking it in! No wonder I saw red."

"You attacked Charles?"

"He's a complete ponce! I wouldn't have thought he was capable – not with a woman, anyway. Then he had the cheek to say I was immature! Me! Immature! Bloody cheek! Do you blame me?"

"And Jimmy?"

Ron sighed.

"Well, I know Sandra liked Jimmy. She was one of the groupies who hung round his disco. I'm not surprised she had it off with him. Jimmy's always pulling the birds. I'm just surprised he agreed to pay the sixty quid."

"I think it was fear."

"Alec was right. We were all mugs."

The Inspector had not expected to like Ron but he appreciated his blunt honesty and his genuine feelings. He felt sorry for him – as he did for all three of the young men.

"Wouldn't it have been better if you'd all had a DNA test?"

"She refused."

"I know."

"It was probably him who told her to refuse."

"Probably. But a DNA test would put an end to all this uncertainty."

Ron nodded.

"I think – in the absence of Mr Stone – I shall insist on all four of you having the test."

"Four? The vicar as well?"

"No, I meant the baby."

"She's got the hots for him, you know."

Raynes nodded.

"He'll learn!"

"I'm sure he will. But, in the meantime, I shall arrange for the tests to be conducted. All three of you will take part."

Raynes looked across to Carlisle. "Make a note of it – in case I forget."

For the first time in the interview, Ron smiled.

"That's great!"

Raynes sighed.

"It may save you a lot of money. On the other hand, it may drop you in it for the next sixteen years . . . But at least you'll know the worst."

15. *Verklarte Nacht*

It was one of those rare occasions when Debbie May found herself unemployed. The appointments book was empty; the telephone did not ring. If she was to achieve anything, she would have to go along to the cocktail bar of *The Green Man* and pick up what she could.

Quite frankly, she couldn't be bothered. So she phoned the Inspector who had now returned from his philandering in Scotland. Perhaps he would be free.

He was.

In fact: "I was going to phone you . . ."

So why hadn't he?

"I've got a baptism video I want to watch."

A baptism video! What a turn off!

"You might be able to identify one or two of the characters. In fact, I'd be glad if you could."

Debbie cheered up.

"I've plenty of videos here," she said mischievously. "Videos which would make your hair stand on end – and other things as well," she added with a touch of vulgarity. "So what's it to be? Bondage, buggery or bestiality?"

Imagining that most of the videos she had on offer would be totally illegal – and, should his cleaner find them, might lead to his career going completely down the plughole, Raynes declined.

He changed tack.

"Just come and look at your picture. It looks particularly lovely this evening. The light's just catching it. But it'll probably be gone by the time you arrive."

With an immense display of reluctance (which was all put on), Debbie agreed to be there in half an hour.

She didn't bother dressing up. She put on a pair of faded jeans, a white shirt and a pair of white trainers. However, she made sure her make-up made her look alluring. She didn't want to be compared unfavourably with her picture.

She appeared at about 8.00pm – having had to turn down a last minute appeal from a doctor-friend. If only she hadn't been so impatient! There was another hundred pounds down the drain!

Raynes was waiting with the video in his hand.

"Whose baptism is it anyway?" she asked.

"A member of the Stone family."

She shook her head.

"I don't know them." But then she paused. "I think I know one of them. Tom Stone . . .?"

"He has a pub. The *Kirby Arms*."

"Yes, I know him. He's had a few wives. I've been to his house once or twice. He's quite a nice guy."

"Well, you'll see Tom. In fact, you'll see all of them."

He slipped the video into the slot.

Mrs May looked at him with some disappointment. Had he forgotten the essential preliminaries?

"You don't expect me to watch all that without a drink in my hand?"

Raynes stood up.

"What would you like?"

"Peach schnapps."

"I don't know if I've got any."

"I brought you a bottle last time I was here."

"In that case, I'll still have it."

Raynes went off to the kitchen cupboard where most of his booze was stored. He made a mental note to buy himself a cocktail cabinet – or pick one up at a sale.

He found the bottle of schnapps and poured her a generous glass. He poured himself a malt whisky. It had some curious Gaelic name: Laphroaig. He couldn't pronounce it but it tasted fine.

He returned with the drinks.

"Now, are we sitting comfortably?"

Debbie stretched out on the sofa, her head on Richard's shoulder.

"Off we go!"

But the tape which rolled was certainly not the baptism at St Benedict's. A team of busty blondes were playing rugby with a horde of randy Welshmen. The titles were in German; the humour gross; the outcome entirely predictable.

Debbie laughed.

"A last minute substitution!"

"We'll watch that later."

"It's one of my favourites."

"Business first."

He changed the tape.

The camera rolled.

"You have brought this child to baptism . . ."

"That's the Reverend Edmund Blazer. He's the new curate at St Benedict's."

"A prat!"

"It's his first baptism. He's naive, articulate, well-spoken, Bristol University."

"He's still a prat!"

The camera moved on to the godparents. "We are willing."

"God! What a shower!"

"That's Charles . . . Ron . . . and Jimmy."

Debbie laughed.

"Check the T shirt! That must have given Mr Blazer a bit of a jolt."

"And that's the godmother – Heidi – and the mother – Sandra."

Debbie took a slug of schnapps whilst the camera featured the main guests, all looking very devout and sincere.

"There's Tom."

"Yes. I recognize him."

"And his brother, Bert . . . that's Mrs Stone . . . and his brother, Raymond."

"Pig!"

"And Donald . . ."

"Boozer."

"And that's all their children, grandchildren, nephews and nieces."

"Not a pretty sight."

"No. They're a rough lot."

Debbie finished her schnapps. It was no use asking for any more at this stage. Richard was intent on watching the video right through.

"I repent of my sins . . ."

"Pull the other one!"

Debbie looked more closely at the godmother.

"Stop! I know her."

Raynes froze the picture.

"That's . . ."

"Heidi. Heidi Houston."

"She was Miss Grasshallows in . . . Oh, I don't know. Three or four years ago."

"Before my time."

"I wonder what she's doing now."

"Hairdresser."

"Of course! I've been there. Reynaldo's – just off the High Street. Well, that's a turn up for the book. I wouldn't have said she was an ideal godmother."

"No," said Raynes. He let the tape move on.

"What about Sandra?"

"Pretty girl. Heart-breaker. How old's the baby?"

"I don't know. Three months?"

"Who's the father?"

"Ah! That's the question! No one knows. That's why he's got three godfathers. It could be any of them."

"Doesn't surprise me."

The Reverend Blazer took the child into his arms.

"A very serious young man . . ."

"He's terrified of dropping the poor kid."

"It all goes OK."

"Mmm."

They watched as Edmund handed the baby back to Heidi.

"Oh, look at that! What a look! I bet he's smitten. Look at the way he lingered over her boobs!"

"Yes, I'm afraid Mr Blazer was well and truly smitten. But you'll be glad to hear he suffered for it. He got knocked out."

"Who by?"

"By Heidi's boyfriend, I believe. He was out cold for a couple of hours."

"Oh! He's lost the candle."

"Has anyone seen the baptismal candle?"

They watched the little girl hand it back.

"Thank you."

"They're all crooks!"

"Who?"

"The Stones. I remember them now. Rape. Indecent assault. Drunk and disorderly. Henslea, of course. They do it for free down there."

"Tom was all right, wasn't he?"

"Money talks!"

"And that's Sandra getting the candle . . . I think she likes him, too. Look at that smile!"

"False."

"Well, in that case, he'd better be careful. He's playing with fire."

The tape rolled unexcitingly towards its end with more shots of the guests.

"That's probably the one who knocked him out – that chap in combat gear. He looks a bit of a bruiser."

"Heidi's boyfriend?"

"Yes."

"I don't think much of her choice of men. Could end up cutting her into little pieces and putting her into bin bags."

"I haven't met him yet."

"So what's it all leading up to?"

"Don't you read the paper?"

Debbie turned and looked at the Inspector.

"Of course I read the paper. I advertize in it. Confidential Escort Agency. Grasshallows 815267."

"It's the missing man . . . Mr Stone."

"Yes, I know. You've searched the river. Dug up the Meadows. Quizzed all and sundry. And you don't know where he is."

"We think he's probably dead."

Raynes switched off the tape.

"He hasn't been seen since Sunday night. After the party, they all went up to the *Kirby Arms*. Bert left at midnight. Vanished into thin air."

"Have you any ideas?"

"No."

"Well, neither have I." She waved her empty glass in his face. "More!"

"More?"

"Well, if we're going to have a cosy evening together, I need to be tanked up. And you can get rid of that blasted tape and put on something decent!"

"You mean the ladies' rugby team?"

"How did you guess! And pull the curtains. This place is a bit public. You can see right in."

"Miss Houston lives at No. 58."

"Well, we don't want her looking in. Or her boyfriend."

Raynes smiled to himself.

It seemed that Mrs May was determined to enjoy the rest of the evening. He went off to collect the bottle of schnapps.

16. *Belshazzar's Feast*

"Are we doing any more searching?"

"No."

It was Tuesday morning and Raynes had a slight hangover. Too much Laphroaig. Perhaps too much Debbie May? No, that couldn't be right. They said sex was good for you.

Carlisle sensed that the Inspector was irritated by the slow progress of the case; but, in fact, Raynes was annoyed because he was obliged to take part in a civic ceremony.

The Minister of Education was due to open the new University science block at 11.00am and then be treated to a civic lunch. Raynes would be tied up till at least 3.00pm, when the wretched man departed. As one of the Police Department's top brass, there was no way of getting out of it.

He supposed – rightly – that the visit of the Cabinet Minister was not unconnected with the impending by-election to choose a successor to Miles Hart who had won the election in June but had then been murdered at his victory party. The general feeling was that the Tories did not stand a hope in hell and that it would be a Liberal Democrat landslide.

Raynes did not care which of them won. What he did object to was these political outsiders coming to Grasshallows and wasting his time. However, he consoled himself with the thought that he would at least get a decent lunch.

He laid the video tape on Carlisle's desk.

"You'd better look at this. It won't add to your sum of knowledge, but I think it gives you a good picture of the principal suspects . . ."

Detective-Constable Carlisle picked up the tape.

" . . . Mr Blazer does rather well – considering all the distractions. Jimmy Watson's T shirt is a hoot and Heidi Houston's dress has to be seen to be believed. I'm told she was 'Miss Grasshallows' about three years ago. Stunning lass. It's rather nice seeing Bert Stone in the flesh.

"He reminds me of Stanley Holloway in My Fair Lady – when he was cleaned up and declared to be Britain's most original moralist. Anyway, see what you think."

"What d'you want me to do?"

"Well, I'm going to this wretched lunch. For me, it's a wasted day. Perhaps you could get all our interviews typed and brought up to date. That would be a help. I'd also like you to arrange for the three godfathers to have their DNA test – before the end of the week. Make sure they each have a definite time.

"Then you'll have the much more difficult task of persuading young Sandra to do the same for her baby. She won't like it – but it'll clear up all this confusion. Use your charm! Say that the uncertainty is impeding our investigations – which it is. If she refuses, go to the district nurse and see if she will help us. And if you have time, you could go and see Tom Stone and ask him the name of that barmaid . . ." Raynes paused. " . . . No, you've probably got enough without that."

"There's still two others we have to see."

"Three!"

"Alec and Miss Houston."

"Don't forget Grace. She knows him of old. She'll probably tell us some interesting tales. It'll be nice to see her again."

Carlisle shook his head. He did not share Raynes' affection for loose women. To him, Grace was just a jaded hag.

Having been given his marching orders, Carlisle went off to find some secretarial help to type his notes. He would watch the video in the rest room after lunch. He would have much preferred to go to the civic lunch. Perhaps, one day, when he became a senior officer . . .

* * * *

The Chief Constable, the Chairwoman of the local Police Committee and Raynes were present when the Minister arrived by helicopter on the University playing fields. They duly escorted him to the big new concrete block funded by the Wellcome Foundation. Ribbons were snipped, speeches were made, a plaque was unveiled and the minister conducted on a rapid tour of the building. After that, there was a lengthy photo session. Ten minutes behind schedule, the motorcade set off for the City Hall.

The seafood terrine with raspberry coulis did not appeal to the Inspector. The colour was off-putting and he discovered only one prawn. The roast beef was tasty but the Yorkshire pudding had been hanging about for a while and was soggy. He avoided the basket of summer fruits and made the most of the cheeseboard. Only one glass of champagne was served and the year of the claret did not suggest that the City was digging deep into its coffers – or its wine cellar. It was no more than he had expected – perhaps even a little less. He left as soon as he decently could.

He was glad to get back to the office and settled down with a large mug of sweet black coffee. Carlisle was still out at Henslea. Whilst he slowly sobered up, he digested the contents of their recent interviews. Really, his colleague took excellent notes – even recording the interviewees' reactions as well as their words. When Carlisle returned, he complimented him on his splendid work.

"Did you have a good lunch?"

"Not really. The menu was unimaginative; the food not very interesting and the wine second-rate. I think the benefactors deserved better. If you're going to lay on a spread, you should do it properly."

Carlisle knew how much Raynes appreciated a decent meal. He would never forget some of the savage comments he had lavished on the food served in the police canteen: "Look! That cauliflower's almost crawling away with shame . . ." "I think that meat's already been through the crematorium!"

"So how was Sandra?"

"Tearful. She started by refusing point-blank; but I told her I had booked an appointment on Thursday. I also told her how unfair it was her taking money from the three young men. None of them was well-paid. It was over one third of Charles' wage; an even bigger slice of Ron's. I told her that during the summer vacation, Jimmy was very hard put to get gigs – depending only on the kindness of people like Uncle Tom. She may chicken out, but at least I gave her something to think about."

"It's better coming from you," said Raynes. "I might have

been swayed by her tears. Anyway, what did you think of the baptism?"

Carlisle smiled broadly.

"I think we all preferred the international rugby."

"Rugby?"

Raynes was puzzled.

"Your popularity has soared. All the junior office staff had a splendid afternoon. You gave me the wrong tape!"

Understanding dawned on Raynes' face.

"The scheming bitch!" he exclaimed. "She did it deliberately! Now I shall get into trouble for supplying porn!"

"Good job I didn't take it home. My wife would have flayed me alive."

"Did you watch the whole thing?"

"Had to. If I'd tried to switch it off, I'd have been lynched. Fortunately, it only lasted forty-five minutes. Everyone went back to work. And I took the tape back to Mrs May and collected the proper one." He looked at it suspiciously. "At least, I hope it's the right one. It could be something worse."

17. *Air On A G String*

Inspector Raynes hoped that his visit to Heidi Houston might be the highspot in his investigation into the disappearance of Bert Stone; and he was not disappointed.

He knocked on the half-open door of No. 58.

A voice sang out: "Come in!"

Raynes hesitated.

Heidi appeared in the doorway wearing a pair of red satin trousers and a loose white blouse slashed almost to the waist.

"Oh?" she said.

"Were you expecting someone else?"

"Yes. My boyfriend."

"Well, I'm sorry to disappoint you. I'm Detective-Inspector Raynes of Grasshallows police."

"Oh, yes. Sandra told me. Come in."

108

Raynes followed her into the house which smelt overpoweringly of perfume. (Mrs May would have identified it as Jungle.) There were highly-polished floorboards throughout the house and an immense sofa sitting invitingly in front of the fire.

Miss Houston slipped a large rubber dildo under a cushion and hoped the Inspector had not noticed. The Inspector did notice. He felt that all that was missing from this temple of seduction was a tiger skin – or even a real tiger.

Raynes sat down on the one chair that did not suggest amorous escapades: a wooden rocking chair. He had begun to think that it had perhaps been unwise not to bring Detective-Constable Carlisle with him.

Heidi hovered before him.

"D'you drink . . . when you're on duty?"

"Not normally. But if you're offering, I'll have a gin."

It would give him time to adjust.

Heidi poured herself a Cointreau with ice.

Raynes took the opportunity to survey her figure. He could easily understand how she had become Miss Grasshallows.

She gave the Inspector his drink and settled herself on the floor, cross-legged, and gazed at him with dark intensity.

"Cheers!" she said.

Raynes took a small sip.

"Your boyfriend is . . .?"

" . . .Karl . . ."

" . . . who knocked out Mr Blazer at the party?"

"He was jealous. He'd been drinking all afternoon. I'd been busy with Sandra and the baby. I think he felt rather neglected. When he saw the Rev kissing me, he just flipped." She laughed. "Poor lad, he didn't deserve it. I don't think he'd ever kissed a woman till that afternoon."

Raynes smiled.

"It seems to have been quite a wild baptism."

"It was rather . . ." Heidi sighed. "Of course, it should never have happened. It was a complete mockery – the whole thing. Sandra doesn't believe in anything – and neither do I. It was just a . . . post-natal publicity stunt. She admitted as much."

"And you're her best friend?"

"I am."

"But you're a bit older than she is?"

Heidi gave him a coy smile.

"A little bit."

"And you keep her on the straight and narrow?"

Heidi almost choked on her Cointreau.

"You must be joking!"

"She does her own thing . . .?"

"Always. But then she tells me what she's done. We have no secrets."

"So you'll know which of the godparents is the baby's father?"

Heidi shook her head.

"No one knows. She refuses to have a test."

"Doesn't she want to know?"

"She's frightened it might be Ron – then she might have to marry him. Both her mum and her uncle Tom think she should. He's even offered to buy them a house. But Ron's as frightened as she is. He's not the marrying type. And her dad agreed with her. 'Take your time,' he said. 'Don't rush it.' So she didn't."

In the course of speaking, Heidi spilt some of her drink down her cleavage. Or perhaps it was a brief distraction put on for the Inspector's benefit?

"Oh, damn!" she said. "It's a new blouse."

She rubbed away the sticky drops of Cointreau. If she meant to arouse the Inspector, she succeeded. One of her breasts nearly escaped.

"So who does she want to marry?"

"No one. She wants to play the field. And who can blame her? She's only nineteen; she wants to have a good time. I say good luck to her." She looked knowingly at Raynes. "Ron and Jimmy – they're both complete scumbags! Marriage to either of them would be a disaster. You take my word for it."

Raynes was prepared to take her word for it. She seemed an honest, outspoken person. Nothing to hide. He looked at her small chubby breasts. Certainly nothing to hide!

"So you go through the motions of a baptism . . . You have a

110

riotous party . . . There are a couple of punch-ups. And then, Mr Stone goes missing . . ."

"Yeah. Creepy, isn't it?"

Raynes thought "creepy" was an unusual word to use.

"I mean, he's just vanished."

"Yes."

"Jimmy thinks he's been seized by aliens."

"He would!"

"So who d'you think he was taken by?"

"Me? I haven't got the vaguest. My first thought was that he'd gone off on the razzle-dazzle. I think that's what Sandra thought."

"And now?"

Heidi was silent.

"You think he's dead?"

"Yes."

"Someone killed him after he came out of the pub?"

She nodded.

"So what've they done with the body?"

Heidi considered.

"Took him for a ride? Dumped him in a ditch? Buried him in a wood? Shoved him into an incinerator? It has to be out of town. If it was in Grasshallows, you'd have found him by now."

"And who would have wanted to kill him?"

Heidi laughed.

"Now you're asking! There's quite a lot of people who'd have liked to get even with Bert. People he's physically attacked. There are plenty of them. People he's cheated. Any number of husbands and boyfriends who have discovered what he did to their partners. His son, Alec. He used to beat him up when he was a child. He hasn't forgotten."

"And what about you?"

"Me? No, he was always very sweet to me. Gave me a great big smacker under the mistletoe last Christmas. Sort of thing a girl doesn't forget."

She smiled broadly.

"And what does Karl think about him?"

"He doesn't really know him. I don't think he'd even met him before the day of the baptism. He's only been in Grasshallows a few weeks."

"Doing what?"

"Labouring."

"So what's his attraction for an ex-beauty queen?"

Heidi uttered a low growl.

"Pure animal! No brains. Sheer primitive lust. I always go for it."

As she spoke, Raynes could almost feel the heat of passion oozing from her body. Not one animal – but two.

Raynes looked at her thoughtfully.

"Not unlike Bert?"

"No, I suppose not. He was a bit of a caveman."

"Did he attract you too?"

Heidi drank the last of her Cointreau and cradled her glass before she spoke.

"Clever!" she said. "Very clever! But you're right. We had it off once or twice, but Sandra doesn't know anything about it. I'd rather she didn't. But I think you could say I knew Bert Stone rather well."

"Indecent assault?"

"The more indecent the better! I can handle it."

"Most people go to the police."

"I know. I don't blame them. Must be terrifying meeting Tarzan straight off the trees. He was lucky to get off with only two charges of indecent assault – and not to be jailed."

"You think it might be one of his victims?"

"Quite possibly. If you're a woman, you never forget such things."

"And where were you on Sunday night?"

"I went home with Sandra and the baby. We got him to bed. Then I took a taxi home, stripped down and waited for my caveman to return."

"And when did he appear?"

Heidi looked the Inspector straight in the eye.

"About midnight. He left the pub with that dreadful Raymond Stone. He was filling his mind with all sorts of revolutionary rubbish. Promising him a job and a flat if he joined the local Communist party. It's an absolute scream, because Karl's a member of the . . ."

Raynes was suddenly conscious of a third presence in the room. Heidi's caveman had returned.

Karl looked down at his beloved in her revealing blouse, sitting on the floor at the Inspector's feet. The empty glasses. The scene was easily open to misinterpretation.

Karl looked at Raynes. The look said: "What are you doing, invading my space, entertaining my bird? Get the hell out of it!"

Raynes found his muscles tensing. If the brute came at him, he was in a vulnerable position, sitting on a rocking chair. It was a blessing he hadn't been sitting on the sofa. Once again, he wished that he had brought Carlisle with him.

Fortunately, Heidi jumped to her feet and put her arms round his neck.

"Karl, this is Mr Raynes. He's a policeman. He's come to ask about Bert."

This information did not seem to calm the savage beast. If anything, the brows lowered and the eyes went colder. Clearly, Karl had a long-standing distrust of policemen.

"Come along to the kitchen and I'll get you a beer."

With a final malicious glance, Karl was led away.

Raynes quickly got to his feet. He would not be caught in a vulnerable position again. He tested his fists in case he might have to use them in self-defence.

Karl returned with his beer and sat down on the sofa.

"D'you want another drink, Inspector?"

"No, thank you; I must be going."

Karl realized there was something lumpy under his cushion. He reached underneath and drew out the dildo. He looked from it to Raynes.

The Inspector laughed.

"That was for your playtime – not mine."

Heidi put her arms around Karl.

"He needs a lot of loving. He had a terrible childhood. Didn't you, love? Come to Heidi for lots of kisses and passion."

She gave him a cuddle and a kiss.

Raynes said politely: "I hope you'll have a lovely evening."

"Beat it, pig!"

Raynes made his way to the door. By the time he had reached the front steps, Heidi was at his side.

"I'm sorry about that. He didn't understand. I'll explain it to him."

Raynes said: "You should have a 'Beware' sign on your gate. That one's lethal. He should be behind bars!"

"Don't be nasty!"

"By the way," said the Inspector, "we were interrupted. What party did you say he belonged to?"

Heidi whispered in his ear:

"The British National Party."

Raynes was surprised.

"I thought they believed in racial purity!"

Heidi giggled.

As they reached the gate, she put a soft brown hand on the Inspector's arm. "I'm sorry you couldn't stay any longer. When he goes, I'll let you know. Then we can hit the hay big time."

Her eyes twinkled and she ran a small pink tongue over her lips.

"Bye, bye, Inspector."

18. *Pastoral Symphony*

Carlisle drove the police Granada into the Picton Dale Caravan Park, pulled up the handbrake and switched off the engine.

"I never expected to be back here again."

"Well," said Raynes, "she's a lady who gets around. She needs the money. And someone who knows how to pull a decent pint or serve a trayful of canapés will never be out of a job. She's one of life's drones."

"She's not exactly a glamour-puss."

"No," said Raynes, "she isn't. But she has great courage, a good sense of humour and a willingness to entertain even the most unlovely sections of humanity . . ." he looked at his

114

younger colleague, " . . . even the police."

They walked over to Grace's caravan.

The lady in question was out on the grass, barefoot, wearing a yellow top and a short red skirt, decorated with butterflies.

"You've got to admit," said Raynes, "she has lovely legs!" To Grace, he said: "It's us again." He gave her a hug and a kiss.

Carlisle kept his distance.

"I'm just watering my geraniums. They're getting a bit dry. I like them to have a little moisture before the sun gets to them."

"Very sensible," said Raynes.

"Would you like a drink?" asked Grace. "I know it's a bit early, but I'm sure you'd like a drop of elderflower wine. There's an old lady in the village who makes gallons of it."

"I bet it's 14% proof."

"At least."

"Well, a glass for me," said Raynes. "But orange juice for Detective-Constable Carlisle. He's driving."

They settled themselves in green plastic chairs outside the caravan. When Grace came back with the drinks, Raynes looked at the empty fields.

"No scouts this year?"

"No. The murder frightened them off. I expect they'll be back."

"Life's not the same without them, is it?"

Grace grinned.

"You're just being naughty."

"Actually," said Raynes, "we're here about something completely different."

"Bert Stone?"

"Yes."

"I read it in the paper. I can't say I'm surprised."

"Why not?"

"Well, he's got so many enemies. The photographer – Mr Beamish – was telling me what that dreadful man did to his wife's best friend."

"What did he do?"

"Indecent assault."

"He's been doing it all his life."

115

"So he has; and now it's caught up with him."

"You think he's been murdered?"

"I hope so."

"D'you have any personal reason for hating him?"

"Yes; but it's a long time ago."

Raynes looked at her. As always, Grace was wearing dark glasses so it was impossible to see her eyes. But a couple of tears trickled down her cheeks.

"You work for Tom Stone?"

"Now and again. Special functions mostly."

"You were at the baptismal party at his house?"

"A little bird's been talking."

"Two little birds."

"Well, I hope they don't talk to the taxman. I just pocket the money I get at functions. Might affect my benefit."

"That's no concern of ours," said Raynes. "What I want to know is whether you noticed anything at the party which might explain his sudden disappearance."

"Well, there was a fight. You'll have been told about that. The poor young man he knocked down. He doesn't know his own strength. And the tricks he was playing. Giving Eric a glass of his home-made beer."

"Who's Eric?"

"He's a young man with epilepsy. Bert told him it was Coca-cola. It went right through him. It was a really dirty trick. We poured about ten gallons of the stuff down the sink. It's a pity he wasn't made to drink his own poison."

Raynes looked at his glass.

"That elderflower's lovely. So refreshing."

"Would you like another glass?"

"If you have it?"

"I've got two bottles of the stuff."

Raynes looked at Carlisle sipping his orange juice.

"Are you getting this lot down?"

"There's not much so far."

"Atmosphere!" said Raynes. "It's always important to get the right atmosphere." He picked up his second glass. "Thank you." He took a sip. "It has a delicious taste . . ."

"And there were those little girls . . . in pink and green dresses. He was chasing them around in the bouncy castle. I don't know what he did to them, but I'm told he gave them money when they left."

Raynes raised his eyebrows a fraction.

"Do you know the names of the parents?"

"No."

Raynes sighed. How often people gave you helpful information – but never gave you chapter and verse. Always it required more hard slog . . . more visits . . . more questions. He turned back to Grace:

"Did Bert approach you at the party?"

"He did; but he didn't get anywhere."

"One of the young men at the party told me that you threatened to castrate him."

"That's putting words into my mouth, Inspector. What I said was that I hoped somebody else would do it. And perhaps they have. Who told you that?"

"The disc jockey. Jimmy Watson."

Grace smiled.

"Oh, he was a lovely lad. So natural. Really helpful. He helped me shift all the crates of bottles at the end. 'No trouble,' he said. 'I'm used to carrying loudspeakers and amplifiers.' I told him all about Bert. He was quite shocked."

"Did you tell him about the little girls?"

"Oh, yes. I wasn't letting him get away with that."

"So what did he do to you?"

"Nothing."

"In the past?"

"D'you really want to know? It was in a pub. Years ago when I was married to Kenny Buchanan. He dragged me into the store room, locked the door and pushed me down on the floor. I started screaming but he bashed my head on the floor. Really rough. When I tried to get up, he punched me in the stomach – completely winded me – and then tore off my pants.

"By the time I'd got my breath back, he was into me. Just animal. Pure animal. He should've been charged. I told him I was going to the police but then he made a great song and dance

117

about his wife and children. What would they do if he went to jail? I should have gone to the police right away – but I didn't. And by then, it was too late. But I've never forgotten. I can still feel him . . ."

Her fists were clenched.

" . . . Murder would be too good for him. He needs to really suffer. I hope he did."

"You seem quite sure that he's dead?"

"Well, people like Bert don't just disappear. They may have heart attacks . . . or get put into mental hospitals . . .. fall down a flight of steps and crack their heads open . . . but they always survive. Bert's got a cushy number, driving that van round the town. He's just become a grandfather. His brother laid on a great party. I bet he didn't pay a penny. Then he went off to that pub. Drinks on the house. Eyeing up that new barmaid at the *Kirby* . . . By the time he left, he was probably plastered. Someone probably volunteered to give him a lift home. But he never made it. They took him for a nice little ride – then topped him. I say: 'And about time too!'"

"You've no feelings for his wife and children?"

"I've no feelings for any of the Stone family. Tom throws his money around but he's as big a shit as the rest of them."

Raynes said nothing.

"His daughter's very pretty. I'll give her that. She's very like her mother when she was young. But Alec's a sourpuss; always mooching around in the background, stirring up trouble. I could see him killing his dad."

"We're hoping to see him this afternoon."

"Well, there's your chance!"

Raynes finished the last of his elderflower wine.

"I have to ask you the obvious question. What were you doing at half past midnight on Sunday . . . no, Monday morning?"

"Asleep. In the caravan. Alone. I start work in the pub at 6.00am. No time for gallivanting."

"And no one to vouch for your story?"

"You'll just have to rely on my good character."

She saw the Inspector's look.

118

"I've never been charged with anything yet!"

Raynes smiled.

"There's still time!"

19. *Sortie*

"That was a complete waste of time," said Carlisle.

"It was very nice elderflower wine!"

"We didn't come out all this way to drink wine!"

"No," said Raynes, "we didn't. We came out here to see someone who has a deep-seated grudge against Bert Stone. She was one of his victims. As recently as ten days ago, she expressed the wish that someone would mutilate him in a particularly horrible way. She has motive – but perhaps not the means.

"And she added another piece of information to our jigsaw. No one else mentioned Bert and those two children. That's another angle we'll have to consider."

Raynes looked critically at his colleague.

"Who are their parents? What do they know? Did they take the law into their own hands?"

Carlisle reached the outskirts of Grasshallows and slowed down to 30mph. Raynes continued to press his point.

"She spoke to Jimmy . . . Did he carry out her wish? Was he playing all night at *The Raging Bull*? And what did he do when he left? She has given us a lot to think about. And," said Raynes, "she also put her finger on Alec – as many others have done. So it was not a complete waste of time."

Carlisle accepted defeat graciously.

As they got out of the car, Raynes asked:

"Did you find out Alec's address?"

Carlisle took out his pocket book.

"159 London Road. Top floor flat. But, at the moment, he'll be working."

"Where?"

Carlisle smiled.

"You'll like this. The crematorium!"

* * * *

Grasshallows Crematorium occupied forty acres of ground on the outskirts of the city. It was a peaceful place with meandering paths, bushes and trees. The memorial roses provided a splendid display of colour. Looking at this tranquil scene, Carlisle said:

"You're not planning to dig this lot up, are you?"

"I hope not."

As they walked over to the office, the first thing they noticed was a large, powerful motor bike. It was a Honda VRF 750 with a double overhead camshaft – quite a new model at that time. They stopped to look at it. Carlisle instinctively checked that the licence was valid; Raynes looked at the mileage on the clock. 5621. Quite a high total for eight months.

Raynes went into the office, flashed his identification card and asked the question to which he already knew the answer: "Do you have a young man called Alec Stone working here?"

"Yes, we do. He's one of the groundsmen."

"Would it be possible to speak to him?"

"He's not in any sort of trouble, is he?"

"No. It's about his father's disappearance. We're making enquiries."

"You'll find him on section T8. He's mowing the lawn."

"Thank you."

As Raynes and Carlisle set out across the grass, the clerk watched them through the leaded windows.

"I thought it was about his bike."

"You heard them. It's about his dad."

"You never know with the police."

Alec saw them coming. He was surprised they had taken so long to find him. He finished off the last few yards up to the path and switched off the mower.

The Inspector introduced himself and his colleague.

"Are you Alec Stone?"

"Yes."

"Is there anywhere we can talk privately?"

Alec led them to a quiet corner, surrounded by high hedges, where there were a couple of benches.

"We're investigating the disappearance of your father."

A contemptuous sneer appeared on the young man's face.

"It doesn't bother you?"

"Not really."

"Glad to see the back of him?"

"Yes."

Alec knew that other people would have told the Inspector what he thought about his father.

"When did you last see him?"

"At the pub."

"On the Sunday night?"

Alec nodded.

Surely they knew this already?

"You had gone there with your dad, your uncle Tom and uncle Raymond, Karl, Ron and Charles. Seven of you. How long did you stay?"

"Till about eight."

"And then?"

"Ron and I went to the snooker."

"He's your best friend?"

Alec did not really have any close friends. He was too prickly a personality. But he liked Ron – so he nodded again.

"Ron says he left you at about 11.00pm. What did you do then?"

"I went home."

"159 London Road?"

"That's right."

"When did you move out of Coronation Gardens?"

"About a year ago."

"Was that when you got this job?"

"Yes."

Raynes' eyes narrowed.

"How did you manage to get this job?"

Alec resented the suggestion that he was incapable of getting a job on his own merits. But he was obliged to admit that his Uncle Raymond had given him a helping hand. He had spoken to someone in the Council.

"Was it him who gave you the bike?"

Alec bristled.

"No. My dad gave me the bike. It was a Christmas present."

"Pretty expensive Christmas present!" said Raynes. "Must have cost at least two thousand quid. And licensed for a whole year."

"It's about the only present he's ever given me."

Alec looked surly and ungrateful.

"So why the sudden generosity?"

"He knew I'd always wanted one."

"That doesn't answer my question."

Alec was perfectly aware of that. He didn't like answering the Inspector's questions. He knew he was trying to make him say things about his relationship with his dad which he would then twist into a suggestion that he was involved in his father's disappearance – or murder. After that, they would take him down to the police station and question him for hours until he broke. He had seen it all on TV.

"I expect he felt sorry about things . . ."

"What things?"

Alec had already been told by Ron that the Inspector knew about his unhappy childhood. So why was he asking? Did he want to humiliate him? Probably.

He looked at the Inspector with cold eyes.

"I know you've already been told about my father beating me. Normally when he was drunk . . ."

"Why was that?"

"Because I stood up to him. He didn't like it."

"He didn't treat your sister like that."

Alec allowed himself a bitter smile.

"No, he didn't. But she was the apple of his eye. Always has been. Everything she wants, she gets."

"Which makes it very unusual that he should have given you the bike."

"I suppose it was meant to shut me up."

He knew the Inspector would jump on that. And he did. But he was ready for him.

"I was very upset about Sandra having the baby. I didn't think she should have it – not at her age. I thought she should have an abortion. I said so. I said it to her. I said it to Mum. I said it to all my friends. I didn't make any secret of my views. Sandra was very upset. So was Mum. Dad told me to shut up. I refused. I caused so much trouble that he did a deal with me. Not another word about abortion – and he would give me the bike. That's the truth – whether you like it or not."

Raynes looked at him in a more kindly fashion.

"I accept that. But it hasn't entirely silenced you, has it?"

"No. I disapprove of what my dad did to Ron – and the others. He insisted that they should all pay maintenance – whether they were the father or not. He threatened them – and they knew that if they didn't cough up, he'd do something nasty to them. He was bullying them like he used to bully me. So I told them they were mugs . . . None of them could afford sixty quid a week. It was a scam. Daylight robbery. But when Ron spoke up at the party, what did he do? He knocked him out!"

The Inspector sounded more conciliatory.

"So there were quite a number of people who hated your father?"

Alec laughed coldly.

"You know that. I bet there's not a single person whom you've interviewed who's said a good word about him. I'm not the only one – not by a long chalk."

"Your mother's put up with him for a long time."

"Twenty-seven years."

"She hasn't left him."

"She wouldn't dare."

"And your sister?"

"She's scared of him too. But she wouldn't admit it."

"You think he had this effect on everyone?"

"You've got your police records."

"I've read them."

"Well, you should know what he's like. Why pick on me?"

Raynes raised his eyebrows.

"I'm not picking on anyone. I'm asking you the same questions that I asked Ron, Jimmy, Charles, Uncle Tom . . . I just want to find a reason why your father disappeared – and, if he was murdered, to find out who killed him and why. There appear to be many good reasons why people might have wanted to kill him – but why should they choose that particular Sunday? I know there was a fight . . ."

"Ron didn't do it."

Raynes noted how quickly he leapt to his friend's defence.

" . . . but that doesn't seem to be a sufficiently strong motive. I'm looking for some special grudge or grievance which surfaced that day – something which may have driven a person to kill your dad."

He looked hard at the young man.

"Well, I didn't do it. It's no use looking at me."

"You could've given him a lift home on your motor bike."

"He was so drunk, he'd have fallen off!"

"No, he wasn't. Tom says that he was quite capable of standing up – or walking. If you'd got him on the back of your bike, you'd have got him home."

"Well, I didn't."

Provocatively, Raynes said: "You might have brought him out here. Plenty of nice places to dispose of a body. I must admit I thought of the cemetery; but I didn't realize the crematorium had so much open ground."

Alec looked at him with disbelief.

"You think I killed my dad?"

"You have to be one of the chief suspects. When you left Ron at 11.00pm, you say you went home. But can anyone confirm that you were in the flat after twelve o'clock?" He looked at Alec.

"Well, can they?"

Very sulkily: "No."

"Well, that's why I have to ask you these questions. Like most people, you have a motive; you had the means. People don't just disappear. Someone has spirited him away. Dumped him; burnt him; buried him; cut him up in little pieces; hidden him in a freezer. I have to find answers. When people tell me lies, I have to be brutal."

"I haven't told you any lies."

Raynes looked at Alec for a long time – running his mind back through their conversation.

"No," he said at last, "I think you have been honest with me. But I still think there's something you know that you're not telling me. And if I knew what it was, I could probably wrap up this case quite quickly."

Alec shrugged his shoulders.

"No one knows whether he's alive or dead. It's a complete mystery to everyone."

"Not to everyone. Someone must know."

Raynes got to his feet.

"Thank you," he said, "for speaking to me so openly. If you think of something later, please have the courage to phone me. It could make all the difference."

He and Carlisle walked back to the office in silence. Raynes went in and said to the clerk: "Would Mr Stone have any access to the ovens in the crematorium?"

The clerk looked shocked.

"Oh, no. He's only a groundsman."

Raynes and Carlisle departed.

When Alec came back with the motor mower and collected his helmet and gloves, the clerk told him what the Inspector had said.

"You'd better be careful, lad! That man thinks you've burnt your dad!"

20. *Scenes From Childhood*

That same afternoon, whilst Raynes was interviewing Alec in the grounds of the crematorium, the Reverend Blazer was preparing his first sermon.

Predictably, he had chosen to speak about love – not that he knew a great deal about it! But it was one of those sure-fire topics with which no one could disagree. Like mother's milk, it was generally rated to be "a good thing". Of course he was not thinking of the "love" dispensed by such wild creatures as

Heidi Houston (which was merely animal passion and therefore sinful); but rather, "love" as displayed on a higher plane – such as duty, care, service and self-sacrifice.

He had enthusiastically plundered St John's epistles, C.S. Lewis, Mother Julian of Norwich and Kahlil Gibran and blended the whole into a tasty mish-mash which he thought the congregation would find acceptable. Certainly more acceptable than the sermon given by the Senior Lecturer in New Testament studies who had waxed poetic about the Qumran community and the Dead Sea scrolls for over half an hour; or the Professor of Philology, who had bored everyone stiff with an explanation of the significance of the "k" sound in Aramaic.

He had just written: "Greater love hath no man than this, that a man lay down his life for his fiend" – and realized he had omitted a vital "r" – when the doorbell rang.

Who could be visiting him at this time in the afternoon? Was it perhaps the police? He hoped not.

He walked down the dark passage and opened the door. He was surprised to see Sandra with her baby. She gave him a radiant smile.

"I was just passing. I thought you'd like to see Mark. He's growing."

Mr Blazer had fervently hoped that he would never see any of the Stone family ever again. But he could hardly be rude and shut the door in her face. This was a moment for gracious hospitality. To invite the young mother in for a cup of tea and to compliment her on the baby which certainly looked extremely healthy.

"Come in," he said. "I'm sure you could do with some light refreshment."

"A glass of wine would be nice. Have you got any red?"

Edmund had a single bottle of expensive Medoc left over from his ordination. It would be a crime to open it. He gritted his teeth. This would be truly sacrificial giving!

The flat was looking fairly tidy – except for his desk which was covered with paper and books. At least it looked as if he was working – which indeed he was.

He turned down the recording of the choir of Queen's

College, who were belting out some anthem by Orlando Gibbons. He reckoned it might upset the baby.

He went through to the kitchen to find the bottle and two glasses.

Sandra put Mark in the corduroy arm chair. He looked very small.

Edmund opened the bottle and poured out the wine. He gave a glass to Sandra.

"D'you know? He's sixteen pounds, two ounces. The nurse weighed him this morning." She poked the baby in a friendly fashion and took a swig of wine. "Oh, look!" she said. "He's smiling at you."

The Reverend Blazer thought it was probably wind.

He sat down in the red armchair. Sandra sat on the floor, casting loving eyes at both Edmund and the baby.

"What are you doing?" she asked.

"Writing a sermon."

"About what?"

"Love," said Mr Blazer briefly.

Sandra suppressed a giggle and took another swig of the Medoc. It seemed good stuff. Thick and strong. Not like some of that cheap muck you got off the supermarket shelves. Probably 14 or 15%.

"When are you going to preach it?"

"Next Sunday."

"Oh, can we come and watch?"

Edmund drank deeply.

"If you must."

"I promise not to breast-feed the baby while you're speaking."

Edmund almost threw up. The thought of his deeply spiritual offering – his carefully crafted words – being interrupted by a steady glug-glug in the back row – or, even worse, in the front pew – was almost too ghastly to bear.

"I hope you'll never breast-feed a baby during a service. It would be most inappropriate."

He looked up at the small reproduction of Raphael's masterpiece of the Madonna nursing the infant Christ to her bosom – and felt instantly guilty.

But Sandra was smiling.

"Keep your hair on! I was only teasing."

She held out her glass.

"That was good stuff. Can I have some more?"

Edmund filled up her glass and changed the subject:

"They haven't found your father yet?"

"No. But you'll be the first to know if they do."

"Why me?"

"For the funeral, stupid."

Edmund considered the grim prospect of a Stone funeral and the inevitable boozy wake that would follow. That was one party he would certainly avoid.

"You're sure he's dead?"

"The police think so. They've dragged the river. Dug up part of Uncle Tom's garden . . ."

"Have they?"

"They didn't find anything." She looked sad. "But they've gone through the Meadows with a toothcomb. Been into every garage and lock-up. Nothing!" She shook her head in disbelief. "It's a complete mystery."

"What d'you think's happened?"

"I don't know. And, quite frankly, I don't want to know. Uncle Tom's promised to look after us. So if Dad doesn't come back, we're going to live with him."

"That's very kind of him."

"I think he's always had a soft spot for Mum."

The Reverend Blazer's mind immediately returned to a darkened bedroom and a dress lying on the floor.

"It'll be a nice home for Mark. A huge garden to play in." She turned to the baby and chatted away. Mark produced another toothless smile.

Before Sandra revealed the real purpose of her visit, she commandeered a third glass of wine. Edmund was anxious. Would she be able to get home safely with the baby?

"If the worst comes to the worst, I'll take a taxi."

Edmund poured her half a glass.

"Oh, go on!" she said. "Don't be a meanie!"

Once the glass was filled to the brim, Sandra revealed the object of her visit.

"I came to tell you some good news."

Edmund's face brightened.

"You're getting married?"

Sandra shook her head, looked at the baby and then gave Edmund a sly look.

"No. I'm pregnant again."

"Again?"

Sandra nodded.

"I was surprised; but it's nearly three months since Mark was born. These things happen. Anyway, I thought you'd be pleased."

For all his sermon about love, Edmund did not greet this revelation with any enthusiasm. In fact, he felt vaguely disgusted. It was another sign of the immorality of the working classes – their insatiable urge to procreate. Yet another social misfit! Yet another baptism! Canon Murray could handle that one!

Overcoming his revulsion, he asked politely:

"So who's the father this time?"

Sandra gave him a beaming smile.

"You are!"

"Me?"

"It has to be. You're the only person I've had sex with since Mark was born. It can't be anyone else."

(This was not strictly true; but Edmund was not to know the wilder shores of her love life.)

The young curate was speechless.

Sandra enjoyed his embarrassment.

"You remember? At the party?"

How could he ever forget that shameful moment? His total lack of self-control? For the last fortnight, he had been trying to blot out the memory of what had happened in that upstairs bedroom. A sin as yet unconfessed and, so, still unforgiven.

It was bad enough to have had sex with an unmarried mother . . . but to have to admit to Canon Murray that he had impregnated a member of the Stone family, would be a moment of utter humiliation. He might be sacked; his priesting delayed; even worse, he might be forced into a shotgun marriage. Everyone would talk about it. They would snigger at him behind his back. He would never become a bishop.

"What do you expect me to do?" he asked, somewhat guiltily.

"What do people normally do when they have babies? They get married. I thought you'd be really pleased!"

She gave him another dazzling smile and drank half the glass of Medoc in one go. She was well aware of the bombshell she had dropped in the young man's life. She could imagine the turmoil in his brain. It amused her. If Heidi had known what she was proposing, she would have had a fit.

"I think it would be really lovely," she added. "We'd have a ready-made family. Mark would have a really caring dad. And I could help you with your work!"

Edmund cast round for a way out of his dilemma.

"Surely we couldn't have done it? Not in those few seconds?"

Sandra reassured him:

"That's the way these things happen. I wouldn't have expected it, but when you don't take precautions, it's a risk you have to take."

"Are you sure?"

"Oh, yes. I saw my doctor this morning. He gave me a urine test and it proved positive."

Anyone with even elementary glimmerings of the process of female reproduction might have doubted whether Sandra could be so sure – so soon. After all, it was only ten days since the party. But Edmund took her assurance at face value.

He still looked appalled.

Sandra smiled – a little more wickedly this time.

"Aren't you pleased? It might be another little priest! Following in his father's footsteps . . . Perhaps both of them?"

Surely she wasn't implying twins?

Edmund struggled desperately in deep waters.

"I don't know . . . I really don't know . . ."

"You don't have to worry about the cost of the wedding.

Uncle Tom'll pay. And Heidi's promised to be my bridesmaid."

"It wasn't that," said Edmund. "It's just that I don't know if I want to get married. I mean . . . we hardly know each other . . . I don't know what Canon Murray will say . . ."

"He can't stop you."

"He might."

The Reverend Blazer thought that this might be his final line of defence. But Sandra naturally took a very dim view of such doubts.

"You couldn't refuse your own child!"

Edmund still cast around for a way out.

Despite the Pro-Life poster prominently stuck on the wall, he said: "Couldn't you have an abortion?"

Sandra looked horrified.

"That's what they suggested when Mark was conceived. But look at him! How could you kill off such a beautiful child? That'd be dreadful! I don't know how you could suggest such a thing."

Almost on cue, the baby began to cry. Sandra put down her glass and cuddled him close to her bosom.

"You don't need to worry," she said. "I can see you're a good, kind, caring person. You're really good with babies. Everyone says so. We'd have a marvellous marriage. Lots of sex. I'd see you got plenty of that."

The horrified look on Edmund's face gave her pause for thought.

"You're not gay, are you?"

"I don't think so; but I never . . ."

"You said you had a girlfriend at Uni?"

"But that was different."

"You mean you didn't have sex with her?"

"Good heavens, no!"

Sandra smiled.

"Don't worry. I'll teach you. You'll love every moment of it."

But it wasn't sex that was troubling the Reverend Blazer. It was her family. He couldn't imagine himself being associated with the Stones. He was perhaps a snob. But the thought of all those coarse, mindless relations – thinking about nothing but drink, money and sex – revolted him. Sandra, herself, was a very sweet girl – but it was the baggage that she brought with her – and the shame. He would be ruining his life. Instinctively, he knew it.

Sandra, of course, saw the whole thing quite differently.

She said: "Most blokes would give their back teeth to marry me – but I wouldn't have them. I've fancied you ever since that first day you came to our house. And now that Dad's away, it'll be much easier."

The Reverend Blazer played for time.

He said he would think about it. The news of her pregnancy had come as a terrible shock. But when he had had time to think about it, they would have another chat. Get to know each other better.

In the meantime, he gave her the rest of the Medoc; he made a great fuss of the baby; she gave him a few drunken kisses; he made her a strong cup of black coffee and ordered a taxi. When the taxi arrived, he carried Mark downstairs, frightened that after drinking all that wine, she might fall down the steps. He saw her into the cab and handed in the baby.

"Bye, darling!" she said.

It was an afternoon Edmund would remember for the rest of his life.

21. *Locus Iste*

Detective-Inspector Raynes was not a man lightly to accept defeat. An obscure clue in the *Daily Telegraph* crossword could irritate him for hours. He would often insert a substitute word until the right one came into his mind. In fact, the very act of filling in the blank space with some fanciful word sometimes prompted his brain to come up with the correct answer within a matter of minutes.

He applied the same technique to his search for Albert Stone. Every possible solution had been considered in an attempt to find the missing man. Not one of them had worked. As he stood looking at the street map of Grasshallows on the office wall, he ruminated on aliens, Martians and little green men. Anyone who might have spirited Bert away.

Mentally, he drew a line from the *Kirby Arms* to Mr Stone's home in Henslea. He had already traced the journey several hundred times – on each occasion casting his eye to left or right. The river . . . the bridge . . . the lock-ups . . . the empty garages . . . sheds and outhouses . . . dustbins . . . boats.

His eye flashed along Riverside Road, over the bridge, up to the roundabout – left to the Meadows, right to Henslea. He knew every detail of that road – the post office, the bus shelters, the street lights. He had covered everything. Everything except . . .

As he completed the sentence, he suddenly realized where Bert's body was to be found.

He shook his head sadly.

How stupid! He should have guessed immediately. It was so obvious!

He went out to the car park and got into his Rover. Without the slightest hesitation, he thrust the car into the rush hour traffic and headed for Riverside Road.

As always, there was a long queue waiting at the traffic lights. He had been intending to write a rude letter to the City Engineer, telling him to adjust his lights to allow more cars through. It was perhaps a blessing that he had been too busy to write; for now he would be needing the help of the City Engineer in a big way.

He sat in the queue – no longer fuming or frustrated – but quietly amused. To think the solution had been right in front of him – and he had never noticed. He had checked everything – everything except the drains.

The reason he had not checked them was because Bert had apparently been so inebriated, he would not have had the strength to lift a manhole cover – let alone fall in.

But along the full length of Riverside Road, there was the new gas main being installed in a deep trench. The Gas Board were moving down the road at about one hundred yards a week. At any given moment, about one hundred and fifty yards of road had been dug up. There were metal barriers, cones, danger signs, sections of pipe, flashing orange lamps, yellow plastic tapes fluttering in the light breeze. Here was a ready-made pit into which any drunk might easily fall.

Just because no one had reported a body did not mean it was not there. He might have been covered with a fall of earth; he might have slipped down the side of a large pipe. He might have been pushed into the trench by some malignant member of the British public. It could have been an accident . . . but, equally, it could have been manslaughter or murder.

It was perhaps surprising that the body had not been seen by any of the workmen – but a light covering of earth might have hidden him from the JCB driver shovelling back the earth. By the time the police had started searching for the missing man, the vital section would have been tarmacked over.

Raynes had no doubt that he was right. Every other possibility had been considered. It had to be this trench, The big question was: how far had the work progressed since Sunday August 13th? Was there a chart or timetable? Would the Gas Board be willing to dig up the trench merely on a hunch? And what would he do if they refused?

The Inspector parked his car in a side street on double yellow lines. It was almost five o'clock and by now, the traffic wardens would have stopped work; so too the Gas Board; they would have finished by half past four.

Raynes dodged through the single file traffic and walked back down the far pavement, so intent on his theory that he collided with an elderly lecturer who was also deep in thought. Raynes helped him to his feet and apologized profusely.

He tried to remember where Carlisle had stopped the car on the Thursday morning, the first day of the investigation, when he had been cursing Rosalind Hayman for stalling her car. Surely it had been near the betting shop?

He measured the distance from the betting shop to the present excavations and divided it by the number of working days. Assuming that the rate of progress was indeed about twenty yards per day, he then paced out sixty yards from the betting shop. It took him to Fagan's, the undertakers. They would not enjoy a second excavation.

The Inspector decided to walk on to the *Kirby Arms*. It wasn't all that far. About six hundred yards. He could imagine Bert giving up his efforts to hail a taxi and setting off home on foot. It would have taken him about eight to ten minutes to cover the ground; which put the time of his death at about 12.30am.

Raynes could not resist popping in to the pub for a drink; but he seemed to have chosen the wrong moment to drop by. The place was full of working people, having a quick one on the way home. It took him nearly five minutes to reach the bar and order a Guinness. Not that there was much room to drink it. He found a small shelf beside a pillar, put down his glass and revelled in his latest discovery.

Through the crowd of bobbing heads, he saw Tom Stone collecting glasses. This was not the moment to conduct an interview but it was perhaps as good a time as any to ask him about the barmaid who had served Bert on the Sunday night. He waited till the proprietor was just a few yards away.

"Evening, Tom."

"Oh, evening, Inspector. I didn't expect to see you here."

"I'm still pursuing the ungodly."

"The ungodly? Oh, I suppose you mean people like me? Is there any news?"

Raynes shook his head.

"Didn't think there would be."

"I was wanting to ask you the name of that barmaid who was working here that Sunday night."

"Elaine. Elaine Sharpe."

"Is she likely to be here tonight?"

Tom's face clouded over.

"No. I had to sack her."

"When?"

"After that Sunday night."

"And why was that?"

"Well, if you want it straight – for having sex in a public place."

"With Bert?"

135

"Who else?"

Tom's lips curled in disgust.

"I don't suppose you've got her address?"

"Phone me later and I'll have it for you."

22. *The Song Of The Earth*

Raynes arranged his visit to the City Engineer early the following morning. He received a warm welcome.

"Inspector, I don't think I've met you before. But, of course, I've read a lot about you in the paper."

Raynes expressed his admiration for all the hard work done by the City Council – especially its efforts at conservation. A pot of coffee was ordered. The Inspector noted the superior quality of china when compared to the police department. Here it was porcelain; there it was earthenware mugs.

"Now, what can I do for you, Inspector?"

"I have a favour to ask. A very big favour."

The Chief Engineer looked eager to help.

"You may perhaps have read in the papers about a missing man. A Mr Albert Stone. He vanished almost a fortnight ago and since then, we've been doing all the usual things – interviewing his wife and family, speaking to his friends; we've dragged the river, gone through the Meadows with a fine toothcomb; but we've found nothing. In fact, we've reached a dead end.

"The man was last seen outside the *Kirby Arms*, hoping to flag down a taxi shortly after midnight. He was trying to get back to his home in Henslea. He was somewhat the worse for drink – but still capable of walking. We've considered all sorts of possibilities – even aliens!"

The Chief Engineer smiled.

"But still no luck?"

"I'm afraid not. Our resident expert in such things tells me that they carry us off to some distant galaxy where they use us for experiments. What they hope to get out of Mr Stone, I don't know.

"Well, I've been racking my brains to come up with some more rational solution; and last night, it came to me. I think that Mr Stone could have fallen into that huge trench the Gas Board is digging in Riverside Road . . ."

The Chief Engineer stopped smiling.

"Oh, no!"

"Oh, yes! We've considered every other possibility. This has to be it. I think he fell into the trench and was partially covered by a fall of earth and then the rest of the stuff was shovelled back over him."

The Chief Engineer was certainly not amused.

"Inspector Raynes, have you any idea how long that trench is? The disruption that work has caused the city – at the very height of the tourist season? It's been absolute hell."

Raynes nodded.

"I know. I've been stuck in the queues almost every day."

"It's the tailbacks that cause all the trouble. Once they reach the High Street, the whole city's in gridlock. You can't seriously be asking us to dig it all up again?"

"No," said Raynes firmly. "I'm only interested in one small section – somewhere near Fagan's. The Gas Board would need to tell us exactly where the trench was open on Sunday, August 13th. If he did fall in, it would have been at the *Kirby Arms* end. If he'd fallen in anywhere else, his body would have been seen. It's a fairly small section I'm talking about – twenty or thirty yards at the most – and they still have all their diggers and equipment on site. At the outside, it would take a couple of days – more disruption, I know – but it can't be helped."

"But suppose you dig down and find nothing? Will you want to extend the work? And what if there's no body at all? All that work for nothing?"

The Chief Engineer was looking desperate.

"Providing the Gas Board are keeping proper records, they should be able to pinpoint the site. I should like fifteen to twenty feet either way. I can promise you – no more than that."

"I don't know if you appreciate, Inspector, how much this has already cost the City? We've had to face financial claims for loss of business – particularly from Fagan's – garaging their cars and hearses elsewhere. The thought of it all starting up again is not going to go down well with the City Treasurer or the Council. If the man is down there, can't we just leave him there? After all, he is buried, isn't he?"

Raynes was not sure whether the Chief Engineer was trying to be funny. Wisely, he assumed that he wasn't.

"I'm sure, sir, that if it was your own wife – or daughter – who was missing and it was suspected that she had fallen into the trench, you would insist on action being taken . . . expensive though it would be."

The Chief Engineer groaned.

"I'll have to make enquiries, Inspector. I can't just say 'Yes' or 'No'. There'll have to be a departmental meeting, consultation with the Gas people, perhaps some discussion at the next Council meeting. You mustn't expect a quick decision. Some very serious thought will have to go into this."

Raynes had attended enough committee meetings in his life to know when a difficult issue was being kicked into touch. He recognized the civil servant's predeliction for stonewalling and buck-passing. He was determined not to give the City Engineer a single inch for manoeuvre. He allowed him a few more minutes of moaning and hand-wringing; then he produced his trump card.

"I'm afraid, sir, there can be no question of public discussion about the opening up of this trench. I have every reason to believe that Mr Stone was murdered and his body thrown into the trench. It is of the utmost importance that the reopening of the ground should appear to be a decision taken by the Gas Board – rectifying a mistake. It has to appear as part of the work in hand. If the matter comes into the public domain, the murderer could be alerted – and might leave the country.

"I'm sure that it would cost the Crown Prosecution Service and the Police Department far more to pursue the culprit abroad than it would cost to dig another hole; especially as the machinery and manpower are all to hand. Another two or three weeks and it might cost a lot more."

Raynes smiled encouragingly.

"Anyway, I'm sure the Police Committee will be happy to chip in." (The Inspector knew this was a complete lie.) "They consider an arrest in this case most important. And we can only secure the evidence by finding the body. I think you will appreciate, sir, the urgency of this case."

* * * *

Raynes returned to his office with a big smile on his face.

"I'm the most unpopular person in Grasshallows!"

Carlisle thought this was probably an exaggeration. Surely the manager of the local football team was infinitely more unpopular? But when the Inspector told him his theory about Bert Stone's disappearance and the need to dig up the road, his colleague immediately appreciated the ructions which would follow – not just in Riverside Road but also in the corridors of power.

"Thy won't like that!"

"They don't. I've just been to see the City Engineer. He tried to fob me off, pass the buck – all the usual ploys – but I told him it was a murder enquiry and the whole thing had to be handled with the utmost secrecy."

"So what's he going to do?"

"Co-operate. What else can he do? Actually, I think he quite liked the idea of digging up a body. Might be quite a feather in his cap. A bit of good publicity for his department." Raynes chuckled. "He's having a private meeting with the Gas Board this afternoon. They're going to look at their plans and find out the position on the ground. He phoned them whilst I was there. They think they can pinpoint the actual place – to within ten feet – so not too much disruption. The work can be done outside rush hours and the City will foot the bill. I couldn't ask for more."

Detective-Constable Carlisle was full of admiration.

"But what if they don't find his body?"

Raynes grinned.

"As I told you, I shall be the most unpopular man in Grasshallows!"

23. *Since By Man Came Death*

To excavate a section of public road is – in the experience of most local authorities – an invitation to open a Pandora's box of human misery. Nothing ever goes according to plan. Very often, the work of one utility causes trouble for another. A water main bursts; someone cuts through a vital cable. So it is no surprise when a completed section of road needs to be reopened. The second excavation of Riverside Road began one warm summer's evening at the end of August.

The Gas Board was there with their JCB. Workers stood around with shovels. Men in hard hats consulted plans, drew lines with chalk and issued a stream of orders. But the police were also present. Ordinary constables redirected traffic and pedestrians. Members of the Forensic Department stood around in blue overalls, trying to look inconspicuous. Detective-Inspector Raynes and Detective-Constable Carlisle stood in a shop doorway, anxiously waiting.

Fortunately, Fagan's had been spared further misery; it was a camping shop that took most of the dirt and the disruption.

"You must be bloody sure!" said Dr Stewart, the police forensic surgeon. "Otherwise, you'll have wasted a lot of people's valuable time."

"If I'm wrong," said Raynes, "I'll give you a dozen bottles of malt."

Dr Stewart smiled happily.

"In that case, I shall be most happy to see you fail!"

But, knowing Raynes' reputation, he felt sure that the Inspector would not have gone this far unless he was positive that the body was really there.

A supervisor from the Gas Board came forward brandishing a large-scale plan.

"We're fairly certain this is the spot. That's where we stopped on Friday 11th. We took photographs – and they confirm it."

He dug into a blue plastic wallet and produced a selection of colour photographs, dated and timed. He pointed to the digger.

"They're going to start about ten feet back. They're going four feet down. Once he's opened up the surface, the men'll dig down."

He rushed off to give his final orders.

Drills broke into the surface of the road; the yellow digger manoeuvred into position and lowered its mechanical bucket; loads of tarmac and red clay were scooped up. But the process of opening up the strip of road was maddeningly slow. Raynes remained outwardly calm – but, inside, the butterflies were doing a clog dance.

Then the men went to work – fast and efficient – even though they had been working all afternoon. Still, it was cooler now and they had had time for a rest and a bite.

They dug deeper and more carefully. They reached the pipe and worked forward towards the place where the body was expected to be. The sound of shovels, clanging against iron, filled the air. A further section of clay was broken into and shovelled away. Then another. The drillers came back to clear another twelve feet of road surface. More red clay was lifted.

It was beginning to look hopeless; but suddenly, there was a shout – and work stopped. Everyone rushed to the edge of the trench.

One of the workers pointed.

"A shoe!"

Carlisle breathed again. At least he would have an excuse for being out so late. His wife had been quite annoyed that he would miss a dinner party she had arranged for her parents.

At this point, the forensic team took over.

Very slowly, the soil was cleared away. At each stage, photographs were taken. The body was gradually uncovered but not without a lot more clay being dug away. The body seemed to have been lying – not beside the pipe – but beneath the level of the pipe – in a shallow grave. There was no chance of the body being moved for a couple of hours. The usual white tent was erected over the trench and metal barriers blocked half the road. The Gas Board, glad that their work had not been in vain, were pleased to call it a day.

Raynes went down to have a look at that part of the body which had now been uncovered. It was male; and the shoe size tallied. He returned to the surface.

He decided to send Carlisle home. He himself would wait until the body reached the mortuary. It was going to be a long night.

* * * *

It was about 1.00am before the body finally arrived on the slab. Despite all the earth and the natural decomposition of the body, it had already been identified as that of Bert Stone. His wallet was still in his jacket pocket but the bank notes had gone.

The forensic department had taken away all his clothes for minute analysis and Bert was as naked as he had ever wished to be, but not in the company he would have chosen.

Dr Stewart tackled his victim with his usual grim humour:

"Good-looking fellow. Well hung."

"I think that was his chief asset."

"Bit of a bruiser. Look at those muscles."

"He was a boxer when he was a young man."

"Still at it from the look of things. Look at his knuckles. Bit of bruising there. Severe damage to the skin tissues. He had a fight with someone."

Dr Stewart looked at the wound in the skull.

"Blunt instrument, I should think. Of course, he could have fallen into the road works head first." He shook his head. "But I think not."

Dr Stewart turned the body over.

"Everything seems fairly intact. No broken ribs. No evidence of bruising. Whatever you say, that clay has preserved him rather well. Filthy stuff. Gets everywhere. Legs and ankles OK."

Bert's eyes, ears, nose and throat were meticulously examined and every detail recorded. Samples from under the finger nails were put in plastic bags. Blood samples were taken; pieces of hair; swabs of all mucous material.

"And now we come to the nasty bit."

142

Dr Stewart cut a neat V around the neck of the victim and sliced the body straight down to the groin.

He looked at the heart, stomach, kidneys and liver.

"Hold your nose. This is going to be pretty vile."

He made a small incision in the stomach. A cascade of brown fluid poured out. The stench was frightful. Raynes turned away and wondered if he was going to throw up. But Dr Stewart seemed quite unaffected. He was filling a small test tube and labelling it.

"As you said, well-pickled. But his liver looks surprisingly good. Not much evidence of food. I shall have to go into the intestines for that."

He looked at Raynes.

"Take a walk. I'll give you a shout when I've sewn him back up."

Raynes took his advice and returned for the final examination of the skull and brain.

Dr Stewart cut through the bone with his Dessouter necropsy saw.

"Bit of a caveman, I'm told," said Raynes.

"So he wasn't called Stone for nothing!"

Dr Stewart laughed – but then looked closer.

"Yes, as I thought, a hefty blow to the skull. We shall have to keep this."

He examined the inner membranes of the skull which cushion the brain. The membranes were torn and several chips of bone had penetrated the brain. Dr Stewart used his forceps and long-nosed pliers to pick out the larger pieces and again put them into a plastic bag. He continued to probe the damaged skull looking for further clues.

"I shall need to look at this through a microscope and take some photographs." He stood up. "But you were right. A hammer blow – or something like it – with considerable force. And then the body pushed into the trench. I'm afraid you've got another murder on your hands."

"I was expecting it."

Raynes was looking a little green. Closer proximity to Mr Stone did not make the heart grow fonder.

"Go home and have a neat whisky. That's what I do. Marvellous disinfectant. Induces total amnesia. Gives you a good night's rest." He smiled. "Doctor's orders!"

When Raynes returned home, he washed his face, mouth and hands – and then poured himself a very large dose of Laphroaig. It seemed a shame to be using such a superb malt as mere medicine. He lay in bed staring at a blank wall. By the time he had drunk the last drop, it was 3.30am.

He fell into a deep sleep.

24. *Walk To The Paradise Garden*

Although he had gone to bed late, Raynes was ready for an early start. He put his alarm on for 7.30am and was in his office by a quarter past eight.

He knew that although the discovery of the body had come too late to make the morning papers, the newshounds would have picked up the exhumation in Riverside Road. Very soon, they would be on Mrs Stone's doorstep. He was determined to get to her before they did.

He had the feeling that, by now, Mrs Stone would be back at work, so he phoned the Royal Infirmary to ask if she was on duty that morning. Discovering that she was on Ward 7, he set off immediately for the hospital. He met Detective-Constable Carlisle as he came through the front door – and took him along with him.

"Was it Bert?"

Raynes nodded.

"Straightforward fall?"

"No. A blow to the back of the head. A hammer or something."

Raynes dived into his car.

"Where are we going?"

"Infirmary."

It was only a few minutes' drive. They bustled through reception where the cleaners were busy with their mops and

144

buckets. By 8.30am, they were on Ward 7. Raynes asked the sister-in-charge if he could speak to Mrs Stone privately – but Betty had already seen the two men and realized that they brought bad news.

"Have you found him?" she asked.

"Yes. Last night. We dug up a section of the road and found his body."

"Where was he?"

"Beside that gas pipe they're laying in Riverside Road. He was down on the left-hand side – covered by a fall of earth. When they put back all the earth, they obviously didn't see him."

Mrs Stone wept quietly. There was nothing dramatic in her weeping. Raynes felt that there must be a sense of relief now that the uncertainty was over.

"He wouldn't have been buried alive?"

"No. We think he may have hit his head on the pipe as he fell in. He would've been dead for several hours."

He gave her time to absorb the information. Time enough later to tell her about the blow to the back of his head. He waited till the crying had stopped and she had wiped her eyes.

"What do I do now?"

"Well, at the moment, his body's in the hands of the police surgeon, Dr Stewart. He's preparing a report, which will give us a clearer picture of what happened."

Mrs Stone's inner fears surfaced.

"He wasn't murdered, was he?"

"We're not sure."

More tears.

Raynes was as gentle as possible.

"We'll find out the full story within the next twenty-four hours. In the meantime, you'll need to go home. But I wouldn't recommend Coronation Gardens. Once the news gets out that we've found his body, you'll be besieged by photographers and reporters. I think it'd be much better if you and Sandra could go to Tom's house. I think you'd be safer there. I'll put an officer at the gate to keep them at bay."

Mrs Stone brooded on this.

"It always happens," says Raynes. "Even if it's just an accident, they're always there. Just like vultures."

"I know what it's like. Last time Bert was in court, they were all at the door. It was terrible."

"We'll do what we can to help. Have you got Tom's phone number?"

Whilst Mrs Stone was getting changed and collecting her things, Raynes phoned Tom Stone and then the police station to arrange for an officer to be on duty in Henslea and then move with the family to Harrogate Drive.

"Is Sergeant Evans available?. . . Good! . . . Send him along. He knows the family."

Uncle Tom asked Raynes the same question as his sister-in-law.

"Was it murder, Inspector?"

"We shan't know until the forensic report comes through."

"I take that as 'Yes'."

Raynes uttered a word of caution.

"I think, for Mrs Stone's sake, we should cross one bridge at a time. He certainly had a blow to the head, but whether this was caused by the fall, we're still not sure."

"You're a good liar, Inspector."

* * * *

By the time they reached Coronation Gardens, the first reporter had already arrived and Sandra was in tears.

"They've found him!" she wailed.

Raynes escorted mother and daughter into the house and left Carlisle to deal with the reporter who was rather a cocky young man from one of the tabloids.

"Was it murder?" he asked.

"There'll be a press conference later this morning."

"Was it a knife? Any drugs involved?"

Carlisle smiled sweetly.

"I haven't seen the report. When we've seen it, you'll be informed."

"D'you think it's one of the family that did it?"

146

Carlisle shook his head.

"Until we know the facts, it would be foolish to speculate."

"Oh, come on! Man to man! You know the score."

Carlisle burst into laughter.

The reporter was surprised by the reaction. He was not to know that Carlisle was thinking of the video of the Welsh Rugby team.

A few moments later, Carlisle was glad to see a police patrol car coming along the road. Sergeant Evans was arriving to take up his post as guardian of the gate. They would get nothing out of him.

* * * *

When Sandra, Mark and Mrs Stone had been safely transported to Harrogate Drive, Raynes and Carlisle returned to the office. Here they found Dr Stewart clutching a bulging file of notes and photographs. He could hardly wait to share his news:

"Blow to the back of the skull. A very strong blow, causing a deep fracture."

"Was it a hammer?" asked Raynes.

"No, I should say something narrower. A spanner or a piece of piping. Chrome – not lead. It's left some clear marks on the pieces of bone. You can see them quite clearly under the microscope. The blow came from the right."

Raynes and Carlisle pored over the photographs of the skull.

"It's more damaged than I thought," said Raynes.

"Were there any fingerprints?" asked Carlisle.

"Impossible to tell with all that earth. The rest of him was untouched – except for his wallet!" Dr Stewart laughed. "You said he should have had about £100 in tenners. Well, he didn't. And it wasn't me who took them!"

Raynes picked up the plastic bag containing the wallet.

"Were there any fingerprints on this?"

"Only Bert's."

Raynes opened the wallet.

A picture of his daughter with Mark – probably taken at the

hospital when the child was born; a betting slip; a receipt from Tesco's; a bus pass – with a very unflattering photograph; a torn cinema ticket and two recent wage slips. Not very revealing.

He looked at the other items collected from Bert's pockets: one pound, eighty-five pence from his right-hand trouser pocket; a handkerchief in his left – with a few smears of blood.

"His blood?" asked Raynes.

"Yes. I checked. Must have come from his knuckles. I told you he'd been in a fight."

Another handkerchief, neatly folded, was in his breast pocket; a couple of cigars – presumably nicked at the party; and a three-pack of condoms from a dispenser – packet opened, one missing.

"Evidence of recent sexual activity?"

"Yes. Smears of semen on his pants and his organ. I've taken samples."

Raynes returned to the photographs. There were thirty-eight of them.

"He looks quite . . . wedged in," said Carlisle.

Dr Stewart nodded.

"He was stuffed down the side of that pipe. Well down. And of course, that protected him. When all that earth was slung back in, there would've been quite a weight on top of him. Couple of tons at least. Then the tarmac – and the steamroller. If he hadn't been beside that pipe, he'd have been heavily compressed."

"Are you suggesting he was deliberately buried?"

"It is possible. But I find it difficult to think of someone being down there – with a shovel – at that hour of night."

"What time was it?"

"As you said, about twelve thirty."

"And no sign of the spanner. He didn't throw it in?"

"No."

"Was there a lot of booze in his gut?"

Carlisle asked the question quite innocently – but Dr Stewart pointed at Raynes. "You'd better ask him!"

The Inspector's face was a study.

"It was vile," he said.

"You weren't there for the best bit!" said Dr Stewart.

Raynes raised a protective hand.

"Spare me! I've seen as much of Bert as I ever wish to see." He shuddered – then recovered. "Is there anything else we ought to know?"

Dr Stewart pointed to the report.

"It's all in there. If you want samples or need to look at things through the microscope, you only have to ask."

Raynes thanked him warmly.

"Your two bottles will be on the way."

"I would have preferred the round dozen."

Raynes smiled triumphantly.

"I knew my bet was quite safe."

After Dr Stewart had gone, there was silencc in the office as Raynes and Carlisle went through his report.

"Could someone have used the shaft of the spanner to dig out a hole beside the pipe?"

"It would've taken them quite a long time. Pretty dangerous too. Anyone could have looked down and seen them."

"Perhaps they were seen – getting into that trench – or getting out of it. We shall have to ask for eye-witnesses. Monday 14th August. About 12.30am."

Raynes looked at the pack of condoms.

"He must have had sex at the *Kirby* . . ."

"Or after?"

"The barmaid perhaps. Elaine . . . Russell, was it? No. Sharpe. Tom's supposed to be giving me her phone number, but he hasn't. You'd better phone him – but don't say why."

"Could that be where his money's gone?"

"One hundred seems a bit pricey – especially when you have to provide your own condom!"

Carlisle laughed.

"Of course, the money could have been pinched by the murderer. It could be a straightforward mugging."

"That's what worries me," said Raynes. "We've been assuming that it was a family quarrel. One of those people at the baptism party. But it could have been someone he met on the street . . . or the barmaid's husband – if she has one."

Raynes sighed. "I must say that all the evidence I've heard seems to ring true. I've been listening for lies – but I haven't picked up anything. Even Alec seems plausible. Much to my surprise."

There did not seem to be much more that could be gleaned from the forensic report. It was filed and locked away.

The Inspector turned to writing a very short communique for the Press. The general implication was that Bert Stone had been mugged on his way home and robbed of a sum of money. His body had been found in a trench dug by the Gas Board. Investigations were continuing.

No mention was made of the nature of Bert's death. Raynes preferred to leave it to their imagination. He put down his pen.

"We'll release it at half past twelve. They won't like it; but who cares!"

25. *The Sorcerer's Apprentice*

It was now Saturday afternoon.

Detective-Constable Carlisle had returned to the bosom of his family whence, it was reliably reported, another child was on its way. It was expected on or about St Valentine's Day. Like most people, the Inspector had assumed that, having suffered so much with their first child, neither of the Carlisles would be in a hurry to repeat the experience.

But memories are short and even the nicest of people can become born-again masochists. Since his colleague was invariably a calming influence and a model of common sense, Raynes was inclined to blame the child's nocturnal tantrums on Mrs Carlisle. Her genetic soup must be over-spiced: her hormonal pudding parboiled. It never entered Raynes' mind that perhaps the long hours Carlisle spent on police business might in itself be a contributing factor.

The Inspector was at a loose end.

Now that the body of Albert Stone had been found, there was

a sense of anti-climax. The people of Grasshallows had yet to be informed of the grim discovery. Most of them were either shopping, sleeping or working in their gardens. A brave few might be supporting the local football team in their first home match of the season; but the crowd would be small and well-behaved. No need for a police presence. Nor were the tourists much trouble. A couple of beat men at either end of the High Street were enough to meet their needs. A patrol ear circled Henslea every half hour.

What could he do?

He had no desire to sit in the house; gardening was anathema. Who could he visit? It was a bit soon to revisit Heidi Houston; he had no desire to meet any of the Stones.

With faint stirrings of malice, he thought of Jimmy Watson – the disc jockey. Aliens! How wrong he had been! So much for the "vibes of eternity"! How pleasant it would be to blast his ridiculous theories. But could he bear the bags of rubbish? The overpowering stench of cannabis? The dirty plates? The bluebottles diving past? The Inspector thought that perhaps, taken unawares, the Sacred Eye of Osiris might sing to a different tune.

* * * *

"God! It's you again!"

Raynes had an immediate sense of *déjà vu*. He was sure Jimmy was wearing the same grotty brown underpants that he had been wearing on Monday. He seemed to have dispensed with the rosary, but the tattoos were still very much "in your face".

"Have you come to arrest me?"

"A guilty conscience?" suggested Raynes.

"It'll happen one day."

"I expect it will. Have you given up the wacky baccy?"

"D'you want to come in?"

"It'd make life more pleasant. And perhaps you might like to put on a few more clothes."

Jimmy twisted his mouth into a lascivious leer.

"Arouses you, does it?"

"Not in the slightest," said Raynes. "But it might add a bit of dignity to proceedings."

"Fuck dignity! I've only just got up."

Raynes walked into the living room and was glad to see that most of the dirty plates had gone. So too had the bluebottle. He sat down on one of the hard chairs and waited for Jimmy to emerge from his bedroom.

"Olé!"

He was wearing a garment that was a cross between a kaftan and a toga with a red woollen cap.

"This do?"

Raynes shook his head.

"D'you want tickets for the seance?"

"The seance?"

"Yeah, man! It's the latest wheeze – once the disco's over. We've been getting the punters to summon up the spirits of the dead. Helping them get in touch with their ancestors. Really scary stuff! Tables moving . . . women fainting . . ."

"But presumably quite profitable?"

"You bet!"

Jimmy found a small bar of Milky Way lying in the folds of his sofa. He bit in to it with the relish of a man who had not eaten for several days.

Raynes smiled.

"Have you tried to summon up the spirit of Bert Stone?"

Jimmy gave the Inspector a sly grin.

"Did he have a spirit? I doubt it. Anyway, as I told you, he's gone hotfoot to the silent planet."

Raynes dismissed the suggestion with contempt.

"I didn't believe you then. And I don't believe you now. I think Bert Stone is still very much down here."

"Still looking, then?"

"No. We've found him."

"Alive – or dead?"

"I think you know the answer."

"Dead. Well, that's a relief. When's the funeral? I'll have to get my black suit cleaned."

Raynes raised his eyebrows.

"Do you have a black suit?"

Jimmy flicked the remains of the chocolate wrapping paper in the Inspector's direction.

"Don't be deceived by all this grot, man. Underneath, there's a successful businessman waiting to leap out."

"Not till you stop paying a certain lady sixty pounds a week."

Jimmy sighed.

"Yeah. That'll be the day." He cheered up. "Have you got the result of that DNA test yet?"

"No. It'll probably arrive next week."

"If it's negative, I'll give you a free ticket to one of my shows!"

Raynes smiled.

"I can't wait."

Jimmy laughed.

"You know – you're pretty cool for a cop! So then – where's Bert?"

"At this moment, he's in the morgue at Grasshallows Royal Infirmary. He's had his post-mortem and we're inviting suggestions from the general public as to how he came to such a grisly end."

There was brief silence.

"You expect me to know?"

"You're as good as any."

"I told you I was at a gig at the *Raging Bull*."

"So you did. And when did it stop?"

"Midnight."

"Did you have to load up your equipment or was it left there for another night?"

Jimmy considered the question carefully. He might be on dangerous ground. This cop-fellow knew more than he did. He pulled off his red woollen cap and scratched his head. It bought him another thirty seconds.

"It'd be better if you were honest with me," said Raynes. "Lies will only make it worse."

"Trouble is, you've got all the cards, man! Whatever I put

down, you'll top it."

"Try me."

Jimmy rubbed his chin thoughtfully.

"Suppose I said I was using their equipment?"

"I would believe you."

"That I got a lift home from the pub?"

Raynes nodded.

"That's possible."

"It's true. I had to get my records back – and my van's off the road at the moment."

"So what time did you leave the pub? Soon after midnight?"

"Yeah. About 12.15."

"And you came past the *Kirby Arms* at about 12.20?"

Jimmy stared at him,

This guy was psychic.

"And you saw Bert?" A harder tone crept into Raynes' voice. "Why didn't you tell me that last time I was here?"

"You didn't give me time. You jumped up and left. If you'd given me time, I'd have told you."

"That's a lie," said Raynes.

Jimmy nodded sadly.

"So you saw Bert?"

"Yeah. And he saw me."

"Where was he? Outside the *Kirby Arms*?"

Jimmy decided that it was better to come clean.

"No. He was walking down the middle of Riverside Road . . ."

"Walking?"

"Well, staggering a bit. I said to Gerry: 'For God's sake, don't hit him!' Gerry managed to pull up the car in time. He rolled down the window and shouted at him: 'You bloody arsehole, get off the road!' 'Scuse the French. Gerry's got a limited vocabulary at the best of times. Bert staggered over to the car. I thought he was going to land him one. He certainly hit the car. But Gerry had his foot on the gas. When he looked back, he said: 'That geezer's hit the deck. But someone's helping him up.' Then we went round the corner and didn't see any more."

Raynes brooded on the picture Jimmy had painted.

"That sounds like the truth."

"Well, you asked me."

"So, who's Gerry? And will he confirm your story?"

Jimmy winced.

"Well, that's the difficult bit. Gerry's a drug-dealer. I can't give you his real name. That's where I get my weed. I owe him quite a bit of money. If I say anything, I'll end up like cat's meat – or floating in the river."

He ran a symbolic finger across his throat.

"All for a bit of wacky baccy?"

Jimmy sighed and sank lower in his battered sofa.

"Don't ask! I can't tell you. If I did, you'd drop me right in it."

Raynes decided not to push him any further.

"O.K.," he said, "we'll leave it there. So long as you can confirm that you saw Albert Stone – alive – on Riverside Road at about 12.20am?"

"Large as life, man!"

Raynes sniffed.

"Well, he was dead by 12.30am. The Good Samaritan you saw picking him up was probably the person who bumped him off."

"Good for him! He deserved it."

Raynes smiled.

"You haven't asked me where he was found."

Jimmy pulled on his red woollen hat. His confidence was returning. "Well, it's obvious, innit? Riverside Road."

"He was found ten feet down beside the gas pipe."

Jimmy was amazed.

"Gee! Earth to earth, ashes to ashes . . . no wonder we couldn't get through to him!"

"Did you try?"

Jimmy grinned.

"No. We didn't want to see his ugly face again."

As he spoke, the telephone rang. Jimmy had to lift several heaps of garments before he could find it.

"Yeah?" he drawled. "Hello, babe, you O.K.? Long time no see." But then his face changed. "Hell, no! When? Thursday night? What a fucking bastard!"

He put his hand over the receiver.

"It's Sandy. She says that bloody weirdo's carved up Heidi. She's in hospital. Smashed in her face . . ."

He turned back to the phone. "You wanna speak to the Inspector? Yeah, he's here. We're just having a snort together. Yeah, he loves it! Sure, I'll hand him over . . ."

Jimmy passed over the phone.

"Raynes here. What's happened?"

"It's Heidi. That thug's beaten her up. She's in hospital."

"Which ward?"

"I don't know."

"When did you hear about this?"

"Just now. Heidi's mum phoned me at home – but I wasn't there. When she didn't get an answer, she phoned Uncle Tom."

Raynes did not hesitate for a second.

"I shall go up to the hospital immediately."

"You will catch him, won't you?"

"Of course. I'll put out an immediate alert."

"I'm just feeding the baby. I'll get a taxi up to the hospital as soon as I can."

"I'll see you there."

Raynes handed back the phone.

This was something he had not expected.

To Jimmy, he said: "I'm afraid I shall have to forgo the pleasure of having a snort! Some other time perhaps?"

He made for the door; but then stopped.

He didn't know Karl's surname. He couldn't put out an alert. He turned back.

"What was that creep called?"

Jimmy shrugged his shoulders.

"King Kong?"

26. *Song Without Words*

The Inspector had expected to see Heidi Houston again – but not in hospital. The news brought him back to the Royal Infirmary – this time to the orthopaedic ward. But Miss Grasshallows 1986 was not immediately recognisable.

First of all, she was wearing no make-up; second, she had a black eye; thirdly, her head was in a sort of metal frame which was designed to hold her jaw in place whilst it healed.

Raynes walked up the ward, looking to left and right. Had Heidi not waved to him, he would have walked straight past her.

What a mess! Even Raynes was appalled.

He sat down beside her and held her hand. Tears poured down her cheeks but she was quite incapable of saying anything, nor could she eat anything. On her bedside cabinet, a glass of orange juice and a packet of protein drink both contained straws. Poor girl! He squeezed her hand.

It would be a long before that little pink tongue touched his.

Whilst he was trying to comfort her, he wondered how he might get some answers to his questions. If her right hand was undamaged, she could perhaps write something down. Anyway, that would come later.

"Was it that brute?"

The cage moved.

He took it to mean "yes".

Some more direct form of communication was needed.

"One squeeze for 'yes'. Two for 'no'."

"Karl whatever-his name-was?"

One squeeze.

"Is he still in Grasshallows?"

Two squeezes.

"Gone back to Leeds?"

One squeeze – but not quite certain.

"Did this happen last night?"

Two squeezes.

"Thursday?"

That was better.

Raynes realized this was going to be slow work.

"Was it in the house?"

One squeeze.

"In the bedroom?"

No, apparently it was in the sitting room. She had tried to phone 999 but she was sure her jaw was broken and blood was seeping out of her mouth. She had been unable to make the operator understand what she was saying. So, holding her face together, she had gone round to her neighbour who had at last got through to the operator and called an ambulance.

It took about ten minutes of trial and error to get this picture. Despite her injuries, she seemed very animated and very angry. Not surprising, really.

She gestured for the orange juice. Raynes held it whilst she drank through a straw.

Raynes said: "You'll get better. It'll be unpleasant. But at least you're alive. He didn't kill you."

More tears. She gave Raynes a very long squeeze.

"You thought he was going to kill you?"

One quick squeeze.

"I'm not surprised. I told you he was lethal. I told you he should be behind bars." Raynes smiled. "One of my friends said he was the sort of person who might cut you up into little pieces and put them in black bin bags . . ."

One squeeze.

She thought so too.

Raynes asked her about the house.

"Was it locked?"

She thought the neighbour would have been in to clear up the mess.

"Would she have the key?"

She thought so.

Had she seen any other policeman?

No.

Would she like him to check the house? He promised not to

158

play with any of her sex toys.

She shut her eyes. Despair at the thought of ever having sex again. More tears.

Raynes assured her that this was an injury from which most people recovered. The most normal place for a broken jaw was a car crash. Accident victims normally made a full recovery.

He gave her another drink.

He realized that it was necessary not to tire her. He explained that when he came back again, he would get her to write down her answers on a piece of paper. She seemed pleased that they had been able to communicate. He put his fingers to his lips and then touched hers. One eye twinkled – the other did not.

As he turned away from the bed, he saw Sandra coming up the ward, pushing Mark in his push chair. If anyone was accused of tiring the patient, better it should be her.

He explained to Sandra that Heidi could not speak and suggested she should use his method of communication. One squeeze for "yes"; two squeeze for "no".

He left them to it. By the time he had reached the exit, both girls were crying and Mark was feebly waving his hands. But then, he could not communicate either.

* * * *

Raynes decided that the best thing he could do was to track down Karl. He needed a name and an address. And if he had a car, its make and number. He decided that perhaps the best person to ask would be Raymond Stone.

Raynes had never met the man but he knew that he worked in the Post Office and was probably a Communist. He said to himself: "Well, nobody's perfect!"

He borrowed a telephone directory from the girl at the reception desk and looked up Raymond's address. Within five minutes, he was at his door.

"Mr Stone?"

"Yes, that's me."

"I'm Inspector Raynes. I'm investigating the death of your brother."

"Is there some news?"

"Not at the moment. I've come to see you about a totally different matter."

"Well, don't stand on the doorstep, Inspector. Come in."

Raynes followed him down a dark passage into a back sitting room where he was introduced to Mrs Elsie Stone, who greeted him like a long lost friend. "I've heard so much about you," she gushed. "It's a real pleasure to welcome you to our home . . ."

Raynes cut short her compliments.

"What I've come to see you about is a young man called Karl . . ."

Mr Stone's eyes lit up; Elsie scowled.

"Him!"

Raynes explained that he was guilty of a serious act of assault – he had broken his girlfriend's jaw and she was now in hospital.

Mrs Stone was quick to say: "I told you so."

Mr Stone expressed his disappointment:

"I didn't think he'd stoop to anything like that. I thought he was a young man with high principles."

"Communist principles?" said Raynes mischievously.

"Well, I think he'd seen the light," said Mr Stone.

"I'm sorry to disappoint you," said Raynes, "but I have it on good authority that Karl is a paid up member of the British National Party."

Raymond looked thunderstruck.

Mrs Stone did not look surprised.

"I told you so! I could see he wasn't listening properly to you. He was laughing at you behind your back. He's made a complete fool of you!"

"Well," said Raynes, "I need to know his surname – and, if possible, his home address."

"He was called Taylor, Inspector. Karl Taylor. And I can tell you where he's living at present. Greenway Gardens. A very good area of the city."

"A very good area," Raynes agreed. "But I was meaning his address in Leeds. That's where he comes from."

Mr Stone nodded thoughtfully.

"I think I might have that."

He stumbled over to a writing bureau and pulled down the lid. He reached into one of the small pigeonholes and drew out a white sheet of paper. "Here we are."

He unfolded the paper with some care as if it were a page of Holy Scripture. It was, in fact, an application form for membership of the Grasshallows Communist Party.

"I don't hold with all that rubbish!" said Mrs Stone. "I'm a Catholic. A lapsed Catholic. But once a Catholic, always a Catholic; that's what I say."

Raynes nodded politely and waited patiently till Mr Stone had delivered his divine message.

"His date of birth was 10.11.66. He was born in Leeds. His mother's name is Marion Taylor. He gives her address as 21 Coldside Crescent. Would that be any help?"

Mrs Stone sniffed with disgust.

"I can't think why he gave you his mother's name."

"It was a contact address. I was going to contact our people in Leeds and see if they knew anything about him. But I suppose there's no point now." Raymond looked sad and miserable. "I must say I'm very disappointed. I thought be would have been a great asset to the Party."

"Stuff and nonsense!" said Mrs Stone. "He was a block-headed fool!"

"He had a very sad family background . . ." Raymond continued. "He told me his father had been jailed – for interfering with his two sisters. A very sad business. Of course, his mother got a divorce; but people don't get over things like that."

"No," said Raynes. "But it's no excuse for attacking Miss Houston in such a violent manner."

"He was just an animal," said Mrs Stone.

"Did he have a car?" asked Raynes.

"An old grey one. A complete banger. I don't think he had a licence. There were no seats in the back."

"Would you have any idea of the model or the registration number in your records?" asked Raynes hopefully.

Raymond shook his head.

"No."

Mrs Stone invited the Inspector to stay for a cup of tea. Raynes politely refused, he stood up to go – but it took him another fifteen minutes before he left the house. The couple were ill-matched and argumentative.

Mrs Stone seemed to rejoice in her husband's discomfiture. Raynes asked if the Communists would be putting up a candidate at the forthcoming by-election? Perhaps he might even think of standing himself?

"They wouldn't put up a candidate," sneered Mrs Stone.

"They wouldn't even save their deposit. They'd be a laughing stock!"

It seemed that Raymond was very much a lone crusader. When Raynes had finally escaped their clutches, he returned to the police station and sent an urgent message to the police in Leeds, asking them to try and find Karl Taylor and hold him on a charge of "assault". When they found him, would they please notify Grasshallows Constabulary immediately.

* * * *

He returned to Greenway Gardens – but not to his own house. He drove along to No. 58. It looked deserted. Raynes' fear was that perhaps Karl had returned. But the door was locked and there was no sign of his grey car. He went to the house next door.

"Yes?"

A very business-like lady.

"I'm Detective-Inspector Raynes of Grasshallows police. Are you the person looking after Miss Houston's house?"

"No, I am not! Try Mrs Ransome at No. 60."

"Thank you."

So round to No. 60.

"Mrs Ransome, I'm from Grasshallows police . . ."

Mrs Ransome's face lit up,

"Oh, I'm so glad you came round. I was going to phone you."

"What were you worried about?"

"The house – being empty. I was frightened someone might

162

break in. You know she's in hospital?"

Raynes nodded.

"She's got a broken jaw. She's in the Royal Infirmary."

"I've been to see her."

"And how is she?"

"Well, she's not able to speak at the moment; but she'll make a full recovery."

"I'm so glad to hear that. When she came round here, she was bleeding everywhere. He hit her in the face, you know!"

"He hasn't been back?"

"No. I've been watching. I've kept my eye on the house. I've been in and cleared up. It was a terrible mess."

The Inspector groaned inwardly.

No chance of fingerprints!

Mrs Ransome saw a shadow pass over the Inspector's face.

"D'you want to come in? I shouldn't keep you standing on the doorstep. Would you like a coffee?"

"That's very kind, but no. I want to go and look round the house. Do you have the keys?"

"Of course. Heidi gave me one set when she moved in; but when she was taken off to hospital, she gave me the others as well."

Raynes took the keys and walked up the steps to No. 58. Once inside, he made a point of locking the door behind him. He didn't want a violent psychopath catching him alone in the building.

He walked through the house. The sitting room looked much the same as it had done when he was there; the kitchen-dining area was quite a good-sized room overlooking the garden.

The bedroom was also quite spacious. He looked round for any signs of blood. There were none. He looked in the kitchen bin: it had been emptied. The bathroom smelt fresh and clean. Mrs Ransome had done her work all too well.

Raynes hunted for any of Karl's belongings – clothes, shoes, shaving kit, toothbrush, photographs, a mention in Heidi's address book or diary. But there was nothing. It was as though he had never been there.

Raynes went through the drawers and cupboards

systematically. He rifled through several drawers of Heidi's underwear. He saw the gold dress she had worn for the baptism, along with several other expensive dresses in her walk-in wardrobe. He noted that Heidi's chief passion - apart from men – seemed to be clothes.

He looked at a picture of her winning the title of Miss Grasshallows in 1986. The banner across her bosom and the small crown on her head. Memories of happier days.

It was all very routine. He went through her packs of photographs but Karl did not figure. There was nothing on her telephone pad. Her attacker was like a footstep in the sand – so swiftly swept away. It was very annoying.

He went out of the house and looked in her dustbin. Even it was empty. Where had she put it all? With the second key, he opened the garage door. Heidi had a red Astra – four years old. It looked very clean. Surely Mrs Ransome had not cleaned that as well?

He shut the garage door, locked up the house and returned to No. 60.

"Did you manage to see everything, Inspector?"

Raynes smiled ruefully.

''I hadn't counted on you giving the house such a complete spring clean.''

"Oh, but I had to. You should have seen the mess! Blood everywhere. On the bed; on the floor; in the kitchen. I felt it was the least I could do.''

"I quite understand, but . . .''

Mrs Ransome put a hand to her mouth.

"You mean . . . I've destroyed all the evidence?''

"Most effectively. You've even cleaned out the dustbin!''

"Oh, I've got that here, Inspector. They don't come till Tuesday; but I've put it together with mine.''

She took Raynes round the corner – and there it was. Two large black bags. The Inspector felt relieved.

"But it's full of all sorts of filthy things. Tissues. Smelly food. Bottles. A lot of bottles. Things with blood on them.''

Raynes smiled.

"That's just the things we need, Mrs Ransome. My

colleagues will be delighted to go through it. There's bound to be one or two fingerprints in that lot."

27. *Morning Papers*

Inspector Raynes joined Mrs May for a late breakfast on Sunday morning. In fact, it was almost afternoon. He arrived with an armful of Sunday newspapers. Debbie looked at them with professional dismay.

"Has the male menopause finally arrived?"

"They're for 'afters'," said Raynes defensively.

"D'you think you'll be in a fit state for 'afters'? Normally, you just fall asleep."

"It's been a hard week – not entirely helped with you doing a switch with those videos."

"I was just trying to make police work more exciting."

"The feminists will have my guts for garters!"

"Tell them there's always a job for them down here."

Debbie cast three eggs into the frying pan. The sausages, bacon, tomatoes and black pudding were all marking time under the grill. The toaster stood poised for its first ejaculation. The hot milk for the coffee was already rising surreptitiously up the sides of the pan. Mrs May prided herself on her high-calorie breakfasts.

"You have a very nice colleague," she said as she put a sizzling plateful in front of the Inspector.

"Young Carlisle?"

"He was most diplomatic. 'I'm afraid you must have taken the wrong video'." She laughed. "I gave him a cup of coffee."

"I hope you didn't give him any more than that?"

"He couldn't afford it."

"You're quite right. His wife's having another baby."

Mrs May looked thoughtful.

"So soon?"

"The last one's still causing problems."

"Poor lamb. Not much fun being married, is it?"

By the time they had reached the second cup of coffee,

Raynes was telling her about Heidi Houston.

"One of my neighbours has been beaten up."

Debbie was not surprised. What else could one expect people to do on these ghastly new housing estates?

"The ex-beauty queen in No. 58."

"The hairdresser?"

"Yes. She had that thug living with her. He beat her up."

Mrs May shrugged her shoulders.

"That's what men do. They can't express their emotions, so they lash out."

"He's broken her jaw. She's in a sort of cage."

"Poor girl. You won't want to see her now."

Raynes put down his cup.

"It's no use looking surprised. I saw the look in your eye. Really set your hormones buzzing, didn't she?" Debbie smiled. "Love always comes at a price. You may find the new dentures a little off-putting!"

Raynes picked up his cup again.

"You really are a complete cynic!"

"Richard," she said, "I know what men are like. My first husband gave me several black eyes, a couple of nose-bleeds. On one occasion, I thought he'd broken my arm."

"Why did he do it?"

"He thought I was playing around."

"Were you?"

Mrs May wrapped her white silk dressing-gown more closely around her whilst she decided how much she wished to disclose.

"Well, I was," she said — a trifle reluctantly, "but he wasn't giving me any housekeeping. He was drinking and gambling every lunch-time. I had to pay for the food, the gas, the electricity and the H.P. He paid the rent."

She sighed.

Those days still cast a long shadow.

"I had to get it somewhere." She cheered up and put on her more confident voice. "But things are better now. In fact, I would say that I am a superb businesswoman."

Raynes laughed.

"You mean the tax man can't catch you?"

Debbie smiled indulgently.

"Well, it is a bit difficult when people insist on paying cash." She put her hand on top of Richard's, knowing how sensitive he could be about her work. "Tomorrow," she said, "I am being paid £100 an hour."

"For what?"

"I am being painted in chocolate. And then he will lick it all off." A wicked smile flashed across her face. "He is providing the chocolate. All I have to do is lie still and not giggle."

"That sounds absolutely disgusting!"

"Doesn't it?" Debbie looked down at the empty plates. "But it pays for the bacon and eggs, the sausages and the black pudding. You are living off my immoral earnings. Tastes good, doesn't it?"

Raynes sighed.

"You're impossible!"

"We aim to please . . . all our customers!" She suddenly looked thoughtful. "I'm sure I've got a little pot of chocolate somewhere. We could practise!"

28. *The Bartered Bride*

Raynes' first visitor on Monday morning was the curate from St Benedict's.

"Inspector, I need some help."

Raynes was surprised to see the Reverend Blazer looking quite so agitated. What sort of help was he needing? Legal? Financial? Theological? He soon found out.

"Sandra Stone wants to marry me!"

Edmund had been agonizing over the problem for almost a week. Even the popular acclaim for his first sermon had barely compensated for the inner miseries he had endured. Mercifully, he had been spared the sight of Sandra breast-feeding Mark in the front pew.

Raynes was not entirely surprised by the news. He had detected vague hints of affection on both sides. But the young clergyman's next remark did amaze him.

"She says she's . . . carrying my baby!"

"Does she?" Raynes raised his eyebrows. "And when did this miracle take place?"

"At the party – after the baptism. I didn't tell you about it because it was very . . . embarrassing."

The Inspector managed to keep a straight face.

"And how did it happen? Was it your idea?"

"Certainly not!" The Reverend Blazer looked mortified at the very thought. "No. She invited me upstairs to see the baby; and then she just grabbed me. It all happened so quickly. I didn't have time to think. But now she says she's pregnant and I've got to marry her."

Raynes looked at the young man, noting the wild, staring eyes and the beads of perspiration standing out on his forehead.

If Mr Blazer had had even the faintest knowledge of the facts of life, he would have known that it was normally a month or two before a woman could be sure she was pregnant – not just a couple of weeks. The Inspector felt that Miss Stone was engaged in a rather neat policy of entrapment, taking advantage of the curate's youth and inexperience. But he did not voice his suspicions immediately.

"What exactly is she proposing?" he asked.

"That we get married before Christmas."

Raynes asked the obvious question.

"Does Canon Murray know about this?"

"No." Edmund shook his head. "He's not back till Wednesday. I daren't tell him. He might block my priesting. He might sack me. If the congregation get to hear about it, it'll be totally devastating. They'll despise me utterly."

Raynes could understand his fears, but there was one question he had to ask:

"Do you have any feelings for Sandra? She seems a nice sort of girl."

The Reverend Blazer hesitated.

"I hardly know her," he said. "I saw her before the baptism, but we've hardly spoken to each other. We've never been out together."

Raynes looked at him thoughtfully.

"Is there anything about her you don't like?"

Edmund burst out:

"Her family! They're so rough. Uncouth. Heavy drinkers. Immoral. I have no time for such people . . ."

Raynes was surprised by the venom of his attack.

" . . . They're just not my type!"

"But Sandra?"

"Well, she's very nice . . . gentle . . . caring . . ."

"Beautiful eyes."

"Yes, she's got beautiful eyes. But you've really got to know a person before you marry them."

"You know she likes sex!"

Edmund sniffed contemptuously.

"With everyone!"

Raynes laughed – and then turned to more practical problems: "Weddings are expensive things . . . Who was going to pay for it? You?"

"No. Apparently her uncle Tom has agreed to foot the bill."

Raynes reflected:

"A very generous man. He seems to have a great affection for his brother's family."

"And his brother's wife!"

The Inspector looked at the young curate with greater interest.

"They're having an affair."

"Really?"

Edmund's mouth puckered with disapproval.

"It was after the party . . . I didn't tell you because I didn't think it was important . . . But, after I was knocked out, I was put in an upstairs bedroom . . ."

Raynes nodded helpfully.

" . . . I slept for a while. Over an hour. When I got up, I went to the toilet. I didn't know which room it was. All the doors looked the same. So I opened one or two doors . . . and there they were. I think it was Mr Stone's bedroom. They were both together. I recognized her dress on the floor."

"What time was this?"

Raynes wished that Carlisle could have been there to take notes.

"About half past six."

"Did they see you?"

"No, they were both asleep."

"So they don't know that you saw them?"

"No. I think they must have forgotten I was still in the house. I left as quietly as I could."

The Inspector looked pleased.

"That's a very useful piece of information."

"You mean it could be a reason why Mr Stone vanished?"

"It provides another motive. I hadn't thought of it. Tom Stone seemed very protective towards Bert's family but now I can see why."

"Sandra said that Tom would pay for everything."

"Guilty conscience!"

Raynes wondered what more the Reverend Blazer might be able to tell him. He viewed the young man in a more friendly fashion.

"But it won't solve my problem."

"Oh, I think it may," said Raynes encouragingly. "There's no way you could think of a marriage – or even an engagement - whilst this murder investigation is continuing. You couldn't possibly enter into any relationship with a family, any one of whom could be responsible for Mr Stone's death. It would be quite impossible."

Edmund breathed more freely.

Of course, the Inspector was right.

"And secondly, whatever this young woman says, you can't really be sure she is pregnant. These are early days. Anything can happen. There might be a miscarriage. Perhaps in a month or two's time, you may have a clearer picture."

Edmund nodded.

"And let's face it," said the Inspector, "she may not even be pregnant. It could all be a trick. Could you be absolutely sure you were the father? Think what happened last time! They still don't know who Mark's father is. I think it would be advisable for you to have a DNA test – just in case. But I wouldn't make any move until the baby was actually born. Once there was clear proof that you were the father . . . Well, a decision would have to be made then. But not now." He looked at Mr Blazer. "Does that help?"

"Very much so. Thank you."

An immense burden was lifted from his mind.

"So you won't need to say anything to Canon Murray."

Edmund felt deeply relieved.

"But if you do have to speak to him, let me know; and I'll have a word with him first."

The young curate was amazed how helpful the Inspector had been. Obviously he had misjudged him. He had thought he was a cold-blooded thug.

"We're old friends," said Raynes, lying cheerfully. "He'll listen to what I say. But nobody will force you into a marriage you don't want. Be kind to Sandra – but firm. If she loves you, she'll respect your views. If she doesn't . . . well!"

The Inspector shrugged his shoulders.

Who was he to give marital advice?

He stood up.

"I'm very glad you came to see me, Mr Blazer. The information you gave me was most interesting. Before you go, I wonder if you'd make a brief statement?" He opened the door. "Carlisle!"

29. *The Flight Of The Bumblebee*

His colleague had been on the phone to the police in Leeds. Karl Taylor had been caught driving a car without a licence.

The car had been fairly safe, parked at the far end of Greenway Gardens – a cul-de-sac not normally visited by the police. But driving on main roads – and through the streets of a large city, he was far more likely to be seen – and he had been.

The elderly nature of the car – a battered old Vauxhall Cavalier – had attracted the CCTV crew scanning the traffic entering Leeds from the motorway. The car seemed to have a loose front bumper. A patrol car was detailed to stop him.

Not only was the bumper loose and the licence invalid, but one of the tyres was bald and the rust on the mainframe was positively dangerous.

Karl had been taken into custody and charged with a number of motoring offences. It was only when he was about to be released that an observant duty sergeant remembered that Grasshallows police were also looking for a young man with that name. Karl was therefore held over the weekend – pending further charges; and steps would be taken to send him back to Grasshallows as soon as possible.

Raynes was quite pleased by the swift and efficient way Karl had been tracked down. If he had abandoned his car and taken a train or a bus into London, it would have taken much longer to find him. He was a fool, going back to Leeds.

Karl would appear in the local Magistrates Court on Tuesday or Wednesday and be remanded in custody till he was collected. When the trial came to court in Grasshallows, Heidi would not be able to appear in court; but she could give written evidence. A doctor would testify to the extent of her injuries. With a bit of luck, Karl would be jailed for at least six months.

Raynes went down to his car and took out the two black bin bags from Heidi's house. He handed them over to the forensic department to see what sordid treasures they might contain.

He also used this opportunity to deliver the two bottles of malt whisky to Dr Stewart. Unfortunately, it turned out to be a bank holiday. Raynes left everything with the caretaker.

* * * *

When he returned to his office, he found a plain white envelope lying on his desk. It was franked "Grasshallows Health Services." Raynes picked it up anxiously. Was he being called in for a colo-rectal examination? That seemed to be the latest medical whim.

But when he opened it, he had a pleasant surprise. The hospital had DNA-tested all three godparents – and the baby, Mark – the previous Thursday and the results were negative.

There was no DNA connection between any of them.

Raynes whistled with amazement.

He had been quite sure it would be one of them. Jimmy, perhaps, had been a little too self-confident. Raynes had had a bet with Carlisle on the other two. He had favoured Charles as the dark horse; Carlisle, playing for safety, had backed Ron. But both of them were wrong.

Raynes was quick to see the implications of this report. He phoned up the hospital department to check whether the details had been communicated to the individuals concerned. The answer was "No." Raynes requested that they be delayed for a week.

"This is going to save some people a lot of money."

"Sandra won't be pleased."

"I don't think she needs to worry. Uncle Tom'll pick up the tab."

Carlisle having taken a statement from the Reverend Blazer, wondered if Tom and Mrs Stone would now get married.

"It would probably be the best solution. A nice home for the baby. Some comfort for Mrs Stone. And a really nice wedding for whichever male Sandra decides to take down the aisle."

"Not Mr Blazer?"

"I think not."

Raynes was silent for a few minutes. He rearranged the pens and pencils on his desk and threw the white envelope into the waste paper bin.

"This won't do her reputation any good."

"No. It means she was carrying on with someone else . . ."

"Perhaps several other people?"

"D'you think the godfathers will ask for their money back?"

"I shouldn't think so. Ron might."

"Charles won't. He loves her."

"So does Jimmy – in his own peculiar way."

"So who could it be?"

"We shall have to ask. It'll be embarrassing. He obviously wasn't important enough to be asked to be a godfather."

"But he might have been at the baptism?"

"You want to have another look at the video?"

Carlisle laughed.

"It couldn't have been Karl. He's only been here a few weeks."

"I don't think he's Sandra's type. Far too brutal. No, I think we're looking for someone more refined . . . Someone more like Mr Blazer. I think Sandra has ambitions for her baby. Certainly not someone like Ron."

And there the matter was left for the time being.

Their next appointment was at 2.15pm – leaving only a brief slot for lunch.

30. *Susanna's Secret*

Elaine had agreed to see the Inspector that afternoon. But what surprised him was the address.

"I didn't realize you were Ron's sister."

The ex-barmaid nodded.

"It's a large family. Six of us. I'm the oldest."

She rubbed her hands anxiously over her red skirt as if she was straightening out some invisible crease. Her face had a lived-in look; her voice was husky – too many cigarettes; her hair dyed blonde but with the dark roots visibly fighting their way to the surface. She had her brother's small, snub nose.

"Mr Stone gave me your phone number. Mr Tom Stone."

"He would."

"You don't like him?"

"He sacked me."

Raynes thought it was perhaps too early in the interview to raise the question of why she had been dismissed. Instead, he asked: "Had you been working there long?"

"A couple of weeks . . ."

She paused.

" . . . this time. But I've worked for him before. Whenever he's hard up for staff, he usually gives me a ring."

"I see. But you don't really get on?"

"Not really. He used me as the way of getting rid of wife No. 2. I thought he fancied me. He pretended he did. Took me round

174

to the house. Opened a bottle of champagne. Did the honours. Then she walked in and caught us. That was it."

"Didn't you get anything out of it?"

"A couple of grand. But I thought he meant it. I didn't realize it was all a big con."

"So why did he object to you and Bert?"

"Jealousy, probably. Doing it in his pub! Doing it in the passage outside his kitchen!" She laughed crudely. "It was a bit much – even for Tom!"

Raynes asked delicately.

"Did you give your consent?"

"Did I hell! I know Bert from of old. Who doesn't? He's just a dirty old man. It's quicker to do it than argue about it. Still at least he paid for it. That's a change."

Knowing that money had gone missing from Mr Stone's wallet, he asked: "May I ask how much?"

"Twenty quid. Helps the housekeeping!"

Raynes was surprised she could treat the matter so lightly.

"But your brother was in the main bar . . ."

"The Lounge bar."

"He might have heard about it?"

"He probably did. Ron must've seen him touching me up. He knows what Bert is like. Bert probably went back and said: 'I've just had your sister' or something like that."

"Wouldn't he have been angry?"

"If he couldn't stand up for himself against Bert, he'd hardly be likely to stick up for me. The little turd!"

Raynes said reprovingly: "You're not very fond of your brother?"

Elaine voiced her disgust.

"Well, he's just clueless, isn't he? Fancy getting that girl pregnant in the first place. She's only nineteen. Bert Stone's daughter! He knows how Bert dotes on that girl. Spoilt her rotten. More than he did his own son! But that's another story . . .

"Then he let Bert go and put his name on the birth certificate! Agreed to pay sixty quid a week maintenance along with those other two blinding fools! Didn't even know whether he was father of the baby! I ask you. He knew Bert would never agree to his daughter marrying him. Bert knew our family all too well. Not good enough for his little princess!

"So what does Ron do? He runs away. Joins the Army. Believe me, he doesn't know what's coming to him. The red caps'll make mincemeat of him."

A casual thought passed through Raynes' mind.

"Where is Ron today?"

She laughed.

"You won't believe it. He and Alec have gone off on their bikes. Hell's Angels. Terrorizing the people of Brighton. He'll probably get arrested! Then see if the Army'll have him. He's just one long disaster."

She reached for her cigarettes and lit one.

"So you don't think he attacked Bert?"

"He wouldn't dare."

"Not even after severe provocation?"

"He's a complete coward."

She drew heavily on her cigarette.

"If you knew our family, Inspector, you'd understand. We seem to have been jinxed from birth."

Raynes was pleased to see the cigarette smoke was going in Carlisle's direction – but the atmosphere in the room was dark and oppressive. He felt there was still more that Elaine Sharpe could tell him. Very soon, she obliged.

"Of course, it wasn't because of Bert that I was sacked."

"No?"

"No. It was because of what I said to his fancy brother when I heard that Bert had gone missing. I said to him: 'Well, now you'll be able to get your hands on Liz . . . like you've always wanted to'."

"Liz?"

"Bert's wife. He's always had a soft spot for her. Some people reckon Alec's Tom's son. That's why Bert gave the kid such a rough time. Jealousy . . . spite . . . call it what you will."

She stubbed out the half-smoked cigarette.

"But it's only hearsay. You mustn't take it as gospel."

Had Elaine been the sole source of this information, Raynes might have taken the story with a pinch of salt. But Edmund had told him what he had seen after the baptism party. It all tied in.

"So what did Tom say to you?"

"He was livid. I've never seen him quite so angry. He said it was a lie and he wouldn't have me spreading gossip about him in his pub."

"He sacked you for that?"

"Well, I said a few more things as well." She lit another cigarette. "I said to him: 'I saw you going out of the pub – just after your brother had left. I know you've told everyone you were clearing up . . . But you threw him out . . . you shut the doors. But, five minutes later, you went out through the back door. You were back in about ten minutes. And you came back looking as guilty as hell.' I said to him: 'If anyone's topped Bert, it's probably you. Just so you can get your sticky mitts on his missus!'"

"I bet that didn't go down well?"

"No. He threatened me with a . . . something legal?"

"An injunction?"

"Yes, that's right. He said he'd speak to his lawyer."

"A frightened man?"

"Very much so. I'm surprised he gave you my phone number. He must've known what I'd be saying to you."

Raynes was grim.

"Yes. But at that moment, we hadn't found Bert's body. We didn't know it was buried only six hundred yards from the pub. It could've been anywhere. He must've felt quite safe. But once the body was found – and so close to the *Kirby Arms* – it must have made him feel nervous. That's probably why my colleague had to phone him up and dig the number out of him."

He looked at Carlisle. "Not looking good for Tom, is it?"

Carlisle drew a neat line under his notes. He imagined that Elaine had given them all the information she could. Quite enough to wrap up the case. They would soon be paying a repeat visit to Harrogate Drive.

Raynes looked at Ron's sister.

"Is there any more you wish to add?"

Elaine Sharpe gave a hoarse laugh.

"Isn't that enough?"

31. *The Gadfly*

"Did she pour out her bile?"

"I'm afraid she did."

Tom was silent.

He was being interviewed – not in his home in Harrogate Drive – but in the back office at the *Kirby Arms*. He was safely ensconced behind a large desk and was smoking a small cigar – probably a Hamlet.

"A bitter woman," he said at last.

"Perhaps she feels that you did her some wrong?"

Uncle Tom took a puff at his cigar.

"Show me the woman that doesn't feel wronged!"

"I think she genuinely thought you were interested in her."

"God! You can pick up better on the street."

Raynes remembered that Mrs May had spoken of two visits to Harrogate Drive. He found himself resenting that remark. "I think she feels she was used."

Tom was callous.

"What else are women for?"

"She says that the reason why you sacked her was not because of her having sex with Bert in a public place, but because of the things she said to you about your relationship with your sister-in-law, Elizabeth Stone."

Some colour came back into Tom's face. Clearly, he had expected worse. This one could be easily dealt with.

"I've always been fond of Betty and her family."

"How fond?"

"Always within the bounds of propriety, Inspector. You don't think I would have done anything to antagonize Bert? Pinched the poor man's ewe lamb?"

That was exactly what Raynes was thinking.

"On the night of the baptism . . ."

"Yes?"

" . . . you came up to the *Kirby Arms* with Bert, Raymond, Karl, Ron, Charles and Alec . . . in a taxi?"

"In two taxis. I told you that."

"So you did. I think you also said that you were at the *Kirby Arms* for the rest of the evening?"

"I was."

Raynes looked at him with the quiet pleasure of an angler about to draw in his catch.

"D'you have any desire to change your story?"

"No. It's true."

Tom's eyes were hard and watchful.

"What would you say if I told you that you had gone back to Harrogate Drive and slept with a lady . . ."

"I would say it was a damned lie!"

" . . . with Bert's wife?"

Red patches appeared on Tom's cheeks.

"I would still say it was a damned lie!"

"In fact, you were seen in bed with Mrs Stone at half past six by the Reverend Edmund Blazer – an impeccable witness."

Tom was once again silent. Clearly, he had forgotten the existence of the curate.

Raynes continued: "He was in one of your upstairs bedrooms recovering from a rather rough afternoon. A large number of drinks and a knockout blow from Heidi's boyfriend. When, eventually, he surfaced, he had a natural desire to go to the toilet. In the course of looking for a toilet, he opened your bedroom door."

"The little shit! I should never have given him the money."

"D'you deny that he saw you together?"

Tom obviously wanted to deny it, but he knew that what the Inspector was saying was true. It was difficult to think of any other explanation for them being together.

Raynes slowly turned the knife.

"Bert was alive at that point . . ."

Tom said nothing.

" . . . wasn't he?"

The Inspector probed a little more deeply.

"How often in the past has Betty come over to you for comfort and support? For a little happiness in a warm bed? It doesn't matter now that Bert is dead – but, as your barmaid was kind enough to point out, it does suggest that you might have had a very good reason for getting rid of your brother."

"Why should I have waited all these years?"

"I don't know."

"He was a greedy fool!"

"I think we would all agree."

"He had a splendid wife . . . twenty-seven years they were married . . . and he deceived her at every turn. She didn't deserve that. I always did what I could for her. She could always turn to me."

Raynes wondered whether this was the moment to stick in the next banderillo.

He said quietly: "Was Alec your son?"

His question produced a violent reaction. Tom threw his cigar into a corner. He smashed down his fist on his desk. He stood up and shouted: "Get out! D'you hear me? Get out!"

Raynes did not move.

Carlisle continued placidly making his notes.

"Sit down," said Raynes firmly. "If I have any more of that nonsense, I shall take you into custody and you can cool your heels in a cell."

"I shall phone my solicitor."

He picked up the phone.

Raynes was coldness itself.

"I wouldn't bother. Long before any solicitor could get here, I could have you arrested and taken to Grasshallows police station."

"Charged with what? Charged with what! Adultery's not a criminal offence."

"Suspected murder?" said Raynes.

"Oh, don't be ridiculous! Whatever stupidities Bert may have committed, I wouldn't have killed him."

Tom sat down again.

Raynes continued to make his case.

"Mrs Sharpe also told me that you went out of the pub after Bert had left. You went out by the back door and you were away for ten or fifteen minutes."

"I think I've already told you, Inspector; I threw him him

out. But then I had a fit of conscience. I went out to see if he was still there. But he had gone. I may have been out for two or three minutes; but no more than that."

"That was about half past twelve?"

"Quarter past, I would say."

"Well," said Raynes, more pleasantly, "when you first told me about this, the time and the place didn't matter. But the police surgeon tells me that Bert died at about 12.30am and his body was found on Riverside Road – only six hundred yards from your pub. I think I'm entitled to ask you some searching questions. It now seems likely that you were the last – or almost the last – person to see him alive. You had a motive. You were in the right place at the right time. I think that even the most sympathetic lawyer would say there was a case to answer."

"So you're charging me with murdering my brother?"

"No," said Raynes, "I'm not."

(At least, not yet, he said to himself.)

"I'm just wanting answers to some perfectly reasonable questions. Such as – how long have you been having an affair with Bert's wife?"

Tom seemed to collapse like a balloon. All the aggression went out of him. He lit another cigar.

"Before she married Bert . . . Of course, I was already married to my first wife . . . so there was no way we could get married. She married him – and, on and off, we've been friends for nearly thirty years."

"Lovers?"

"All right – lovers."

"And Alec was your son?"

Tom swallowed. This was the difficult one.

"I don't know. We've often speculated. Bert accused me of being his father. I've always denied it. But we've had a lot of rows . . . a lot of bitterness. Alec's very like Bert. Aggressive. Moody. Not particularly bright . . . but I suppose the Stone genes run in his blood. I always did what I could for Alec, but Bert resented it."

"Who paid for the bike?"

"I did."

"He says his dad did."

"Well, I put up the cash. Bert wouldn't have let on."

"And why did you put up the cash?"

"To shut him up. He was making everyone's life a misery saying that Sandra shouldn't have the child. She should have an abortion. Betty begged me to do something to quieten him down. She knew he longed for a bike; so a deal was done." Tom stared sadly at his desk. "Sandra was very hurt."

"So you coughed up?"

"I put the money into Bert's account."

"And Alec got the bike last Christmas?"

"I don't see it's important."

Raynes said patiently: "It's important because I've got to understand the background to Bert's death. The tensions, the aggro, the bitterness of all the people involved; the things that could have driven someone to put the boot in.

"When we first met, you told me that you were in between marriages – waiting for wife No. 4. I took that to mean that you were looking around. I didn't know that you had a ready-made family – wife, daughter and grandchild – just waiting to tie the knot. I would say that Bert's death suited you rather well."

"Don't malign my few good deeds."

"I most certainly won't. I think you are basically a kind, good man. But I also think you despised and hated your brother – primarily for the way he treated the woman you loved. You did all you could to help, but there were times when you were totally exasperated, angry, wanting to get rid of him.

"What I am suggesting is that on the night of the baptism, all these feelings came together. You threw him out of the pub, went after him, assaulted him, pushed him into that trench, covered him with soil – then or later, and hoped that would be the end of him. No body, no proof.

"You sacked Elaine because she spoke the truth. She knew you only too well. You use people, Tom. When you have finished with them, you dispose of them. Give them a divorce; give them money. You should have given her a couple of hundred to keep her mouth shut. But she isn't the only one who has pointed the finger at you. Others can put two and two together. You had the motive and the means. So long as there was no body, you were sitting pretty. Now the body has turned up – virtually on your doorstep – and you're the No. 1 suspect."

Tom Stone listened to the Inspector calmly. Eventually, he uttered a deep sigh.

"I hadn't realized that the case against me was quite so cut and dried. I shall most certainly consult my solicitor; but I can assure you, Inspector, that although I am guilty of adultery – over many years, with many women – I am not guilty of murder.

"Bert's behaviour on the day of the baptism was quite unforgivable. He was vicious, spiteful, cruel; he was looking for trouble. He had absolutely no self-control or decency. He was a foul creature but I would never have lifted a hand against him. I would far rather have seen him in jail. Frankly, I'm surprised you lot have never put him away.

"I've had to live with it – for years. I've had to bail him out, bind up the wounds, pay off his debts, find him jobs, lie for him – and got nothing but abuse in return. I shall certainly benefit greatly from his death – but I didn't do it and you'll have a hard job proving it."

His face was grim. "Is that enough?"

"For the moment," said Raynes. "But before I go, I would like to look around the premises. The kitchen first, I think."

Tom was thankful to get the Inspector out of the office. It had been a hateful experience. He had felt like a cornered animal.

He led the two officers down the passage.

Raynes stopped.

"Is this where Mrs Sharpe was assaulted?"

"Yes."

"And are these the condoms dispensed in your gents' toilet?"

He showed Tom the packet which had been found in Bert's pocket.

Tom nodded.

"I'm surprised he used them. Must be getting respectable in old age. Probably frightened of catching something."

Raynes did not comment.

They continued down the passage and entered an impressive

modern kitchen filled with stainless steel sinks, ovens, burners and huge extractor fans. Everything looked spotlessly clean.

"We're inspected regularly by the Environmental Health," said Mr Stone proudly. "We have one of the highest standards of hygiene in the city."

"Better than *The Green Man*?"

Tom laughed. A scornful laugh.

"You should see their kitchens! Antiquated isn't the word. The Pest Control have to be called in regularly to deal with the rats. It's the old drains and the holes in the floors. They should have dealt with them years ago."

Raynes was slightly taken aback by this unexpected attack on his favourite hostelry. Perhaps things were rather grim behind the scenes; but their food was excellent.

If it was good enough for the Rotary Club, it was good enough for him!

But the Inspector did not let Tom Stone bask in his pride for long.

"Where d'you keep all your equipment?" he asked. "Your knives, your choppers and cleavers?"

Mr Stone pulled open several drawers.

The Inspector drew out a hefty marble rolling pin. He weighed it carefully in his hands and looked significantly at Carlisle.

"Could be?" he said.

Carlisle nodded seriously. The rolling pin bore no resemblance to a chrome-plated spanner; but it was a formidable blunt instrument and could do a lot of damage. Raynes' junior colleague kept up the charade.

"Do you want me to take it back to the station?"

"No. They'll have scrubbed it down by now."

The owner of the *Kirby Arms* looked at the Inspector with some alarm. "You don't think . . .?"

Raynes inspected all the kitchen equipment, lingering over the sharp knives and meat cleavers.

"Quite a little arsenal you've got here."

"It's all used."

"And kept under lock and key?"

Tom Stone began to feel uneasy. He didn't know exactly what the Inspector was looking for. He began to offer a series of fatuous excuses. Raynes ignored him.

"I believe you have a beer garden?"

"Yes, out at the back. A very popular venue for our customers in summer."

And indeed it was. Sheltered by high walls, a broad patio surrounded by flower beds and tubs of geraniums. There were the usual quota of tables, chairs and parasols.

"And who does your gardening?"

"A Mr Peterson. A retired bloke. Comes in once a week and mows the lawn. Does a number of small jobs whilst he's here."

"And where does he keep his equipment?"

"In the shed."

A small white wooden building just outside the kitchen. Raynes noticed that the key was in the lock.

Tom Stone opened the door. The first thing the Inspector saw was the motor mower, cable, seed boxes, plant food, pots of paint and a bag of cement. Behind the door was a selection of forks, spades and rakes. And a large metallic blue tool box.

Raynes picked it up and took it outside. He looked at the comprehensive array of tools, including a large chrome-plated monkey wrench and a claw-headed hammer.

"I think we shall have to take this away with us," he said.

But there was something else niggling at the back of his mind. Something else that he had seen, but not completely registered. He went back into the shed and looked again behind the door. All the tools had clean, shiny surfaces but on the spade, there was a crust of red clay. No, his eyes had not deceived him.

He invited Carlisle into the shed to have a look.

"Could be?" he said again.

He came out of the shed and looked at the flower beds Dark black soil. Not a trace of red clay.

He looked at Carlisle.

"We'd better take it with us. I saw one or two black bin liners in there. Make sure you don't touch it."

Raynes gave Tom Stone a piercing look.

"The motive. The means. And now – the murder weapons! You'd better make sure you get a good lawyer."

"It's Derek Coates-Smythe."

Raynes raised his eyebrows.

"I said 'a good lawyer'!"

32. *The Nutcracker*

Raynes looked at Carlisle.

"I fear we may be barking up the wrong tree. Or, even worse, being led up the garden path . . ." He paused. "I really cannot believe that Alec is Tom's son." He shook his head.

"He's far too like Bert. Tom is a smoothie – he oozes with charm." He thought back to the scene in the *Kirby Arms*. "Well, normally he does . . . But Alec is dour and graceless. Agreed?"

"Agreed."

"If anyone is Tom's child, it's Sandra. She has charm. Quite unlike her father."

"But they didn't quarrel over Sandra . . ."

"No. She was his 'little princess'. He adored her. Protected her. I can understand why."

"Perhaps he didn't have any suspicions at that time?"

"No. But the affair's been going on a long time. What did he say? 'On and off for almost thirty years'. Bert must have found out eventually. No wonder there were harsh words. His own brother!"

"Tom would have bought him off."

"Of course he would. Every man has his price. The Reverend Blazer gets a hundred quid for church funds. Alec, a motor bike. Elaine Sharpe, two grand. Yes, Tom can be quite generous."

"I wonder if Bert ever beat him up?"

"Tom was a boxer as well – he told us that."

Raynes gave Carlisle a reproachful look. He was the taker of notes; he should have remembered that.

Carlisle ignored the look.

He couldn't remember everything.

"It must have really riled him when Tom suggested that if Sandra didn't marry Ron, he might marry her himself. Wife No. 4. Especially when he was still sleeping with her mother."

Raynes agreed.

"The whole thing's a complete mess. The bloodlines are hopelessly entangled. But would he really think of marrying his daughter?"

"He wouldn't be allowed to. He'd be breaking the law."

"But who's to say? Who's going to spill the beans?"

"Alec?"

Raynes was silent for several minutes. He stared out of the window deep in thought.

"Yes," he said. "Alec. He would've heard the rumours. The rows between Bert and his wife. It's not much fun discovering you're illegitimate and the person you thought was your father utterly rejects you. And not only rejects you, but beats the hell out of you when he's drunk. He knows that Sandra is his father's favourite child; but perhaps he suspects that she too could be Tom's daughter. If so, why is she being treated so differently?"

"He doesn't like his sister."

"He doesn't like her being pregnant. What was it that woman said? 'Bringing shame and dishonour on the family!' That's a laugh. After all that's gone before. I should have thought the family were quite used to shame and dishonour!"

"And what would he have thought about his mother having an affair with Tom? He would have despised her."

Raynes smiled.

"If Alec had known his Greek classics, he would have murdered his mother – not his father. Oedipus had killed him already."

"But Alec says he didn't kill his father. And you said you believed him."

"Well, if Tom is his real father – or if he *thinks* Tom is his real father – then he obviously hasn't killed him. But, maybe – I say, maybe – Bert is his father after all. For years, he's been told he's someone else's son – so when I ask him: 'Did you kill your dad?' he quite honestly says : 'No'."

Carlisle shook his head in despair.

"Is there anyone who could sort out this mess?"

They both came up with the same answer:

"Mrs Stone."

33. *Pieces Fugitives*

However, for the moment, all investigations were temporarily suspended whilst the Inspector and Carlisle went up to Leeds to charge and arrest Karl Taylor. They left early on Tuesday morning.

Raynes decided to take Sergeant Evans with them. He was a tough, no-nonsense sort of fellow who would keep Karl under a close eye and would not hesitate to lash out if the prisoner caused any trouble. The Inspector had no desire to share a car with Karl so they took a van and a police dog with them.

The journey up to Leeds took about two and a half hours and they arrived shortly after 10.00am. But Karl was appearing in the local court that morning to face a series of charges under the Road Traffic Act. Naturally, he would be pleading "Not guilty" and a date would be fixed for his trial.

The three officers from Grasshallows therefore had another two hours to hang around the court until the case had been heard. During that time, Raynes was confronted by Ms Busby, Karl's social worker.

"Do you know anything about Mr Taylor's background?"

"No," said Raynes, who took an instant dislike to the woman.

"Justice cannot be administered without full reference to his social background."

Raynes did not agree with this assertion but he let it pass.

"Have you known him for a long time?" he asked politely.

"I've been working with his family for the past five years. I know them extremely well."

Raynes wanted to ask if they were all "nut-cases" but felt that such a question would be regarded as politically incorrect.

188

Instead, he asked: "What does the family consist of?"

"His mother and two sisters."

"And do they have problems as well?"

Ms Busby bristled.

"The whole family was deeply traumatized by the behaviour of Mr Taylor senior. Both girls were abused by their father. One of them has attempted suicide. Both of them are still receiving outpatient psychiatric treatment."

Raynes tried to look caring and sympathetic.

"And what did he do to Karl?"

Ms Busby looked severely affronted.

"He did nothing to Karl. Karl has been the one person who has held the family together. He has been the chief breadwinner. Do you know that he has been sending back one hundred pounds a week from his work in Grasshallows to help clothe and feed his family? No, of course you don't. If you arrest him, they are all going to suffer."

"I'm very sorry to hear that."

"No, you aren't. You just don't care."

Raynes sighed.

"All I know is that a young woman is in hospital in Grasshallows with a broken jaw and two black eyes. Her head is held together in a metal frame. She can't speak and she can only be fed through a straw. There is not the slightest doubt that Karl assaulted her."

"She probably provoked him."

"They've been living together for the past six weeks."

"A lovers' tiff."

Raynes raised his eyebrows.

"If you had seen the amount of blood over the bed, the floor and the furniture, I think you would have rated it a pretty serious assault." (Of course Raynes had seen no such thing, but he had a vivid imagination.) To Ms Busby, he said:

"Does he have a problem with women?"

Ms Busby stoutly defended her charge.

"I would say that he is very protective towards women. He idolizes his mother and he is very gentle and supportive towards his sisters. They love him very much and now you are

189

trying to put him behind bars – far away from Leeds, where they will not be able to visit him. They just couldn't afford it."

"Are they here today?" asked Raynes, looking around him.

"No," said Ms Busby.

"Not very supportive!" said Raynes. "I am surprised."

"It would be far too distressing for them – seeing their brother in court – being taken away in handcuffs."

Raynes looked at Karl's charge sheet.

"It's not exactly the first time, is it?" he said accusingly. "Theft, theft, theft, assault, assault, theft, assault. He's already spent two periods in detention. With a track record like that, he should expect to be put away. He's a public nuisance. Have you seen the car he was driving? A rusty frame. A loose bumper. Untaxed. And probably no insurance. He could easily have killed himself – and his sisters if they had been travelling with him. He could have done them even more harm than their father!"

Ms Busby was almost in tears.

"Oh, what a heartless brute you are! Those two girls have suffered quite enough. You have no idea what they have been through. You are breaking up a family; taking away the one person on whom they depend. You police are all the same! You are blinkered. Once a man is labelled as a criminal, you regard him as a criminal for life! You make no allowance for human factors. You give people no chance to start again."

Raynes was icily polite.

"I think Mr Taylor has been given quite enough chances to reform. If he chooses to beat up defenceless women, he'll get longer and longer sentences. He has only himself to blame. Now, if you would excuse me . . ."

Raynes turned on his heel and walked away, heading for the court room. Behind him, he could hear Ms Busby berating Carlisle and Sergeant Evans.

"I think you should be ashamed of yourselves. Working with such a man!"

* * * *

By comparison, the court was quite peaceful.

The offenders behaved quietly and respectfully; the lawyers spoke in low voices; the magistrates listened attentively and made their decisions in an apologetic tone of voice as if they regretted having to punish and fine.

"Thirty days . . ."

"Fined two hundred and fifty pounds . . ."

"Licence endorsed . . ."

And then Karl Taylor was brought into the dock. He too seemed quiet and self-controlled. His face was pale and inscrutable. He stood immobile, looking straight ahead. He confirmed his name and address. His charges were read out. A young lawyer rose to his feet to say that he was representing Mr Taylor who would be pleading "Not guilty". All in all, the hearing was over very quickly and Karl was taken away.

Raynes returned to his colleagues in the passage.

"I think he's ready for us."

Carlisle looked doubtful.

"I wouldn't be too sure. That Busby woman's gone to see him. And his lawyer will want to speak to him . . ."

Sergeant Evans was thinking about lunch.

"Are we having a bite of lunch before we set off, sir?"

It was going to be a long day.

* * * *

Karl was taken back to the police station. In one of the small interview rooms, he was formally charged with assault. Karl said nothing but his eyes remained cold and watchful. Raynes remembered his frightening presence in Heidi's house. His own vulnerability. "Beat it, pig!" Karl had no time for the police.

They did at least give him some lunch. Raynes and his colleagues had steak pie and chips in the staff canteen. Then Karl was escorted out to the van. The police dog sniffed at him and barked loudly. Here, Sergeant Evans came into his own, making sure that the wire cage was properly secured and that there was no way the prisoner could escape. Dog and sergeant would watch him every inch of the way.

In Grasshallows, the process was reversed. Karl was escorted to the police cells, given another meal and a cup of tea. The police dog was fed and rewarded for his vigilance.

More legal documents were signed; another legal aid lawyer approached to represent the offender; and arrangements were made for a further court appearance on Wednesday morning. There, predictably, Karl would again plead "Not guilty" and be remanded in custody. It would probably be a case for the Crown Court. Raynes was glad to see him behind bars.

As they walked back to their office, Carlisle mimicked Ms Busby: "Oh, what a heartless brute you are! You make no allowance for human factors. Never give people a chance to start again."

Raynes turned to his colleague.

"Would you give that one a chance to start again? That Busby woman was lucky he never laid into her!"

34. *Fur Elise*

It was only four days since Betty Stone and her daughter had moved into Tom's house in Harrogate Drive, but already there was a visible improvement in the state of the kitchen.

Everything was clean, tidy, polished. Coffee was served in cups – not mugs. Raynes complimented Betty on the transformation.

"Last time I was here," he said, "the place was a tip; unwashed plates; sugar out of a packet; dog-ends everywhere."

Mrs Stone smiled indulgently.

"He looks after his pubs. He keeps them spotlessly clean."

"Yes. I noticed."

She would have been told about his visit to the *Kirby Arms*. He looked at her thoughtfully.

"Are you intending to move in – permanently?"

There was a longish pause.

"We're thinking about it."

"Wife No. 4?"

"We're not exactly strangers."

"No. You've been lovers for quite some time. Thirty years, I'm told."

Betty Stone said nothing.

Raynes said: "The first time we met, you were accusing Bert of chasing after anything in a skirt. You said it was his great weakness. But you seem to have been doing precisely the same thing with Tom."

Mrs Stone chose her words carefully. "It wasn't all that often," she said. "Months might pass. But when I was down, he was always there to help me."

"Did he have down patches too?"

Betty Stone laughed.

"Not half. Those wives of his led him a merry dance. He didn't know the half of what they got up to."

"But you did?"

"I heard about it – on the grapevine."

"And told him?"

"Of course."

"And then he got a divorce?"

"Sometimes." Betty Stone poured herself a second cup of coffee. "Other times, he just let it be. It suited him. They were both doing their own thing. But, eventually, he got tired of them."

"And he used people like Elaine Sharpe to provoke the break?"

"She hates him."

"Why does he employ her?"

"She's a good worker."

Raynes said quietly: "She seems to have been Bert's last conquest."

"So I hear."

"D'you think she might have killed him?"

"Not really. All she was interested in was his money."

"He didn't normally pay."

"No. But I daresay she was finding things a bit tight. Because Ron was paying all that maintenance, he wasn't paying his rent. I expect she was glad to get a bit of her own back."

Wheels within wheels.

Raynes and Carlisle accepted a second cup of coffee. With some delicacy, the Inspector said:

"She seems to think Tom was Alec's father."

"Quite a few people have said that."

"But is it true?"

Betty shrugged her shoulders.

"How should I know? They didn't have those new-fangled tests when he was born. I always thought he was the spit and image of Bert – but without the charm!"

She smiled sadly.

Raynes said: "We shall need to find out."

"Why?"

"Because it might be a clue to your husband's murder."

"Oh, Alec would never have laid a finger on him. He's a coward – like the rest of them. He didn't mind humiliating his dad in public; but he'd never get involved in an actual fight."

"He'd suffered enough?"

Betty rose to her husband's defence. "Alec was a difficult child. Threw tantrums. Screamed a lot. Woke us up at night. Bert didn't have much time for him. 'Gurning little bastard!' he used to say. He'd just go out and leave me to it. But then Sandra came along. Totally different. Lots of smiles. No trouble at all. He adored her. Spoilt her rotten. And, of course, Alec resented her getting all that attention. He used to attack her. And then Bert would take it out on him."

"You think he's always been jealous of her?"

"I'm afraid so. Anyway, we see less of him now . . . Now he's got his own flat . . ."

" . . . And his motor bike?"

"Yes."

"Which Tom paid for?"

Mrs Stone nodded.

"He seems very generous?"

"Well, we had to do something. He was upsetting Sandra terribly. She wanted to have the baby – but Alec didn't. I think he was put up to it by Ron. They're close, you know. Thick as thieves. Everyone said Ron was the father but Bert believed

194

Ron was using Alec to get him off the hook. Ron had a motor bike but Alec didn't. You can see how their minds worked. Something in it for both of them."

"And Tom paid up?"

"He always does."

Raynes smiled – a deceptively sweet smile.

"Well, I suppose if he really loves you, he'd do anything for you, wouldn't he?"

Betty Stone was silent. Perhaps she doubted whether Tom, after all his affairs, would be capable of loving anyone. Even if she married him, was there any chance of him being faithful? Probably not.

Raynes returned to the events of Sunday August 13th.

"You didn't go back to Coronation Gardens with Sandra and Mark?"

"No."

"You stayed on here in Harrogate Drive?"

"I was tidying up – after the party."

Raynes raised his eyebrows.

"Would it not be more accurate to say that you were waiting for Tom to come back from the pub? Both of you hoping to spend a little time together? Wasn't that how it was?"

Mrs Stone said nothing.

"You will have heard there was a witness . . ."

Betty's lips tightened.

" . . . The Reverend Blazer. He saw the two of you upstairs."

Mrs Stone could not contain herself.

"He had a brass neck, complaining about us! Only two hours before, he'd been having it off on that bed himself! With my daughter!"

"How d'you know?"

"I saw them!" Raynes said nothing so Betty continued: "I heard the baby crying so I went in to see him. And there they were – on the bed – hard at it!"

"You didn't try to stop them?"

"Of course not! Don't be stupid!"

"Did they know you were there?"

"No. I just slipped out and shut the door."

Raynes could imagine that Mr Blazer would be mortified if he knew that Sandra's mother had been watching them. He observed tartly: "Your daughter seems pretty free with her charms!"

"She has a lot of love to give."

Well, that was one way of putting it!

Raynes returned to his investigations:

"And how long were you and Tom together?"

"About an hour."

"Till seven o'clock?"

"Perhaps a little longer."

"And then, what did you do?"

"I went home."

"On foot?"

Mrs Stone showed some irritation. "Of course not! We got a taxi. Tom took me back home and then he went on to the pub."

"But he wouldn't get a taxi for Bert."

"No. He was fed up with him. We all were."

Raynes looked at her.

"So you had no alibi?"

"Sandra was in the house. And Heidi."

"But not after midnight?"

"No. She went home at about nine o'clock. Sandra gave Mark his last feed about ten. Then we both went to bed."

"You expected Bert to appear later?"

"I didn't know what to expect."

Something in the way she spoke gave Raynes pause for thought. It was not quite the reply he was expecting. He looked at Carlisle. He too looked thoughtful. A picture was beginning to form in the Inspector's mind. An unexpected picture . . . but not impossible.

He looked more closely at Mrs Stone.

He said quietly: "You could have been out in Riverside Road, waiting for him, couldn't you? Carrying an offensive weapon? Just biding your time? You could have arranged with Tom – not to get him a taxi, so that he would have to walk home? You could have been lurking in the shadows . . . No one would have known . . . would they?"

196

35. *Madame Butterfly*

Their conversation was interrupted by the return of Sandra and Mark. They had been out for a long walk. Mark was now asleep but Sandra was longing for a cup of coffee and a chocolate biscuit.

Mrs Stone sent them through into the sitting room whilst she made a fresh brew of coffee. Carlisle asked Sandra how the baby was getting on. How much did he weigh? Had he had his jabs yet? Was he sleeping the whole night? Raynes said nothing. This was very much Carlisle's department.

But once the fresh cups of coffee had been brought through, he turned to more serious matters. With a friendly smile, he said to Sandra:

"What's this I hear about you being pregnant again?"

The question shocked Betty Stone.

"Oh, no!" she said. "You can't be!"

Raynes continued to smile.

"I have it on excellent authority. From Mr Blazer."

Sandra blushed and tried to hide her embarrassment by fussing over Mark.

"It was all a joke," she said.

"He took it very seriously," said Raynes.

"Tell me it's not true?" said Mrs Stone.

"I'm not pregnant."

"Thank God for that! One grandchild is quite enough."

"He came to me for advice," said Raynes, sipping his coffee and wishing Mrs Stone had put more sugar into his cup. "I think you told him that he was the father?"

"Oh, Sandra!" said her mother. "Not the curate! What will Canon Murray say?"

Raynes was pleasantly amused but Carlisle thought he was being rather cruel bringing up such an embarrassing matter in front of the girl's mother.

A more forceful Sandra emerged.

"I didn't have sex with him and I'm not pregnant."

Raynes knew she was lying – but he didn't challenge her.

Instead, he said: "I believe you were hoping to marry him?"

Sandra went very red.

Mrs Stone was obviously delighted.

"Did he propose?"

"No, he didn't!" said Sandra with some venom. "He's a wimp! I gave him the chance but he turned it down. I think he's gay. He's frightened of having sex with me." She looked at Mark. "He liked the baby, though."

Raynes was at his most disarming.

"I don't think it was the sex that bothered him. Rather the family connections . . ."

Sandra and her mother both looked puzzled.

"You see – it may not matter to you – but the Stone family is under investigation for a most serious act of murder. Much as he may have liked you – and the baby, he could never give his consent whilst such a cloud of suspicion enveloped the family."

"Of course not," said Mrs Stone.

"Once the investigation is over, and we know who killed your dad, then the matter might well be considered in a more friendly light. But you put him in an impossible position. There was no way he could say 'yes' however much he wanted to."

"I don't think he wanted me. He tried to get me drunk on some cheap plonk and then bundled me into a taxi and sent me home."

Raynes continued to present the possibilities in the most favourable light.

"I don't think you've really had a chance to get to know each other," he said. "I mean, you've never been out for a meal together or gone to the cinema or anything. The only times you've been in touch have been in connection with the baptism."

Sandra was not convinced by Raynes' fine words.

"He's a hypocrite," she snarled. "He said that if I was pregnant, I should get an abortion. He was quite willing to kill his own child. That's what they said about Mark."

"That's what Alec said."

"He wasn't the only one."

Sandra was bitter and stinging in her reply.

Raynes said quietly:

"I thought you said that you didn't have sex with him. So he couldn't possibly be the baby's father."

Betty Stone understood the point the Inspector was making. She knew her daughter.

"Stop lying, Sandra! Tell the Inspector the truth."

"Not in front of you, Mum."

Mrs Stone got to her feet.

"Very well. Discuss it among yourselves. I'll go and get lunch ready." She picked up the baby. "And I'll feed Mark."

As she left the sitting room, she very firmly shut the door. As she did so, Raynes adopted a slightly harsher tone.

"Let's have a bit of honesty, Sandra. I believe you had sex with Mr Blazer at the baptismal party. Is that true?"

Sandra looked flustered and angry.

For a moment Raynes thought she was going to get up and storm out of the room like her mother. But she stood her ground.

"Yes, we did."

"I believe he didn't have much choice in the matter?"

"It was very quick."

Raynes looked at the very beautiful young mother sitting on the very edge of the sofa.

He said: "You're a young woman who tends to get what she wants . . . You like to have your own way . . ."

Sandra nodded hesitantly.

" . . . But why did you concoct this cock-and-bull story about being pregnant? You couldn't possibly know that you were pregnant in so short a time. Were you trying to trap him?"

Sandra decided to tell the Inspector the truth.

"You have no idea," she said, "what this past year has been like. It was bad enough being pregnant – and not knowing who the father was. Then I had Alec telling everyone I should have an abortion. I was under a lot of pressure. Dad was against me marrying Ron or Jimmy. But I didn't want to marry anyone.

"But now that Dad's gone missing – now he's dead – I feel quite free. Mark's a lovely baby. No trouble. I'd like to give him a better life. Find him a decent dad."

"Someone more educated?"

"Yes. Someone who'd get him out of Henslea. I thought for a moment Edmund might be the right person. He's gentle. He's kind. But he showed himself in his true colours. He's bigoted. He's a snob. He's not interested in helping me."

Raynes thought that whatever her reasons, she had not gone about it in quite the right way. Handled differently, Edmund would have been putty in her hands.

" . . . I mean, he's got absolutely no sense of humour. I was teasing him. I said we'd come to St Benedict's on Sunday morning when he was preaching his first sermon. I said that I hoped he wouldn't mind if I breast-fed Mark in the front row." She laughed. "I thought it was quite funny but he was horrified."

Raynes said he wasn't surprised. A first sermon must be quite a nerve-racking experience. The thought of such a distraction – in the front pew – would be devastating.

"It was only a joke," she said.

"He doesn't seem to like your jokes," said Raynes.

"No," she said, "he doesn't. And, anyway, why did he come to you?"

Raynes was brutally honest.

"He came to see me because he had failed to report an important fact during our first interview. He wished to tell me that when he left this house, after the baptismal party, he saw your mother in bed with Uncle Tom. He thought this was a material fact we ought to know."

Sandra was silent.

She bit her lip.

"You knew about their relationship?"

She nodded.

"It's been going on for a long time. Since before you were born."

She still said nothing.

Raynes decided to go further.

Looking at Carlisle, he said: "Have you ever considered that Uncle Tom might be your father?"

Sandra took the suggestion on board.

"Alec . . ."

"Yes, everyone thinks Alec is Tom's son. Your dad was convinced that Tom was his father. And Alec believes it. He thinks that was why your dad beat him and treated him so badly, But I think Alec is very like Bert, whereas you seem . . ." he paused thoughtfully, " . . . much more like your Uncle Tom."

Sandra breathed deeply.

There was a look of relief on her face.

"It has crossed my mind. But my dad loved me very much. He was always very kind to me."

"He called you his 'little princess'?"

She smiled.

"He spoilt me rotten."

"But would it worry you if it was true?"

"Not now."

"You'd expect Tom to pay for any future wedding?"

Sandra laughed.

"He pays for most things."

"So he does." Raynes looked round the sitting room. "And I suppose this is now going to be your home?"

"Every cloud has a silver lining."

Raynes guessed that Sandra saw her new home in Harrogate Drive as the first step in getting a better life for Mark.

He decided to puncture the balloon just a little.

"So are you going to marry Charles . . . or Ron . . . or Jimmy?"

"I don't want to marry anyone."

"Not even the father of the baby?"

"We don't know who it is."

Raynes sat back. This was the moment for the conjuror to produce the white rabbit out of the hat.

"Well, we've had the results of the DNA tests."

Sandra's face became tense.

"Oh?"

"And which of them d'you think is the father? Jimmy?" He paused. "Charles? Ron?" He let her wait. A long, long wait. Then he said: "It isn't any of them!"

Sandra looked amazed.

"It's got to be one of them."

"Has it? Well, I'm telling you, young lady, it isn't. You won't be able to claim any more sixty pounds. You can't claim money under false pretences. In fact, you may have to pay money back . . . but I don't suppose that'll bother you now."

"So who is the father?"

"You tell me!"

Sandra looked quite bemused.

"Tell me the names of every single person you had sex with between September and November last year. Even if you don't know their names, give me an idea how many there were."

"Why is it so important?"

"Because I think the person who was responsible for fathering your child was involved in the death of your dad."

"That's impossible!"

Raynes raised his eyebrows.

"Let me be the judge of that. You just give me their names."

"I don't know their names – it's so humiliating!"

Sandra began to weep.

Carlisle wondered how much longer the Inspector would keep going. It was becoming embarrassing. It was obvious that the girl did not want to reveal that she was a complete slut.

But Raynes waited patiently.

Slowly the picture emerged.

"There was a boy I met at Jimmy's disco – I don't know his name . . . There was a chap called Bill at the University. He's a research student. Then there's a friend of Heidi's – Graham or George. I can't remember. He had red hair. And there was someone I met at work. He's married. I can't think of his name. Four of them."

"Is that the lot?"

"Yes."

There was an element of defiance in Sandra's reply.

"Are you sure?"

"Yes."

Raynes looked at her with some irritation.

"I think there's one name missing from that list."

"Well, obviously you know more than I do."

Raynes said quietly: "I think I do."

At that moment, the door opened and Betty Stone walked in. "That's your lunch ready," she said. "And remember, you've got an appointment at the dentist's at 1.45pm."

Carlisle had an unpleasant suspicion that Sandra's mother had been listening at the door.

36. *La Donna E Mobile*

Whilst Sandra was visiting her dentist, Raynes paid a return visit to the hospital.

The beauty queen looked much improved. The black eye was now yellow and purple but there was once again a twinkle in her eyes that had not been there on Saturday.

She looked pleased to be having visitors but was still unable to speak.

Raynes introduced his colleague.

"Are you feeling any better?" he asked.

She shook her head and pointed to her left shoulder which was strapped up.

Raynes handed her a Biro and a pad. He hoped she was right-handed.

Heidi scribbled on the pad:

"They think I've dislocated my shoulder."

Raynes held her hand.

"We've brought some good news. Karl's been caught up in Leeds. The police noticed that his car hadn't got an up-to-date licence, so they took him in for questioning. We went up to Leeds yesterday and charged him with assault. He appeared in court this morning and now he's being remanded – in prison – until his trial." He squeezed her hand. "You'll be interested to hear that he pled 'not guilty'."

Heidi shut her eyes and then put a hand up to her cage.

"I know."

He looked across the bed to Carlisle.

"We shall need to take a statement . . ." He looked back to

Heidi. "When you feel ready to help us."

Heidi shrugged her shoulders and then winced in pain.

Raynes said: "I think that means she's willing to give it as soon as we wish. Is that right?"

The cage nodded.

Raynes said: "We've got some more good news. Mrs Ransome has cleaned your house beautifully. Everything's been washed and tidied up. Every drop of blood has been cleared away; the rubbish put out in the bin. Of course, she's destroyed all the evidence but your house is now quite habitable."

Tears rolled down Heidi's cheeks.

"She's a good neighbour. The one on the other side wasn't much use. In fact, she seemed a complete bitch."

A single squeeze of the hand.

"A third bit of good news. We've found Bert's body. Yes, Sandra will have told you. He'd fallen into that large trench the Gas Board have been digging in Riverside Road. We had to dig up the road to find him." Raynes looked across to Carlisle. "It was Friday, wasn't it? I've lost count of the days."

Heidi reached for the pad.

"Was he murdered?"

Raynes guessed her question before she had finished writing. "Yes."

"How?"

Raynes smiled. "Well, we haven't told people yet; but you're hardly likely to speak to anyone. So I can tell you, it was a blow to the head."

She looked sad. She picked up the Biro and wrote:

"No more kisses under the missletoe!"

It was a difficult word to spell.

Raynes laughed.

"You don't have much luck with your cavemen!"

A wry smile – and then more writing.

"Do we know who did it? No, not yet. But we've had some evidence from Jimmy. Real evidence, this time. You may remember he thought Bert had been seized by aliens. Well, Jimmy was driving home from his gig when he saw Bert staggering down Riverside Road, very unstable on his two pins.

"They stopped to have a few words. Bert was his usual forceful self. Aimed a blow at the driver . . . missed . . . then collapsed in the road. When they looked back in the mirror, they saw someone helping him to his feet. We think that may have been the person who killed him.

"Why? Probably because Bert attacked him. He was in a very bad mood that night. He was capable of attacking anyone."

There was a long silence at the bedside.

Heidi indicated that she would like some orange juice.

Raynes handed her the packet and the straw.

Carlisle doodled on his notepad. There wasn't very much to record thus far; but Raynes was about to change that.

He had decided that this was as good a time as any to take a statement. He would ask the questions. She would write the answers. Carlisle would record both in his notes. It sounded easy; but, very quickly, both men discovered that some of the answers might be quite lengthy. The questions would have to be broken down into smaller sections.

Heidi seemed quite happy to co-operate but Raynes cast an anxious glance over his shoulder at the staff nurse. She might think he was overtaxing her patient.

First of all, the time of the assault?

She thought it was about 11.00pm.

Yes, on Thursday night.

Karl had been out with Raymond Stone. He had been seeing a lot of him since the baptism. She regarded him as a thoroughly bad influence. Capitalists, property owners, the middle class, anyone who had secure jobs, homes and pensions – he was against them.

And yet Raymond was supposed to be finding Karl a flat in Grasshallows and another job. He'd had enough of labouring. He aspired to better things. Perhaps a cosy niche in the Schools Maintenance Department? Raymond had promised to see what he could do.

When he came back on Thursday night, he had been drinking. He had accused her of various things – which were untrue. He had twisted her arm, rammed her head against a door, thrown her on the floor. Later, he kicked her.

Then there had been a lull whilst he had his supper. She had taken off her knickers and tried to make up to him. But he repeated the accusations. She had got angry. He had been like an animal. Shaken her; thrown her against the wall; punched her in the face; burst her nose. There was blood everywhere. The final blow had completely rocked her – smashing her jaw.

She had thought he was going to kill her. But he left her in a heap on the floor. She saw him packing his bags; taking money out of her purse; she heard the slam of the door; the roar of the car engine. After that, she had passed out.

When she came to, the clock said 1.40am. She had tried to phone 999 but couldn't make herself understood. They must have thought she was drunk. With a great deal of effort, she had got on to her feet and made her way to Mrs Ransome's who had phoned for an ambulance. Mrs Ransome must have thought she had had a fall because she didn't contact the police.

So she had been taken to the hospital, been operated on – and missed most of Friday. Her mother had been notified on Saturday morning. The Inspector knew the rest.

Raynes thanked her for giving them the information. He asked Heidi whether she knew that Karl had a criminal record? She nodded. He had told her he had been inside twice. Raynes wondered whether he had told her anything about his family? A little. His sisters? Yes, he had told her about them. They seemed to have had a terrible childhood.

Remembering Ms Busby, Raynes asked whether it was true that Karl had been sending them £100 a week? She knew he had sent them something but she didn't know how much. He always seemed to have plenty of money. But why he should rake through her purse, she did not know.

The staff nurse appeared at Raynes' shoulder.

"Miss Houston will be very exhausted after all your questions. Perhaps you could come back another day?"

The Inspector flashed his identification card – but the staff nurse was not impressed.

"You've been here an hour. That's quite long enough."

Raynes turned on the charm.

"If you could give me just a couple more minutes, we shall

206

be finished. There are one or two more questions I must ask."

Heidi looked appealingly at the staff nurse – who relented. "Well, five more minutes, but no more than that."

Raynes once more took Heidi's hand. He caressed it.

"This is going to be the difficult part," he said. "Will you give me an honest reply?"

Heidi nodded.

She trusted the Inspector. In fact, she had already signed him up as a future lover. (If anyone ever wanted to be her lover again!)

A few more tears ran down her cheeks.

So what was the question?

Raynes took a deep breath.

"Do you know who is the father of Sandra's baby?"

Heidi looked shocked.

On her pad, she wrote:

"It's a secret."

Raynes said: "I know it's a secret. But do you know who it is?"

A long pause.

Slowly, Heidi nodded her head.

"I need to know. Sandra won't tell me. I know it isn't Ron, Charles or Jimmy . . . But I have to find out who killed Bert and I can't help thinking there's a connection."

But, future lover or not, Heidi was unwilling to break her promise to Sandra. She knew her reply would cause a lot of trouble. But did it matter any more? Had she been silent for too long?

Raynes took her pad and wrote a name on it.

He looked at Heidi.

"Is it him?"

With great reluctance, Heidi nodded again.

"You're quite sure?"

Behind him, the staff nurse said:

"That's enough, gentlemen."

Raynes looked down at Grasshallows' former beauty queen – with a gentle, kindly look. He gave her hand a final squeeze.

"And I think you have already told someone else?"

Tears poured down Heidi's cheeks.

He knew . . .

She knew . . .

It was all her fault.

37. *A Policeman's Lot*

It was an almost silent journey back to the police station.

"You were right," said Carlisle.

"It had to be him."

"What do we do now?"

"Wrap up the case."

"The usual?"

"They deserve an explanation."

Raynes was mindful that although he now knew all the answers, there were many loose ends to be tidied up before the case could be described as complete.

His first port of call would be the forensic laboratory. Further samples would have to be taken; fingerprints to be compared; there would have to be phone calls to more than a dozen people; a re-examination of Bert's body; a double-check of the DNA tests already done – including those of the baby – and fresh ones to be sought. Above all, there must be a complete ban on any further visits to Miss Heidi Houston.

She must not tell others what she had told him.

He tracked down Dr Stewart and told him all he knew about the case. More work would be required from his department – and quickly. Dr Stewart wondered if the Inspector had any more of that splendid Highland malt. Raynes realized that he was once again being subjected to blackmail – but in a good cause.

"You can have a whole boxful!"

"You are a most generous man."

As they left the laboratory, Raynes said: "That man must be a complete alcoholic. I think his blood must be 80% proof!"

On their return to the police station, the duty constable offered the Inspector a timely warning:

"There's a lady upstairs waiting to see you. A Miss Godfrey. She's been here about forty-five minutes. Wanting to know where you were."

"I don't know anyone called Godfrey."

The constable smiled.

"I think you do. You had lunch with her last Tuesday."

Realization dawned in the Inspector's eyes.

"Ah? You mean the Chair of the Police Committee? What does she want?"

"I think she has a complaint . . ."

As Raynes continued to look puzzled, the constable leaned forward conspiratorially: " . . . Videos, sir."

* * * *

It was one of the strange quirks of Raynes' professional life that whenever he was on the verge of some great personal achievement, he should always be brought down to earth by some ridiculous, trivial matter about which he had completely forgotten but which now seemed set to trip him up.

He remembered how the Chief Constable had tried to sack him over the issue of obscene phone calls when he was about to solve the murder of Sophie Jack.

Once again, fate had intervened.

"Miss Godfrey, I'm sorry to have kept you waiting."

"Where have you been?"

"At the hospital, interviewing a young woman who has had her face smashed in by her lover."

"I thought you were investigating the death of Mr Stone?"

"I am. But this young woman was almost killed. The case had to be dealt with promptly – and it has been."

The Chair of Grasshallows Police Committee put on her most forbidding look.

"You know why I am here?"

"I've been informed."

"It has been brought to the attention of the Police Committee that you have been supplying and circulating pornographic videos to the staff in this building . . ."

Raynes tried to intervene but was silenced.

" . . . I do not need to tell you that this action is quite reprehensible in a man in your position. One might expect such stupidity from a young constable – but to have items of this sort being distributed by a senior officer is quite inexcusable."

"I . . ."

"Hear me out, Inspector. There are women in this building who are deeply offended by your behaviour which amounts to the grossest form of sexism and harrassment. You have been in serious breach of the guidelines and statutory regulations governing police working practices."

"There is a perfectly reasonable explanation."

"I do not wish to hear your excuses, Mr Raynes. This matter will be brought before the next meeting of the City's Police Committee and you will be most seriously reprimanded and perhaps even demoted. You may save your explanations until then."

At no point in the exchanges did Miss Godfrey sit down. As she delivered her final blast, she walked over to the door – and then stopped – almost as if she had forgotten something.

"What did you say the name of the young woman was? The one in hospital?"

Rather shell-shocked, Raynes replied:

"Miss Houston. Miss Heidi Houston."

Detective-Constable Carlisle smiled helpfully.

"Your niece, ma'am."

* * * *

After Miss Godfrey had gone, Raynes looked at his colleague, speechless with admiration.

"How on earth did you know that?"

"I keep my ear to the ground, sir," said Carlisle modestly. "I seem to remember a reception – last Christmas I think it was. I don't think you were there. She was boasting that her niece had been Grasshallows' beauty queen a couple of years earlier. It seemed a good moment to remind her."

There was a knock at the door.

"Yes?" said Raynes brusquely. "What is it now?"

"A young man to see you, sir. A Mr Alec Stone . . ."

38. *Enigma Variations*

The time had now come to bring everyone together. A meeting was arranged for 4.00 on Thursday afternoon. The Inspector gave Tom Stone a choice: The *Kirby Arms*, the police station or his own home. Tom opted for Harrogate Drive.

Eleven people were expected to be present: himself, Betty and Sandra, Alec and the three godfathers, Raymond Stone and Grace, Elaine Sharpe and the Reverend Blazer.

Tom was unhappy about Elaine being there but Raynes told him she was a key witness. Sandra was worried about the baby. The Inspector arranged for a policewoman to look after Mark. There must be no interruptions.

The chief problem seemed to be getting Jimmy Watson to appear. He was said to be unhappy at being seen so frequently in police company. It was beginning to undermine his reputation. Raynes explained that was why he had chosen Tom's home; it was neutral ground. But there was still a chance that Jimmy might not turn up, so a police car was sent to collect him.

Tom Stone tried to make his guests feel welcome. A wide selection of drinks was set out in the hall – but most people didn't feel like drinking at that time in the afternoon. Ron had a beer and Grace had a brandy – "a large one, please". But the rest of them preferred to remain cold sober whilst the Inspector related his picture of all that had happened since the baptism.

Once everyone was seated, Raynes began:

"My colleague would tell you that I approached this case with very little enthusiasm. I am not really interested in missing people. Either they turn up of their own accord – having wasted a lot of people's valuable time – or they are found dead, in the Meadows or in the river – some of them suicides, others dying from natural causes.

"To begin with, it seemed that Mr Albert Stone had gone off with some woman. He had done it before but not for quite so long without contacting his family. We searched the river, the Meadows, the local garages and lock-ups – but without success. Mr Watson suggested he might have been seized by aliens. We were open to any suggestions; and certainly, the general impression was that Mr Stone had vanished into thin air.

"Of course, the answer was staring us in the face. That deep trench opened up by the Gas Board along the whole length of Riverside Road. Once you thought about it, it was the natural place for his body to be found. Failing to find a taxi, Mr Stone set off to walk back to Henslea. Even though the Gas Board have gone to great lengths to prevent anyone falling into the trench, it was the most obvious solution. I'm sorry it took me so long to see it.

"With the prompt assistance of the City Engineer and the full co-operation of the Gas Board" (perhaps a little poetic licence there!), "we were able to pinpoint the area of road which would have been open on Sunday 13th August, the night of the baptism. The ground was dug up and Bert's body was found. We all hoped it might have been an accident – a tragic accident, but the damage to his skull suggested otherwise. He had been attacked; he had been robbed; eighty pounds had been taken out of his wallet. His body had not just been pushed into the trench; it had been carefully buried to one side of the new pipe, so that it would not be seen by the workmen who would be filling in that part of the trench the following day.

"Once the body had been examined by the police surgeon, it was clear that we were investigating a murder. I had already considered this possibility and in the course of my inquiries, discovered that Mr Stone was a man with many enemies.

"He was a forceful, aggressive man – a bully – who enjoyed arguments and provoking people. Over the years, he he has assaulted many women – often quite violently; and he had been found guilty of several acts of indecent assault. One of his victims has said that he could be so violent that it was better to give in to him rather than fight. Throughout his life, he has been a man whom people feared.

212

"Even before his body was found, I had identified no fewer than six people who had bitter grudges against him. Since then, the number has steadily increased. Although it is possible that Bert was mugged by some passing stranger – I was inclined to think that the cause of his death would be related to matters nearer home. Much nearer home.

"First of all, Mrs Betty Stone has suffered many years of humilation and pain. Even though she was proud to have reached her Silver Wedding anniversary in 1987, she had no real love for Bert. The person whom she loved was his brother, Tom, who had been her lover – on and off – for almost thirty years. Bert's death would have given them both the opportunity to marry.

"Alec hated his father. He had been beaten and bullied as a child. He couldn't understand why he was treated so differently from his sister. It was rumoured that his real father was Tom Stone, but I have to say – from the DNA test taken this morning – that Alec was indeed Bert's son. It is a mystery why Bert treated his son so badly.

"The godparents – all three of them – had plenty of reasons for hating Bert. They were all very fond of Sandra but she did not know which of them was Mark's father. Mr Stone had no wish for them to find out. He was determined that each of them should pay for the upkeep of the baby – sixty pounds a week – and he would pocket the cash. This was a heavy burden for someone like Charles who was on a low wage; and for Jimmy who had to find extra gigs during the summer months. Each of these young men was bullied into paying maintenance. When Ron had the temerity to challenge Bert about this, he was knocked out at the baptismal party. Small wonder he decided to get out of harm's way and join the Army.

"Later, I heard evidence from Grace Lawrence and Elaine Sharpe, both of whom had suffered at Bert's hands – one of them many years ago; the other on the night of his death. Grace said publicly that she hoped someone would castrate him. 'Death was too good for him.' We might also remember Mr Beamish, the photographer. His wife's best friend was one of those indecently assaulted by Mr Stone.

"So all these people were suspects. Where were they on the night after the baptism?

"Sandra, we are told, went home with Heidi and the baby. She had given Ron the brush-off; so he and Alec went to the snooker club till about eleven. Charles was home by 6.00pm and claims to have been in bed by midnight. Heidi had read the riot act to her boyfriend after he had assaulted Mr Blazer, so Karl went off with Raymond Stone. They were together discussing politics and jobs till after 10.00pm."

"It was much later than that," said Raymond. "We must have been drinking till well after eleven."

"But not in the pub?" said Raynes.

"No, at home."

"We are told that by midnight, Grace was tucked up in her caravan in Picton Dale. We might also hope that Mr Blazer was also fast asleep. He had had a very traumatic day."

Edmund lowered his head.

"There were only three people whom we know for certain were close to the scene of the murder – Jimmy Watson, Elaine Sharpe and Tom Stone.

"Jimmy was running a disco at the *Raging Bull* till midnight when he was given a lift home. On their way up Riverside Road, they saw Bert staggering home down the middle of the road. The driver stopped to deliver some choice words to Mr Stone who then lashed out at the driver, hit the car instead and fell on to the road. This was at about 12.20am.

"Elaine and Tom were clearing up the pub. Tom had ushered his brother out of the *Kirby Arms* at about midnight, hoping he would find a taxi. According to Mrs Sharpe, a few minutes later, he went out through the back door of the pub; he was away for about ten minutes and came back 'looking as guilty as hell'."

"Don't believe her. Inspector. She's got it in for me."

Elaine laughed coldly.

"Your whole family are liars!"

"Enough!" said Raynes. "What I am seeking to do is to prove that everyone – even Betty Stone – could have been in or around Riverside Road after midnight. Not one of you have a satisfactory alibi. But it would have to be someone connected with the *Kirby Arms* who did the murder because . . ." Raynes paused " . . . because the spade used to bury Bert Stone's body beside the gas pipe was found in the gardening shed at the back of the pub. There was red clay on the blade and a fine pair of fingerprints on the shaft!"

He looked around with quiet pride.

"The murderer forgot to wear gloves!"

If he looked for a glimmer of guilt on the faces of the assembled company, he was disappointed.

"Now it seems to me that whoever killed Bert never expected his body to see the light of day again. They thought that once he was buried deep in the trench – with all the earth piled back in and the steamroller pressing down the tarmac, that was it. No alibi would be needed – because no one would ever know where or when he died.

"But now we know 'where' and 'when'. We still have to find out 'why' and 'who'. As I have said, there is a clear connection with the *Kirby Arms*. The police have also discovered a tool kit in the same garden shed. The police surgeon tells me that Bert was probably killed by a spanner blow to the skull. Small specks of chrome were found imbedded in his skull.

"It seems, therefore, that the murder weapon and the spade were readily available. They were known to be in the shed. And they were not only used, they were returned! This suggests to me that the murder was not done on impulse – not a casual mugging – but was definitely premeditated.

"So then, who are the most likely suspects?

"We return to Mr Tom Stone – the richest member of the family – always prepared to buy himself out of trouble. On the night of the baptism, he invited a number of people back to the pub and provided them with free booze for the rest of the evening. He claims that he was short-staffed that night, but he still found time to come back to this house to spend an hour or two with his sister-in-law, Betty.

"By the time he returned to the *Kirby Arms*, Charles Costello had gone; Ron and Alec were about to leave; but Raymond Stone and Karl were still there. And so was Bert, eyeing up the barmaid and preparing for his grande finale later in the evening.

"During the baptismal party, the two brothers had fallen out. Tom had told Bert to get a move on and encourage Sandra to marry Ron so that Mark could have a proper home. If Bert didn't show some initiative, he might marry Sandra himself! Not surprisingly, Bert took great offence at that. Tom had already pinched his wife; would he pinch his daughter as well?

"Tom must have asked himself how much longer Betty could live with this brute. Perhaps the constant sight of those road repairs in Riverside Road gave him a bright idea. Once buried in that trench, Bert would be gone for ever. He would remain a missing person. No one would ever know where to dig up the road. It would be the perfect murder.

"So he threw Bert out at midnight – but then he went out through the back door, carrying the spanner. He pursued his brother down the road – six hundred yards down the road; killed him and pushed his body into the trench. Later, when everyone had left the pub, he took the spade and dug Bert more deeply into his grave."

Tom looked white faced.

The case seemed damning.

Raynes paused.

"The only flaw in this argument is the red clay left on the spade. Having been shown round the *Kirby Arms*, I noted the spotless condition of the kitchen. I cannot believe that a person so concerned with cleanliness and hygiene would leave such damning evidence on a spade."

Tom Stone relaxed.

The Inspector's visit to the kitchen had not been in vain.

Raynes turned to Alec.

"Quite a number of people have pointed the finger of suspicion at Bert's son. They detected in him the same spirit of aggression and troublemaking. They knew how his father had treated him over the years – and they could see there was no love lost between them. They could still remember the family row – last Christmas – when Alec demanded that Sandra have an abortion. Alec was given a motor bike to shut him up.

"I am told that at the baptismal party, it was Alec who stirred up the godparents by telling them what mugs they were to be paying Bert sixty pounds a week. Ron had thought it was just him who was paying the money. Alec's revelation led directly to the fight in which Bert knocked out Ron.

"This could have been the straw which broke the camel's back. I can see Ron and Alec going off to the snooker club – but I can also see them returning to the *Kirby Arms*. According to Elaine, Ron was present in the Lounge bar when Bert was forcing his attentions on her in the kitchen passage."

Raynes looked at Elaine.

"What time would that have been?"

"After eleven."

"So there we have it. These two young men came back to the pub. They were familiar with its layout. They could see that Bert was the worse for drink. They knew it was close to closing time. They knew that the top end of Riverside Road was not a good place to try to stop a taxi. They expected him to walk home. So they made plans to waylay him just where the road works began.

"Jimmy said that when he and his friend drove away from Bert, the driver saw in his mirror, someone coming forward to pick Bert up. But suppose Jimmy had seen Ron or Alec lurking in the shadows, would he have split on them? Jimmy is very loyal to his friends. Perhaps too loyal?"

Jimmy grinned – but said nothing.

Raynes continued:

"But suppose, instead of picking Bert up, they laid into him with the spanner and then chucked him into the trench. I can imagine them hiding the body and returning the spade. I can also see them overlooking the tell-tale traces of red clay. After all, it was dark!"

Alec looked his usual grim self – but Ron was shaking his head. There was no way he was involved. But Sandra had her doubts.

Raynes moved on.

"Let us now pass to the other man of violence. A thug who was not frightened of using his fists; who had a monumental hatred burning inside him. Not for Bert Stone, but for his own father. He had already punched Mr Blazer and, this week, he has assaulted Heidi Houston so viciously that she will be in hospital for several weeks. If we had to choose a likely candidate for the murder, Karl would be our first choice. He has already been jailed twice for assault. But I notice from his record that all his attacks have been with his fists – not with a blunt instrument. If we had found Bert with a broken jaw, we could be fairly certain that his assailant was Karl.

"But did he even know Bert? Had he ever met him before the baptism? I am told that Karl has only been in Grasshallows for a matter of weeks. At the baptismal party, Karl was very much on his own. He didn't mix with anyone. The only person he was interested in was Heidi and when he thought she was devoting too much time to Mr Blazer, he let fly. He may have been invited up to the pub by Tom but he spent most of the evening chatting to Raymond. I do not think he would have exchanged more than a few words with Bert." The Inspector looked at Raymond.

"Did he?"

"Not that I can remember."

"Karl is certainly a man of violence; but it is difficult to find any motive. The two men were complete strangers."

Raynes had now reached the most delicate part of his exposition.

"So what *was* the motive? Money? Revenge? One of the most bizarre things about this case – the one that was brought to my attention almost immediately – was the choice of godparents for the baptism. Three men were chosen, any one of whom could have been the baby's father. Sandra has told me of four other men who might have been involved – but Charles, Ron and Jimmy were the most likely.

"For one very good reason, Mr Stone refused to permit a DNA test. Money! He had forced each of these young men to cough up sixty pounds a week for maintenance. Once the real father was known, that bounty would cease. So it was in his interests to prolong the uncertainty for as long as possible. It also gave Sandra more time to decide whom she would marry. If anyone . . .

"So, from the beginning, our attention was focussed on these three young men. Which of them was it? As long as we kept posing that question, no one would ask: 'Could there have been someone else?' But already there were pointers in that direction. Alec had demanded that Sandra should have an abortion. He declared that she had 'brought shame and dishonour on the family.' In what way? Was he talking about the arrival of an illegitimate baby? In this day and age! Surely he was being a little extreme? Or did he know something we didn't?

"Whilst Bert was alive, nothing could be done; but when I came on the scene, I immediately insisted on a DNA test for Charles, Ron, Jimmy – and also for the baby. To my surprise, none of these young men were Mark's father. This was perhaps a bit of a blow to Jimmy's pride. After all, he had claimed that he possessed 'the highest sperm count in Grasshallows!'" Raynes laughed. "But at least the test spared him and the others any more payments of sixty pounds.

"Who, then, was the father?

"This morning, we have tested Tom, Alec and Sandra herself. We have not tested Karl or Mr Blazer because they are both newcomers to our city. Neither Tom nor Alec was the father – but two other people have confirmed my suspicions and a further sample was taken over the weekend. I am sorry to be the one to reveal it publicly – but it is a certain fact. Bert Stone was the father of Sandra's baby."

39. *O Mio Bambino Caro*

There was normally some part in Raynes' expositions when a hitherto unrevealed fact caused upset or uproar – and this was it.

Sandra shrieked and ran out of the room, weeping. Betty went after her – closely followed by Tom. The three godfathers sat back in their seats and looked at each other. Raynes could sense their relief – a heavy burden lifted from their shoulders.

Elaine took out a cigarette and tapped it on her knee. She felt there was some justice in the world – Bert Stone, having fouled everybody else's nest, had now humiliated and abused even his own daughter.

Grace felt sorry for Sandra; Edmund pitied her but was glad that all thought of marriage had now been dissolved. The Inspector had been right. A few days had changed the picture entirely.

Alec had been expecting the screams and the tears.

They had been a long time in coming. He remembered his father boasting – sometime the previous autumn – that no woman could resist him. Not even his daughter. He had caught her in the bathroom just after she had got out of the bath – wearing only a towel. There had been a bit of horseplay but soon they had been hard at it on the floor. Sandra had been crying out: "Oh, Dad!" but her protests were ignored and her resistance was of short duration.

Of course, his father had been drunk when he told him all this. Later, he denied all knowledge of ever having said such a thing. When he had questioned his sister, she had not evinced any shame. She had just shrugged her shoulders and said: "Well, he's a man – just like the rest of you."

For his mother's sake, he had said nothing but, when Sandra became pregnant, fearing the worst, he had demanded that she should have an abortion. That hadn't made him very popular. He had threatened to go public; but the motor bike had bought his silence. Every man had his price.

Of course, he could not be sure that his dad was the baby's father. It might very well be Charles, Jimmy or Ron. Sandra was sure it was one of them – but she didn't want to find out. He could understand why. He had hated the hypocrisy of the baptism, his father's total contempt for the three godfathers, meekly paying their sixty pounds per week. His father called them "spineless mugs" – and so they were. He had come very close to spilling the beans at the baptism party but he prided himself on keeping the family secret – especially from his friend, Ron.

He had reconsidered his position when Inspector Raynes spoke to him in the grounds of the crematorium; when he said:

"There's something you know and you're not telling me. If I knew what it was, I could wrap up this case."

He had been thinking about it a lot. When his father's body was discovered, he had decided that he would tell the Inspector in confidence what he knew. That was why he had gone to see him on Wednesday afternoon, but Raynes had said that Heidi had already told him. So she knew as well.

Alec wondered how long Sandra would be weeping and wailing in the kitchen. So did the Inspector. He gave her five minutes and then sent Carlisle to bring her back. This was a murder inquiry – and there was more to come.

Carlisle was not very successful – and neither was the young policewoman. Sandra's crying had woken up the baby and she refused to be parted from him. Eventually, Raynes decided that his presence was required. He said to Sandra very quietly:

"If you don't return to the main living room immediately, I will transfer this whole meeting down to the police station. There, I will charge you with obstruction of police business. And I will then place your baby in foster care until this case is over."

Sandra found the Inspector's words so offensive – so utterly inhuman – that she stopped crying and weeping. Instead, she was consumed with an overpowering anger towards this wretched policeman who could even think of taking Mark away.

"You beast! You beast! You can't take him away!"

Carlisle assumed that Raynes was bluffing – and perhaps he was.

"The choice is yours, Sandra," he said. "I will give you two more minutes."

He looked at his watch and walked out of the kitchen without another backward glance.

Four minutes later, Sandra returned to the sitting room. Wild and red-eyed, she sat hugging her mother on the sofa. Raynes looked at her with some compassion and said:

"Thank you. We will now resume."

The Inspector picked up the threads of his narrative:

"Before the break, I was saying that Bert Stone was the

father of Sandra's baby. We have taken a DNA sample from his body and the test has proved conclusive. There can be absolutely no doubt."

Raynes spoke as gently as he could.

"How this happened, I do not know. Only Sandra can tell us. Did they have relations over a period of time? Or did it just happen one night? Was it done with consent – or by force?"

Sandra snuggled closer into her mother's arms.

"Knowing Bert, one would assume it was the latter."

Raynes looked at Carlisle. "Alec told us that Sandra was scared of her dad but would never admit it. I would imagine that he pushed for an abortion not so much to humiliate his sister – but rather to expose his father."

Alec nodded.

"This has been a very well-kept secret; but once Alec found out what had happened to his sister, others must have been told. Her mother . . . her uncle Tom . . . After all, he put up the money for the bike."

Tom bristled.

"I didn't know anything about this, Inspector; and neither did Betty. We didn't even guess."

Raynes accepted his words with a pinch of salt. He hadn't forgotten what Elaine had said:

"The whole family are liars!"

Raynes continued:

"Had the godfathers known, they would never have paid a penny in maintenance. So we can exclude them."

Charles, Ron and Jimmy exchanged grateful looks.

"In fact, the only person who was party to the secret was Heidi – Sandra's best friend. I think she must have been told just before the baptism. Anyway, as you will appreciate, this narrows down the field considerably. Because I believe the fact that Bert was known to be Mark's father was the trigger for the murder."

Raynes paused.

"Sandra knew. Alec knew. And Heidi knew . . .

"But there was – unfortunately – a fourth person who knew that Bert was father of the baby. Someone completely outside

222

the family. The moment Heidi received the information from Sandra, she passed it on to her boyfriend. She did not think the information could be of any consequence. Karl was an outsider. He had never met Bert. But this information would certainly have prejudiced Karl against him.

"Remember Karl's own family background. A father who had abused his two sisters – one of whom attempted suicide; both still receiving outpatient psychiatric treatment. His social worker, Ms Busby, told me that Karl was very caring and supportive towards his sisters. Whether this was true, I don't know. But what he had been told by Heidi would certainly have aroused his deeper feelings.

"Once Karl met Bert at the baptism, he would have been watching him carefully. He would have noticed Bert's interest in the two little girls playing in the bouncy castle. I am quite sure nothing happened at the party . . .." Raynes caught Grace's eye. " . . . Well, who knows? But that may have convinced Karl that Bert would be better dead. The rough house later in the afternoon would have shown him what sort of man he was up against.

"Karl bided his time. He went up to the pub. He chatted to Uncle Raymond. Or perhaps Raymond lectured him?" Raynes smiled. "Teaching him the finer points of Marx-Leninism? During this time, he had an opportunity to watch Bert at close quarters and the family friend provided him with a useful alibi. He left the *Kirby Arms* and went home with his new-found comrade – much to the disgust of Mrs Stone. But all the time he was plotting.

"He knew when the moment of execution would come. It would be when Bert left the pub. He had the means – a really hefty, old-fashioned spanner in the back of his car. I'm afraid I misled you about the spanner in the tool box. Karl used his own weapon. The police found it in his car; it was taken for examination by the forensic department in Leeds; and they have confirmed that this was indeed the object which killed Bert.

"Karl had also decided how he would dispose of the body. One thing that no one seems to have realized – myself included – was that Karl was a contract labourer for the Gas Board. He was brought down to Grasshallows to work on the laying of the new gas main in Riverside Road. The trench was familiar territory to him. He worked on it – and in it – every day. He knew precisely how Bert's body could be hidden away.

"However, his working tools would have been locked away over the weekend; so he needed a spade or shovel. During his time at the *Kirby Arms*, he probably had a quick look round the back regions. The garden shed is just beyond the kitchen. The key is often left in the lock. It would not have taken more than a few seconds to pinch the spade and hide it in his car – or perhaps in some corner of the pub where he could collect it later.

"I think that, after leaving Raymond and his wife, he must have collected his car and driven back to the pub. He would have needed to check that Bert was still there. Of course, Tom might have ordered a taxi for his brother; but Karl had accurately sussed out the atmosphere. Bert would get no more favours from Tom that night. So, sitting patiently in his car, he waited for Bert to emerge. As Bert staggered slowly down Riverside Road, he stalked him – waiting till he reached the nearest excavations. He probably had the spanner tucked into his waistband.

"As the two men neared the vital spot, Karl suddenly saw Bert stagger into the path of a passing van or car. He would have witnessed the harsh words exchanged between Bert and the driver. He would have seen the blow which missed its target; and he would have seen Bert sprawling in the middle of the road. Karl rushed over – not to help him – but to administer the *coup de grace*."

Raynes paused.

"I suspect – I cannot be sure, but I suspect – that Jimmy saw Karl lurking in the shadows as they drove away from Bert. Jimmy told me that the driver had seen in his rear mirror someone running towards Bert – as he thought, to help. But Jimmy would perhaps have guessed – when he heard that Bert was missing – that Karl was involved.

"All that talk about aliens was not complete garbage. There had been an alien waiting to zap Bert. As far as you were concerned, Karl was an alien." Raynes looked at Jimmy. "Is that true?"

Jimmy nodded.

"Sort of."

Raynes said: "If you had told me, you could have saved me a lot of time."

Jimmy laughed.

"We aliens stick together!"

Raynes shook his head. It was no joke.

"Karl is quite a strong lad. He would have had no difficulty holding Bert up – or moving him. If anyone asked him what he was doing, he could always say that the man had been knocked down by a car. He would have shifted Bert to the edge of the trench and then lowered him down. He didn't throw him in. Hence the lack of any further injuries to Bert's body.

"After that, he would have returned to his car for the spade. He would have used that time to see if there was any police activity – anybody who had noticed the murder. Once he was sure that his attack had attracted no attention, he would have gone down into that trench – the part that was likely to be filled in the following morning – and carefully dug a small grave for Bert which would not be apparent in the clear light of day.

"Karl then returned to his beloved, who was by now becoming a little anxious. Heidi was very fond of her caveman. She had been angry with him for attacking Edmund, but now she was wondering where he was. She told me that Karl did not return to Greenway Gardens till midnight.

"That was a lie. It was probably after 1.00am. But I didn't have a chance to challenge her because, at that moment, Karl walked into her sitting room. I found his presence very intimidating and it brought my visit to a rapid end."

Carlisle shrugged his shoulders. That should teach his boss not to go visiting on his own!

Raynes continued: "In the course of the murder, Karl pinched £80 from Bert's wallet. Later, he returned the spade to the garden shed at the *Kirby Arms*. He was not too particular about cleaning his tools – hence the crust of red clay. But, of course, the real giveaway was Karl's fingerprints on the shaft of the spade.

"From that moment onwards, Karl was a little twitchy. He thought he had pulled off the perfect murder. The body was now safely entombed. No one would ever find it. New sections of the road had been opened up. But Heidi might have had her suspicions. Where had Karl been that night? Did she notice any earth on his clothing or his shoes? She knew that he was working for the Gas Board in Riverside Road, but she never mentioned it. Certainly not to me. In fact, it took a great deal of heart-searching for her even to admit that she had passed Sandra's secret on to Karl. She now regards herself as responsible for Bert's death. And, in a way, she is."

Sandra disagreed.

She roused herself out of her mother's arms.

"Don't blame her. She didn't know what he was like. He was an animal . . ."

Raynes smiled. "I think we would all agree with that. But, soon after my visit to Heidi, the order was given for the road to be dug up. Karl must have heard about this at work. He realized what it meant. He suspected that Heidi had told me something during my visit. He challenged her. She denied it. He was sure she was lying. So he battered her; punched her; kicked her. It is a wonder he didn't kill her. Then, unwilling to face the police at the very scene of his crime, he rushed back to Leeds – back to his family and friends – and there, he was caught by the police. Yesterday, he was charged with assault and remanded in police custody; this morning, he has been charged with the murder of Albert Stone."

If Raynes expected a round of applause, he was disappointed. There was a complete silence as people digested the facts of the case and their own part in the drama. For most of them, the murderer was not who they thought it was. It was not one of the family but a complete stranger who had committed the deed. Jimmy might have guessed . . . Heidi might have guessed . . . but neither had conveyed their suspicions to anyone else. From a few, very slender clues, the Inspector had managed to track down the murderer. Even if there were grounds for congratulations, there was no great pleasure in discovering the truth. Too many nasty facts had been revealed about the Stone family – the lies, the greed, exploitation, adultery, bribery, theft . . . even incest.

But Raynes thought he could at least mitigate that charge.

"There is one point I have so far omitted. Deliberately, I may say. As a result of our DNA testing, one final fact has come to light. And that is that, contrary to all expectation, Sandra was not Bert Stone's daughter. Tom is her father. This will come as a complete surprise to all her family because, as you know, Bert idolized his daughter. She was the apple of his eye; his 'little princess'. It is perhaps all for the best that we now know she was not his child."

Sandra moaned: "Oh, my God!" and wept copiously in her mother's arms – the baby forgotten. In fact, she was almost like a baby herself. Tom looked proud and happy. Alec still sulky and sad.

Raynes reckoned that it had been a very tough afternoon for Sandra – and he had not helped.

He turned to Carlisle.

"Have I left anything out?"

His colleague shook his head.

"No. I think you've told them everything."

Carlisle seemed disappointed that there were no more arrests to be made. Normally, at this point, the handcuffs came out and extra officers flowed in from outside. But, today, the company was strangely subdued – even reluctant to depart.

Grace sidled up to Tom.

"Tom, darling, can I have another brandy?"

"Another large one?"

"Yes, please."

She turned to Raynes:

"I'm really looking forward to the funeral. To hearing what Canon Murray says about him. I'm told he simply loathed him."

Raynes smiled.

"Yes, it should be a fascinating moment. Greek meets Greek. Sinner meets sinner." He put his arm round Grace's shoulders. "Remember to bring your hip flask with you!"

40. *The Trojans*

Canon Murray had returned from his Greek cruise tanned and refreshed. It was his first proper holiday for several years. He had renewed his acquaintance with the heroes of the Greek classics. He had sailed in the wake of Helen and Paris on their voyage to Troy. Trodden on the very stones where Achilles had bared his heel; explored the maze where Theseus had worsted the Minotaur; hoped for some comforting words from the oracle at Delphi – but had seen mostly ruins. He had climbed the Acropolis but had been almost choked to death by Athens' toxic fumes.

During his time on the boat, he had met a charming widow – a former school teacher – who had shown enormous interest in his work. They had dined together every evening; visited the ancient sites hand in hand; and (if the truth be known) slept together for the last ten nights. They had exchanged addresses and Canon Murray hoped that his inamorata would soon be paying a private visit to Grasshallows. He thought he could hear the distant sound of wedding bells.

So he was in a good mood when he met his curate, the Reverend Edmund Blazer, on Friday morning for their first staff meeting since his return.

The first thing on the curate's agenda was to congratulate his boss on the visible success of his holiday. He could already detect a new vigour, a renewed sense of purpose, a fresh twinkle in his eye. (But enough of that!) His real object was to report on the events of the past six weeks and to present them in the best possible light.

The German choir had given an excellent performance of Pergolese's 'Stabat Mater' in St Benedict's. Visitors had said what excellent acoustics the church had. There had been an excellent crit in the *Grasshallows Echo* and over eighty CDs had been sold.

The preachers had all delivered excellent sermons, but perhaps the Professor of Philology had been a little over the congregation's head. He himself had enjoyed the Senior

Lecturer in New Testament Studies on the Dead Sea Scrolls. He smiled modestly. He had also preached his first sermon – a mere trifle compared with these heavyweights – but it had gone down well and many people had expressed their appreciation.

The congregation had been well-visited, especially those in hospital. He had taken services in three residential homes. He had given the housebound their communion. He had gone with the Ladies' Guild on their summer outing to Norwich. He was organizing an autumn pilgrimage to Walsingham and he had written an article on St Seraphim of Sarov for the September magazine. So much for the good news!

He made no mention of the stolen paschal candle (a new one had been bought); nor the shattered Christ (it had been repaired). The broken tiles had been restored as best they could. With commendable restraint, he mentioned that during the Rector's absence, there had been a baptism: "Mark Stone".

He made a point of looking at his notes as if to remind himself of the event: "28 Coronation Gardens. On Sunday August 13th."

The name "Stone" electrified Canon Murray.

"Whose child is he?"

"His mother is Sandra Stone."

"But she's not married!"

"No."

Canon Murray's face changed. "You know perfectly well that, at St. Benedict's, we never baptize any child if the parents are not married!"

The Reverend Blazer was able to look suitably surprised.

"But we've never discussed it . . . sir."

(He thought it better to add the "sir".)

The elderly Canon thought about it. The curate had only been ordained at the end of June and he had gone off for his cruise on July 20th. They had only worked together for three weeks. Perhaps Mr Blazer was right? They had not discussed these things. More charitably, he asked:

"Did the baptism go all right?"

Lying heartily, Edmund said: "It went very well. Mr Stone gave a donation of £100 to St Benedict's." (He was careful not to say which Mr Stone had given him the money.)

Canon Murray was impressed. In times past, St Benedict's would have been lucky to receive even five pounds from any member of the Stone family. But such largesse was equally distasteful.

"It's simony, of course. Believing that the sacraments can be bought with money." With some gravitas, he added: "I shall go and see Mr Stone."

"Are you going to give the money back?"

"Certainly not. But I shall insist that his daughter marry the child's father."

"But that's quite impossible!"

(For two very good reasons.)

"Nothing is impossible, Mr Blazer."

The curate played his trump card with aplomb.

"But Mr Stone *was* the father!"

The elderly Canon perceived a moral abyss opening before him. Not only had an illegitimate child been baptized in St Benedict's, but there had also been a gross act of incest.

"Did you know this? I mean, before you baptized the child?"

"No, sir. I did not."

"You were deceived?"

"Totally."

Canon Murray had rarely encountered such wickedness amongst his parishoners – if indeed the Stone family could ever have been considered members of his congregation. None of them were on the electoral roll.

Summoning up all his spiritual strength. Canon Murray decided that he must confront Mr Stone and condemn him for his shameless deed. He quietly rehearsed some of the rebukes he would deliver.

Edmund waited with some pleasure for the inevitable denouement.

"I shall go and see Mr Stone right away."

"I'm afraid that's impossible, sir."

"Don't keep saying things are impossible, Mr Blazer!"

"Well, in this case it is. Mr Stone is dead."

He handed over that morning's copy of the *Grasshallows Echo* with the prominent headline: "Man arrested for Stone murder."

Edmund gave him time to read the first few lines. Then he said: "He was murdered after the baptism. The police have now released his body. The funeral's on Tuesday."

Canon Murray tried hard to grapple with the consequences of this fast-moving drama. Clearly, Mr Blazer was more in touch with events than he was.

"Would you like to take the funeral?" he asked.

"No, sir. I think it would be inappropriate. The Stone family have particularly asked for you. They feel your experience and knowledge of the family would be of inestimable value."

Canon Murray sighed. There was no avoiding it. But he could not help feeling his curate had run rings round him. He revised his opinion of the young man. Very shrewd. Very worldly-wise. He wondered if perhaps he might give him an inkling of his future matrimonial hopes.

He smiled benignly.

"Well, we've had a baptism; next week, we've got a funeral. All we need now is a wedding!"

A look of horror came into Edmund's eyes.

"Oh, no, sir! That would be quite impossible."

"Impossible?" Canon Murray was taken aback.

"I've discussed the matter with Detective-Inspector Raynes and he was quite against it. No such step should even be considered. It would upset the congregation. It would bring the ministry into disrepute. I mean, you can hardly say you know a person when you've only known them for a few days."

Canon Murray was speechless with embarrassment. To think that his relationship with such a charming widow – conducted with such complete discretion – could already be public knowledge.

Mr Blazer smiled helpfully.

"Inspector Raynes said that he was an old friend of yours. I'm sure he'd be willing to speak to you and give you the best possible advice."

Canon Murray recovered his powers of speech.

"Thank you, Mr Blazer. I can think of nothing more humiliating."